Published by Tate Publishing & Enterprises, LLC
127 E. Trade Center Terrace | Mustang, Oklahoma 73064 USA
1.888.361.9473 | www.tatepublishing.com

Tate Publishing is committed to excellence in the publishing industry. The company
reflects the philosophy established by the founders, based on Psalm 68:11,
"*The Lord gave the word and great was the company of those who published it.*"

Book design copyright © 2016 by Tate Publishing, LLC. All rights reserved.
Cover design by Dante Rey Redido
Interior design by Jake Muelle

Published in the United States of America

ISBN: 978-1-68301-931-2
1. Fiction / Christian / Fantasy
2. Fiction / Action & Adventure
16.05.12

S0-ABB-079

GRACE

CALVIN DE

GRACE

Gra
Co

N
in
w

TATE PUBLISHING
AND ENTERPRISES, LLC

I will exalt you, Lord, for you lifted me out of the depths and did not let my enemies gloat over me. O Lord my God, I called to you for help, and you healed me. You, Lord, brought me up from the realm of the dead; you spared me from going down to the pit. Sing praises of the Lord, you his faithful people; praise his holy name. For his anger lasts only a moment but his favor lasts a lifetime; weeping may endure for the night but joy comes in the morning. When I felt secure, I said, "I will never be shaken." Lord, when you favored me, you made my mountain stand firm; but when you hid your face, I was dismayed. To you, Lord, I called; to the Lord I called for mercy: "What is gained if I am silenced, if I go down to the pit? Will the dust praise you? Will it proclaim your faithfulness? Hear, O Lord, and be merciful to me; Lord, be my help." You turned my wailing into dancing; you removed my sackcloth and clothed me with gladness, that my heart, may sing your praises and not be silent. Lord my God, I will praise and give thanks to you forever. (Psalms 30)

Prologue

August 2, 2010

"David, wake up," Amy said shaking her husband's leg. "David Grace, it's almost seven and you need to get going if you want to be first in line at the courthouse."

"Almost seven!" Oh crap, I overslept. I could have sworn I set the alarm for six," he said, shuffling to his feet while reaching for the clock.

"You did," Amy replied. "But I turned it off around six fifteen because you slept right through it. Besides, you needed the rest anyway."

"I guess you're right, love, because I've been up all night studying God's Word. By the way, thanks for standing by my side to move forward in the ministry for Christ."

Today is a joyous day for the Graces. Even though lately they've been going through some perilous times, it seems like light always shines through the darkness. Standing in the mirror as he brushed his teeth, David reflects on his two years of marriage and what has brought about this day. After spitting and rinsing his mouth out thoroughly he begins to groom himself while smiling thinking about his unthinkable love for his wife Amy. The same courthouse he is going to get his DBA license at is the same courthouse they were married on Valentine's Day in 2008. "God is good," he said to himself as he walked out of the bathroom to give her a morning kiss.

"What time is it, love?" Pulling her by both her arms he looked into her blue eyes and gave her a kiss before she could answer.

"Honey," she chuckled slightly with endearment. "You need to stop and get going before you start something you are not able to finish."

Rubbing his hands through her blond hair, he replied, "Okay, Mrs. Grace, but you have to promise to give me a rain check at my discretion."

Amy shakes her head because her husband's mind is always in the gutter. As she went to the bathroom to get ready for work, she thought about when and where David was going to cash his so-called "rain check." And most of all, will she be ready when he does?

The clock read seven thirty-six when David sat down on the foot of the bed to put on his loafers. Cook County's courthouse in Markham is twenty minutes away, and from the looks of it, he is going to be late. Rising swiftly, he grabbed his keys off the nightstand and poked his head in the restroom door.

"Baby, I'm gone. I love you and have a great day at work."

"I love you too and don't be speeding because we can't afford any tickets right now."

"Okay. See you, babe, when you get off work. Wish me luck."

Opening the door to his apartment daylight slaps him in the face and wakes him up out of his morning sluggishness. Their apartment is on the second floor, so he takes the stairs two by two until he reaches the bottom and jogs to his car. It's summer time so David decides to skip warming up his old faithful Honda Accord and drives off heading for Expressway 57.

Monday mornings are always no good to drive anywhere in Chicago, Illinois. The traffic completely slipped his mind because the last two weeks he's been laid off awaiting his transfer to the Coca-Cola plant in Beaumont, Texas. Seven months ago in January, Chicago's plant said they were closing his department down and granted those with seniority to choose first on the list of three plants which had positions available, since he has been with them for over ten years he chose Beaumont because Amy had a friend named Tabitha who recently just moved there.

Bumper to bumper, he sat on the expressway contemplating on the two names he is going to name his church. One was the Temple of Christ and the other is God's Temple. He didn't tell his wife, but in his heart he secretly wanted to name his church the Temple of Grace after himself. Turning the gospel station on, he looked down on the passenger seat at his bachelor's seminary degree. The four years he took online at a Chicago's seminary school has finally come to an end and it's time for him to show the world that hard work pays off.

Deacon Samuel, a man who knew his grandmother and watched him grow up, is the one who prophesied this day over his life during lunch at work late December. He said, God put it on his heart to tell him that he would someday lead a great number of people and to never let pride find its way into his soul. "Pride is what got Lucifer," Samuel would always say. "It's a sneaky sin, David. You never realize it's there and when you finally do, it's too late because you have sinned."

David Grace has always been great with people. Everyone who knew him said great things about him and continually asked his input on matters concerning the Bible. Ever since he was a child people would call him blessed because of what he endured during birth. His mother died while bringing him into this world prematurely. She was a virgin when she was raped by his unknown father so that made two parents he would never get to meet.

Pastor Thelma Grace, his grandmother, is the one who gave him the name David because his mother's name was Ruth. She professed from the day he was born that even though he was only three pounds at birth, he would grow up to be a handsome strong man of great valor. David loved his grandmother because she always believed in him and in her eyes he couldn't do anything wrong. When she passed away, she passed away in peace knowing that she raised him the best way she knew how. All he could say is, "Thank you, Jesus, for my grandmother Grace." Each day he looked in the mirror at what a healthy man he has become.

"Finally," he said aloud as the cars began to give him some space to drive. With his foot on the gas pedal, he accelerated pass the speed limit disregarding his wife's last statement. Time is of the essence because its eight fifteen, and he is still ten minutes away from his destination. It's not like he had something else important to do, it's just the fact of waiting in those winding lines if you're not first in them. Exiting 159th, he speeds a little more with only the courthouse on his mind. It's as if he is a racing horse with side shields on because his vision is only straight ahead.

The arrow in which was green turned yellow a few seconds before he reached 159th. Just before he approached the yellow light, it changed to red before he crossed the white lines on the pavement. A loud snap from a red light camera followed by a wailing horn and screeching brakes overpowered the day-to-day city noise. Burnt skid marks dig into the asphalt following behind the vehicle that tried to suddenly stop for the car that turned in front of it. All four of David's windows shattered as he is T-boned on the driver's side by an old pickup truck. Motionless, he lay hunched over toward the passenger seat with only his seat belt keeping him up.

"Someone call an ambulance!" a woman shouted in tears. "Hurry, someone call an ambulance!" she repeated over and over while staring at the blood from David's forehead dripping down his face onto the broken pieces of glass all over his pants leg.

1

The year is 2014 and the month is November. It's Thanksgiving Day and the homeless people of the community are lined up outside the church banquet hall with actual members of the congregation. As the famished faces come through the doors, they are warmly greeted with a smile and a firm handshake.

Pastor Grace is what the small city of Beaumont, Texas, called him and he is the pastor of the Temple of Christ. From the time the doors of his church opened, miraculous growth spans of members began to join in numbers in which no church has seen in ages. Amazed at how fast the church has grown, Christians throughout Texas commence to come and see Pastor Grace preach the gospel.

"Good afternoon, Pastor Grace, and thanks for today's Thanksgiving dinner," a homeless man said with a loud stench barely giving David eye contact.

"Good afternoon to you too and you're welcome. By the way, what's your name?"

"Cain but everyone calls me Abel because I'm able to do a lot of things with my hands when it comes to work," he said, nudging pastor as if he is interviewing for a job.

David Grace chuckles while putting to the side the man's verbal job application. The line going inside the hall has nearly stopped so David smiles and says, "Let's just say I like your nickname too. Enjoy your Thanksgiving meal, Abel, and church starts at nine every Sunday morning.

Finally, the banquet hall is full and the first lady of the church, Amy Grace, gives the last dinner plate to Deacon Cotton. "The Bible says, the first should be last and last should be first. Ain't that right, first lady?"

"Amen to that, but it's time to bless the food, Deacon Cotton, so we'll talk later," Amy replied softly.

Pastor Grace walks to the front of the gathering with his heart merry from a great turn out.

> Dear heavenly Father, we gather here today hand in hand, members and nonmembers, knowing that it is you who has brought us together on this Thanksgiving Day. Everyone in here are equal in your eyes and I pray that no one here feels out of place as we partake of the blessings before us. Lord everyone here also knows I'm long winded and can

stand up here all day long praying unto you. But out of respect for those who came who are less fortunate, I'll close by saying, thank you Jehovah Jireh Lord my provider for the food we are about to receive. In Jesus name I pray and let the church say, amen.

Amen came from every corner of the vast hall as they all let go of each other's hand and sat at their tables. Its two so everyone present showed no shame when it came to eating. For a brief moment, you couldn't tell the members from the homeless people because the wait of being served and seated caused everyone's stomachs to grumble.

Turkey, ham, corn, greens, yams, cranberry sauce, dressing, and everything else Thanksgiving dinner has to offer is on everyone's plates. Bite by bite they all ate until all you heard is clinging from the silverware hitting the empty plates. When noticing that everyone were nearly finished, Amy and the women's ministry served dessert while the men went around refilling everyone's cup with sweet red punch the elders mixed together the night before.

"This is the day that the Lord has made. Let us rejoice and be glad in it," a lady by the name of Miss Nancy said before eating her last piece of sweet potato pie.

Time went by quite quickly while everyone was eating but slowed down as soon as all the food was gone.

Fellowshipping among each other about how good of a church the Temple of Christ is, the homeless people started to exit to get back to the little property they have before their belongings come up missing. On their way out, they gave a nod here and a thank-you there toward those left to clean up. Pastor Grace could tell all of their bellies were full because not a soul asked for a take-home plate.

"Well, love," Pastor Grace said, grabbing his wife's hand. "It looks like a job well done."

Amy clinched her husband's hand tighter. "Yes, Pastor, and we have it all on videotape for those who won't believe what we've accomplished here today."

The women ministry are hard at work cleaning the hall as thoroughly as possible. Amy joined in shortly after her husband decided to retire to his study to review today's videotape. She could tell he was excited to watch it so she caught the hint and went to help the ladies finish getting everything back in order. After seeing that everyone's hands were busy working for the Temple of Christ, she found the nearest garbage can and began to assist Miss Landry with all the tables. Immediately, one of the newer members of the ministry tried to stop her because of her being the pastor's wife but Amy nicely refused her amiableness with a hand gesture.

"Sorry, Sister Sweat, but I too must be a good steward for our Lord and savior Jesus Christ."

Pastor Grace's Maserati is not in his assigned parking space when the lights shut off one by one throughout the sanctuary. Deacon Cotton stayed to watch over the ladies and to make sure all the doors were locked. Amy had to drive her Range Rover because she had to get to the hall early to set up. Also, she had to govern all the progress for the first Thanksgiving dinner in which everyone from the community would be under one roof. Deacon Cotton walks her to her SUV after he sets the alarm on the church.

"Thanks, Deacon Cotton, for always making sure we are safe on the nights we get out of here kind of late."

"No, thank you for that wonderful meal the sisters put together today," he replied with a smile. Closing her door he said, "Drive safe, first lady, and be blessed."

Half an hour later, Amy is reaching for the remote to her garage. When the garage door got halfway up, she notices that David has not made it home yet. *Now where can he be?* she thought. *He left before me.* She shrugged her thoughts off because she didn't know exactly how long it was before she left did David leave. Anyway, she knew he would be home shortly behind her.

David left the sanctuary early to surprise his beloved wife with some flowers for all the persistent work she put into the Thanksgiving dinner. He decided to duck out of the back door when he finished reviewing the videotape of today's event. The cameraman captured everything he needed, and more so in the days to come he will give it to the church's editing crew first chance he gets. He had a week to have it ready for the mayor so it really isn't any rush to have it edited as of this moment, and besides the hard part is over with.

Walmart is the closes store to the Temple of Christ so that is the first place that popped up in his mind when thinking of a love offering for his wife. *I know it doesn't have the best flower department but something is better than nothing,* he thought while parking his car perfectly between the yellow lines. Stepping out of his Maserati, he pauses and takes a deep breath of the night's cool fresh air. The parking lot lights shined down upon the hood of his royal-blue car and he smiles because of all he has achieved since he decided to leave Chicago. Beaumont is not as nearly as big as the great windy city but he can honestly say that this is what he now calls home.

The electric doors to Walmart automatically opens when David is four feet away. As he walked through the double doors, the store's heat grabs him immediately and dissipates the tiny chill bumps all over his arms. He knows the store floor layout so he heads straight for the floral section near produce. When he approaches what's left of the rose bouquets, a store attendant on her way to clock out recognizes him and goes over to see if she can be of any help.

"Hello, Pastor, and what's the special occasion?"

David turns around and looks down at Ja'Nice Walker who is one of the members of his church. "Oh, nothing really. I'm just trying to surprise Mrs. Grace for all the hard work she did for the Thanksgiving dinner."

"You're so sweet, Pastor, and first lady is a very blessed woman."

"Thanks, Sister Walker."

"Well, Pastor, I'm about to get off so if you'd like I can check in the back to see if we have any flowers that looks prettier than those," Ja'Nice said, scrunching her nose while pointing at the end of the day roses.

"That would be nice of you if it's no trouble."

"It's okay. Just think of it as a gift from me too since I couldn't make it today because I had to work." Ja'Nice smiled from ear to ear and hurried off.

While waiting, David began to browse the aisles letting his eyes take mental notes of specials Walmart have on sale in produce. Mrs. Grace loved a good sale and couldn't help but to purchase something when she found one. Promising to let her know chicken leg quarters and potatoes had an unbelievable price, someone tapped him on the shoulder from behind.

"Hello, David," a soft woman's voice said before he can turn around.

David knew who it was so he tried to step away from her before giving her his full attention. "Good afternoon, Princess," he replied looking left to right to see if he sees any familiar faces.

"Good afternoon," she sassed standing akimbo. "Is that all you have to say to the woman who would be your wife if you were not married to Amy?"

Princess Jackson has always been head over heels for Pastor Grace. It started shortly after she was nominated to be his secretary three years ago when the Temple of Christ was getting off the ground. David tried his hardest to ignore her seductive ways behind closed doors but her long dark curly hair and milky chocolate skin didn't make it any better. After a year of dodging her she finally cornered him in his office and they shared a kiss they both would never forget.

The next day and the days to come were never the same. Lying is something David was never good at, so he demoted her to treasurer before anyone could suspect them for having an affair that wasn't there. Even though she wasn't around him as much as before, it didn't stop her from trying her hardest to take the pastor from his wife.

"Hello, Princess." David unbuttons the top of his shirt as a bead of sweat formed on the side of his head. Scanning the aisles, he looks for Ja'Nice to return with his wife's flowers. It's been over ten minutes so she should be coming back any second now.

"Don't be nervous, David. I promise to be good in public." Princess smiled while wiping the sweat from his face with her thumb. Staring into his gray eyes, she said, "Sorry I couldn't make it today for the dinner. It's just that I feel so uncomfortable every time I see you and your wife together."

"I totally understand, Princess, but nothing happened between us so please don't let my marriage stop you from coming to church."

Ja'Nice came around the corner out of nowhere with a fresh bouquet of flowers. When she walked up, David lumbered, and his six-foot-two-inch frame shrinks a couple of inches. His smile is still there but Ja'Nice could tell his mood has changed from earlier. Silence and bewilderment filled the air, so she decided to break the ice between the three of them.

"Hello, Ms. Jackson." Ja'Nice extended her hand for a friendly handshake, and Princess accepted it not ashamed at all to be seen with the pastor.

"Hello, Ja'Nice. Nice to see you tonight," Princess replied. "Sorry I can't talk long, I have to get going because I have a friend coming over later. With that said, I guess I'll see the two of you at church Sunday morning." Princess scampers off with a smirk on her face before disappearing around the corner.

Ja'Nice's facial expression is blank because of how Princess Jackson departed from the two of them. Not wanting to pry, she continues with what the Pastor came for. "Here's your flowers, Pastor Grace. I handpicked them and wrapped them myself. Sorry it took so long but I love Mrs. Grace and she deserves nothing but the best."

Saying his wife's name brought the color back into his ashen skin. Smiling with his glossy white teeth, he thanked Ja'Nice for the beautiful flowers and told her not to be late for Sunday morning services. Looking down at his gold watch, he realizes it's getting late so he waves good-bye. "Have a blessed night, Ms. Walker," he said as he walked off to be checked out on line seven.

Pastor Grace races home after checking the time again on his dashboard. Using his remote, the buzz of the garage opening startles Amy while she is washing clothes. Their dog Lux begins to bark and runs to the door that joins the house to the garage. Jumping in a joyful tantrum, Lux spins, barks, and wags his tail to his master's arrival. "There's my boy," David said bending over to rub his fingers through Lux's hair.

Lux is a black Tibetan terrier, and when you rub him he makes sure you don't miss any spot of his long-haired body. Especially when it's not cut like it is as of this moment.

"Hey, love," David said, handing his wife a dozen of red-and-white roses.

"Ooh, and these are beautiful, David," she replied with surprise. Amy always called him David outside the church and Pastor Grace when around members. "What's the occasion?"

"Love is the occasion, and guest what?"

"What now, David?"

"I love you, Amy Grace. Since the first day I met you, eight years ago, I knew I would be standing at this washing machine tonight telling you I love you!" David said emphasizing the words, "I love you," in his sentence.

Friday morning came as if night never existed. After making passionate love, they both fell fast asleep from the long hours they put in all day yesterday. The house phone's blaring ring from the kitchen awakens them from the deadness of their sleep. Pastor Grace tried his hardest to ignore the phone, but a small kick to his ankle caused him to jump out of the bed and drag his feet to the kitchen.

"Hello and good morning." David's eyes are barely open when his greeting falls from his lips.

"Good morning to you too, Pastor." Tabitha Thomson, who is Amy's friend from Chicago and also a leader of the women ministry, is on the other end of the line with a sense of urgency in her voice. "Sorry to bother you at such an early hour, but our treasurer Ms. Jackson's heel on her shoe snapped on the steps of her apartment and she took a terrible fall last night.

"What? I mean, are you serious, Ms. Thompson?" David wipes the sleep from his eyes and fully wakes up recalling his last night's encounter with Princess.

"Yes, I'm serious, Pastor," Tabitha replied surprised at his response to the harsh news. "As of last night she's in Baptist Memorial Hospital with a concussion and a broken ankle. I talked to her right before I called you, and she wants to know if you can go visit her because she needs all the support and prayer she can get to get through this. She's in room 826 if you want to call first but please know she is on a lot of pain medication so some of the things she is saying doesn't make any sense.

"Okay, Ms. Thompson, I'll keep that in mind when I go to see her. By the way, thanks for the news and sorry for not answering sooner."

"Good-bye, Pastor, and see you Sunday."

Pastor Grace held the phone a few seconds before placing it back on the kitchen wall receiver. Distraught about the news he's just heard, he ponders on how quickly an unfortunate accident can happen to a person. It's a little after eight so he lies back down turning opposite of Amy while meditating on his change of plans for today.

Amy snugs up against him and asks, "Who was that, love?" David is in deep thought because of his pastoral duties he must tend to the sick and shut in. But he's also cynical to the fact that this may not be as severe as Princess is leading it on to be.

"David honey, who was that on the phone?" Amy asked for a second time.

"Huh? Oh, that was your friend Tabitha letting us know that our treasurer Ms. Jackson has had a terrible accident putting her in the hospital."

"Sorry to hear that. Is she going to be okay?"

"From the looks of it, yes, but her ankle is broken and she has a concussion." David turns over and lets his wife put her head on his chest. "I'll be going to visit her later after I stop by the church to check on things. She's in room 826 if you want to call and see how she is doing."

"I think I'll do that later when I think she's feeling up to par for a conversation. If it's not too much, love, I'll send her some flowers from the two of us."

Amy rolled over to finish the last of her beauty rest. Taking most of the cover, she closed her eyes hating the fact that her schedule wouldn't allow her to go with him to the hospital. A woman's intuition is never wrong so she knew Princess has a fling for her husband but never had any evidence to bring it to David or Princess's attention. A woman of God is what she is and woman of God is what she is going to stay. All she can do is trust her husband because without trust their love wouldn't be anything.

2

Pastor David Grace stepped inside of the Baptist Memorial Hospital elevators not knowing what to expect from his visit today with Princess Jackson. Reason being is because whether sick, injured, or on her deathbed, Princess will always be Princess no matter what. No one occupied the elevator, so straight to level eight the elevator will go, unless someone from another floor is going in the same direction.

Inside the elevator, mirrored walls surrounded him which gave him time to look at his appearance with more scrutiny. Adjusting his necktie on his collared shirt, he then brushes the crumbs off his slacks from the cheeseburger he ate in the car. Gravity pulls down on his stomach when passing the sixth floor and causes his knees to buckle and shift a little bit. A courtesy bell lets him know he's arrived on Princess's floor and the door opening makes him feel like he is John Coffey about to walk the green mile.

"Excuse me, Ms. Acu'na." David glances at the Hispanic lady's name tag again to make sure he pronounced her name correctly. Clearing his throat, he says, "Could you please tell me which way is room 826?" Mrs. Acu'na is sitting behind the nurses' station doing paperwork and simply points to her left without giving him any eye contact. "Thanks, I think," he said thinking, *I'll just find it myself.*

The numbers on the doors to his left and right began to increase starting at 810 so he knew that he was going in the right direction. Some of the rooms have balloons taped to the doorknobs while others have ribbons and congratulation signs indicating a baby has been born. Room 820 is at the end of the hallway so he picks up the pace when realizing Princess's room is shortly around the corner. As he walked to her room, he wondered why Princess's door is not decorated like the majority of the rooms on the floor. Especially since she's the type who wants the world to know she is a princess.

Princess's door is slightly ajar when David said, "Knock, knock," in a low voice while giving it a light tap.

"David, is that you?" Princess's voice sounds weak and weary but that doesn't stop her from raising the back of her bed to sit up.

"Good afternoon, Princess. I pray I didn't wake you and that you're up for a visit? I'm sorry I didn't call first." David walks over to the side of her bed and looks at the bandage wrapping around her head. "How are you feeling?"

"I'm okay I guess," she said barely lifting up her broken right ankle. "Hopefully I'll be able to leave tomorrow or the next day. It depends on what the doctor says about my concussion."

David pulled a chair to her bedside, and they began to talk about the accident and how scared she was when she went tumbling down those stairs. Princess rolls over to her left side to show him the bruises that covered her back. He could tell there were more bruises because most of her body was exposed underneath the nightgown that only covered her front. Princess's actions were done intentionally but she didn't want to go any further with exposing herself because it might have ran the pastor off.

Shaking her unbelievable figure from his mind, he asks, "How long will you have to be in that cast?"

"Eight to ten weeks, I think. Really and truly, I don't know. Once again, it depends on what my doctor says." Princess smiled while looking him over from head to toe.

"What are you smiling about?"

"You being here sitting by my bedside with me." She didn't hesitate at all when answering his question.

David returned the smile but let her response roll over his head. "The reason why I ask is because the church is going to have to fill your position as treasurer until you get back. And the money from the state will be here next week for the prison ministry."

"Well, I'm sorry, Pastor, for not having any suggestions. Honestly, you have to admit, David, there's only one Princess Jackson and you're looking at her in the flesh." Princess raised her hands and smiled cheerfully.

David paused to take in her comment carefully. Not because of the fact that she was boasting about her physical qualifications but because she was very good at handling the church's money. Every cent since he gave her that position was accounted for and every dime was spent on something that edified the church. Also, from being his secretary in the beginning she knew things about him that not even the closest people who knew him did. Including his wife. He had to admit, replacing Princess Jackson would not happen overnight.

A knock on the door startled the both of them. Princess doesn't know who it can be because she isn't expecting any visitors until tomorrow. She made sure her day was clear from friends or family in hopes that Tabitha's message would seem urgent enough for David to come to her aid. This is the reason why her door, or inside her room, isn't decorated with flowers and get-well-soon decor.

"Come in!" Princess yelled in her loudest voice while making sure every inch of her body is covered.

"Excuse me," a male's voice said entering her room. "I have some flowers from Lillie's flower shop for a Ms. Jackson."

Princess's eyes grew big because she doesn't know who they could be from. Her excited expression explains it all when she said, "That's me! That's me! Please come in."

The delivery guy placed the beautiful crystal vase filled with a variety of different-colored flowers on the stand on her bedside. A digital pad is pulled from his back pocket and a plastic pen-like stick is handed to her so she can sign on the dotted line. "Enjoy your bouquet, Ms. Jackson, and whenever you think of flowers, think Lillie's." A faint smile came from the delivery guy's mouth after he quoted the store's slogan. As he turned to leave, David got up and saw him to the door.

"Thanks um…"

"Frank."

"Okay, Mr. Frank, thanks for your services. Here's a tip so you can get yourself some lunch from Ms. Jackson."

Frank said, "Gracias, Mr. Jackson," over and over when noticing he was given a twenty-dollar bill.

David laughed and closed the door behind him. Taking his seat again, he smiles because despite Princess's devious ways she did deserve some sunshine on a cloudy day every now and then. Watching her open the card, he looks over to the beautiful assortment of flowers and sees that they are not cheap.

"So who are they from? Because whoever it is cares a lot about you."

"I don't know. If you'll be quiet I'll tell you in a second when I read the card. And for the record, Pastor, jealously is not a good look on you so please stop because you're too handsome for that."

Princess slit the pink envelope open with her manicured nail and rubbed the red velvet cross on the front of it.

The card read:

> Surely He took up your pain and bore our suffering, but He was pierced for our transgression. He was crushed for our iniquities; the punishment that brought us peace was on Him, and by His wounds we are healed.
>
> Isaiah 53:4, 5
> AMY and David Grace

Princess's smile turned into a frown when seeing that Amy meticulously made sure her name was in all caps. The fire that burned inside her made her want to toss the card across the room but being that she considered herself a lady, she faked her happiness and set it next to the flowers.

31

"Thanks for the flowers and cards," she said calmly while purposely leaving it open for David to read.

"Card! What card?" he asked obliviously.

"That card." Princess points to the card standing next to the vase.

David picks up the card and lets his eyes scan over the familiar verse of Isaiah 53. He doesn't catch the all caps of Amy's name in the closure at first, but after reading it carefully for a second time, he understands why Princess's hairs on the back of her neck are standing.

Six years he's been married to his wife and eight years he has known her. Everything is making complete sense now as he recalls the numerous phone calls throughout the day from Amy to see how he is doing. He had just got off the phone with her when he pulled into the parking garage so that told him that the bomb that just exploded in Princess's lap was meant for the both of them.

"So like I said, thanks for the card and flowers."

"Oh you're welcome." David stutters a little but catches himself in midsentence. "I'm sorry but it completely slipped my mind that Amy were sending you some flowers from the two of us. I probably would have remembered if you would've had some flowers from some of your other friends around here."

"Don't worry, my other friends and gifts will be here tomorrow and however else long I have to be in here,"

Princess snapped back. "I'm not feeling too good and all this talking has made me tired. I think it's about time for me to press this little red button for pain because the sound of your voice is making my head hurt."

Taking the hint clearly, David gets up quietly and tucks in the side of the blanket underneath her. To his knowledge he hasn't done anything wrong but Princess had to find something to get mad at him about besides the card his wife sent her. Before leaving he pours her a cup of water and says, "Thanks for all that you do for me and the church. Hurry up and get well soon because I'm going to truly miss you. Good-bye, Princess, and keep me updated on your progress."

The visit with Princess Jackson went half as bad as he expected. Everything he wanted to accomplish he didn't but at least he let it be known that he cared about her by showing his face for over an hour. One thing he learned for sure is that he never planned for his main prospect in his business to ever go down for the count. Especially not at this time of the year when such a great lump sum of money is about to come in from the state.

Princess and David are the only two people able to deposit or withdraw from certain accounts in the church, so with her being hurt he is going to have to take on the treasurer position all by himself. The only problem is having to explain to Amy and the church why the leaders of the Temple of Christ cannot elect someone else who is well qualified to be treasurer until Princess gets back.

Amy calls as soon as he presses the start button in his Maserati. Her voice through his car speakers sounds angry while she explains how she's been trying to reach him for the last hour. David realizes that the hospital must have dropped his signal on his iPhone and lets her know what had happen. He laughs inwardly because of her flowers and card but doesn't let her know that he and Princess got her message loud and clearly. Really and truly, her being angry is very sexy to him.

"So what happened today, love?" David puts the car in first gear and holds his foot on the brake for a few seconds.

"What happened is that I drove all the way to the county jail to pick up our new badges for the outreach prison program and they said I couldn't get yours because I am not the one who usually picks them up. I told them I was your wife and let them see we have the same last name but they were not trying to hear it." Amy's voice got louder and louder as she expresses her disbelief.

"Calm down, baby. I'll swing by there first thing Monday morning and pick up mine." David is relieved to know that the county jail didn't tell her that Princess is the person from the church that picks up the badges regularly. "See, love, problem solved." He quickly changes the subject.

"Now on to important matters. What are we going to eat tonight because I'm famished?"

The calmest of his voice always soothes her spirit when she takes a walk on the dark side because of anger. Forgetting all that she was mad about, Amy replied, "How about we meet up at Olive Garden on Calder at my expense. I recently saw a commercial with this new shrimp pasta and I am dying to try it." David giggles aloud into his car speakers because Amy's expense means that he is the one going to be paying for the dinner.

Dinner was great. David and Amy enjoyed each other's company talking about the busy church schedule they are about to endure for Grace Ministries. Amy felt she made her point with timing the flowers to be delivered while her husband was in the hospital with Princess. Therefore, she just listened to what the women's ministry had to do to make sure the Word of God be manifested in the lives of all those the ministry came into contact with.

At the end of the day, with Princess being out of the picture for a while will be good for the both of them. Good for Amy because she didn't have to worry about keeping her eyes full time on Princess flirting with her husband; and good for David because he didn't have to worry about his wife giving him the googly-eyes and cold shoulder when Princess is around.

Day one of David's prison outreach ministry titled "Grace Ministries OPAT" started two weeks after the state's financial funding was deposited in the church's account. OPAT which stood for One Prisoner At a Time began last December with the help of Mayor Freeman's campaigns support letters to the state of Texas. The program granted the Temple of Christ $250,000 a year for the next four years to help prisoners who are being released get back on their feet.

For ten months, the church is supposed to go throughout the state of Texas dispensing the funds with smaller programs, and for two months they are to stock back up on supplies needed for the next trip out. Mayor George Freeman is a direct shoo-in for next Texas governor so with his name backing the proposal no one detested it not being something great for the men and women coming out of jail.

One hundred twenty-five thousand dollars to the church is what the state dispersed every six months to Grace Ministries. In order for the rest to be dispersed, the proper paperwork showing where and to whom the fundings had went had to be sent in every three months. This was Princess's job and no one knew how to account for a dollar better than her.

Debra Paxton and her team of women were over the uniform ministry for the entire church. Their job is to make sure anytime the Temple of Christ stepped outside the doors of the church, all members will be in a professional attire for whatever they were called to do. All T-shirts, bumper stickers, buttons, pens, and wristbands were completely out from the last mission Grace Ministries went on so Debra had to reorder everything. The company they ordered all their gear from misprinted their slogan by putting 1PAT instead of OPAT as their abbreviation. All the ladies of the church were mad and wanted to send them back but Pastor Grace said 1PAT is different and different is what the ministry needed.

Jefferson County Correctional Facility (JCCF) is the first jail of twenty-one on their schedule to visit. When entering, the guards gave them a quick pat down and glanced over all of their badges. After being cleared, Sgt. Maxwell came from his office to personally thank David Grace for his return to the facility and for the support he's blessed the inmates with when they were released. Chaplain Harris is there to greet them when they exited the main building and to escort all of them to where the offenders are housed.

"Nice to see you again, Pastor Grace, and thank your church for coming out tonight."

"No, Chaplain, thank you for having us again." David gives him a firm handshake and pats him on the back.

Walking a few steps further, the group of men and women came to a fork in the facility's walkway. "I'm pretty sure everyone here remembers the routine from last year. The men's chapel is down there to the left and the women's dormitories are at the end of this walkway."

"Sorry, ladies, but the women's chapel won't be finished until next year. You will have to use an empty dormitory for services tonight. The good news is that tonight the majority of the men and women turned out in great numbers when hearing Grace Ministries is coming."

"God is good and our Bible tells us that we are God's temple. I'm pretty sure our ladies here tonight know how to praise the Lord throughout any circumstances," Amy said this recalling how the Temple of Christ started in their two-bedroom apartment when she and David first moved to Beaumont, Texas.

Jefferson County Chapel is filled with inmates awaiting to hear God's Word for them tonight. An inmate by the name of Big O who's been awaiting his trial for two years is a strong believer in Christ. He is the one who helped pass out Bibles, pamphlets, and bookmarks stamped Grace 1PAT. He also was incarcerated the first year Grace Ministries got started and is the main reason tonight's turn out is so great. When the last piece of reading material is handed out, Big O got the entire church to shout "Jesus" before a choir of three men started to sing the praise song, "Jesus Can Work It Out."

Pastor Grace stepped to the podium as soon as the song ended. Motioning with his hands, he asked everyone to come forward for altar prayer. The deacons and members who came with him stood in the midst of the offenders and grasped their hands until everyone were linked in a big circle.

Pastor Grace prayed,

> Our Father which art in Heaven, Lord of all things and through your Son all things are made. It is for this reason alone we are able to stand at your footstool and bring to you our petition of thanks. Lord, we thank you tonight for your mercy. Lord, we thank you tonight for your grace. Our prayer is that you continue to keep your hedge of protection around us and our families as we walk this walk of faith in your son Jesus Christ our Lord and savior. Please, Father, forgive us for abusing your long-suffering each day we sin continually before your holy eyes. We thank you Jesus for dying on that rugged cross and shedding your sinless blood. God, you are awesome and your judgment is awesome. In my heart and in these men's hearts we fully understand that it is you who has the last say so in all matters in this world and in the world to come. You know what we are asking for Father and most of all you know all that we need. With that, we

close by saying thank you, Lord, with the utmost of
our faith. In your son Jesus Christ's name we pray.
Amen.

Tears were in some of the men's eyes as they turned to
walk back to their seats. Some of their tears were from the
joy of them knowing that God is in control of everything
and loves them unconditionally. Others had tears of regret
for the crimes they committed and prayed for forgiveness
of their sins. A few of the deacons sat with the men who
needed an ear to listen because the Holy Spirit is definitely
moving behind the barbwire fence tonight.

Pastor Grace couldn't stop God from moving throughout JCCF's chapel so he held the message he set out to
preach for a later day. Instead, he went among the brethren laying hands and praying with them one by one as
they brought their prayer request to him. The three-man
choir sang old hymns from the hymnbook starting with
"Amazing Grace" and that started a chain of inmates asking
to be led through the sinner's prayers.

At the end of the service, Grace Ministries told all the
men present that the doors of his church were open to any
offender seeking to better themselves when released. A
clipboard is passed around for anyone who wanted to sign
up for Grace 1PAT. When the clipboard made its way back

to the deacons, they praised God because 80 percent of the congregation had signed up for their help.

"God is good," Deacon Cotton said looking over the sanctuary.

"Yes, Deacon, God is good," David replied amazed at how the Holy Spirit took over the service tonight. "Excuse me but tonight's service is over!" he shouted. "Be blessed and have a Merry Christmas and a Happy New Year!"

Amy and the women's ministry met up with the men back at the church's shuttle bus. The men were still at awe from the power of God that they couldn't wait to share with the ladies all that had happened in the chapel. No one could keep quiet long enough to listen to one another, because the women had awesome praise reports as well. Brother Chuck, their driver, didn't go inside but wished he had after seeing the joy in all their faces.

Grace Ministries has begun once again, and from the looks of it, God will have his hands fully in control of it. In three weeks they are to be in Beeville, Texas, at Garza East and West. Christmas and New Years are a few days away, so afterward the team better be ready for the long ten months ahead of them.

3

This week was a tiresome week for Grace Ministries. Not only this week but also the months that led up unto today. The good news is that everything has been running smoothly except for the fact that fatigue has set in on the men and women from traveling so much. David promised the team that Easter Sunday will end their journey for the first part of the year and they would get back on schedule at the end of May.

Since everyone was looking forward to today, their motors began to shut down when Grace Ministries had to appear at two unscheduled events in the panhandle of Texas at the beginning of last week. Bro. Chuck, however, got everyone home safely Good Friday night and that gave the elders of the church time to prepare for one of the biggest turn outs for the Temple of Christ.

Easter morning Pastor Grace made it to the church around seven because he needed some alone time to fully prepare for the message he is bringing today. Soothing music echoed off the walls of his office as he sat behind his desk with his eyes closed. Saturday night, he jumped deep into his studies so he knew what word he is going to preach but God never revealed to him the title.

While carefully meditating, David's short lifespan passes before him, and he questions his preferred choices he's made in the thirty-six years he's walked this earth. One thing he hasn't been able to shake from his spirit is that God still uses him in miraculous ways, but for some reason God's love doesn't feel the same as the day when he decided to become a pastor. A buzz from his door interrupts his thinking right when he was about to put his finger on the answer to his question.

"Good morning, Pastor Grace, and sorry for disturbing your studies but it's time."

Pastor stands and looks at his wall clock shaped like the thorns that was placed on Jesus's head as a sarcastic crown. "It's eight forty-five already, Deacon Cotton?"

"Yes, Pastor, and the church is waiting for you to start the Easter Sunday's program."

Deacon Cotton closes the door and walks back to the sanctuary. David looks in the mirror and straightens his tie before opening the door to follow him. The tiled floor he walked upon ended at the side entrance to the pulpit. David steps onto the small carpeted staircase and emerges on stage underneath the big cross that loomed over his beautiful glass podium. Loud shouts of praise and claps from the audience uprooted through the building sending soft vibrations beneath his feet.

"Happy Easter, everybody!" David shouts and waves in all directions.

"Happy Easter, Pastor Grace!" The Temple of Christ yelled back all at once to let him know how much they love and adore him.

"First of all, I want to say please forgive first lady Mrs. Grace for not being here for early-morning service. Today, she decided she wanted to make me an Easter dinner with all the trimmings so she said she will not make it until eleven. At first, I wanted to tell her I'll take her out for dinner after service, but then I thought about it, who am I to get in the way of any woman wanting to cook a meal for her man? Amen."

The congregation let out a low laughter to their overseer's humor. "As we all know church, today is the day that we, the body of Christ, celebrate the day Jesus our Lord and Savior rose from the dead with all power over sin and death. Being that today is a joyful day for the Christians around the world, I would like to start our Easter program doing something joyous. If everyone can get up and meet me and the elders outside at the main entrance, we have a special treat for our youth ministry today."

Parents and their children exited the church as quickly as possible when Pastor Grace gave them the signal to leave. When everyone is outside, a pink-and-yellow Easter bunny came out of the gym and started mingling with all the kids. Tabitha, who had put today's program together, announced that an Easter egg hunt will be on the playground in approximately fifteen minutes for the kids twelve and under.

She also let the teenagers know that the church had Easter cupcakes and candies for those who wanted to participate in the gym. Blowing her whistle, she told everyone to get to where they are going so that they can all be back in the sanctuary to hear today's message when it's over.

Princess Jackson invited her twin brother Prince to church today. The two of them are standing alongside the fence of the playground watching the kids search for the hidden eggs throughout the black mulch. Prince and Princess are getting a lot of attention this morning because no one knew up until this morning that she had a twin brother. Especially not the ladies, and that's probably why, because Princess had to have all the spotlight at all times.

"Good morning, Princess," David said slipping her a note while shaking her small hand. "And who might this handsome fellow be escorting you this beautiful Easter morning?"

"Hello, Pastor Grace." Prince extends his hand and the two of them act like they are trying to see who has the strongest grip. "The name is Prince Jackson. I'm Princess's big brother by two minutes."

"Oh you don't say," Pastor Grace replied. "I didn't know she had a brother." David looks at her wondering why she never mentioned it to him.

"Sorry, David, but I didn't think me having a brother was so important to you."

Pressed for time, he glances at his wristwatch and realizes the eleven o'clock service is coming up shortly. Princess also acknowledges the time and reads the short note he slipped her while David and her brother continue what they would call male bonding. The note read that the second half of the states fundings will be in May 15th, so she needed to be free to work the books to show where the first half of the $125,000 had went. Before the pastor got a chance to leave, she hugged him while whispering in his ear everything is going to be taken care of and for him not to worry about a thing.

"What was that all about?" Prince asked when seeing how his sister perked up while hugging the pastor.

"Oh nothing," she answered softly with a dreamy look in her eyes.

"Now come on, Sis. You know we know each other better than we know ourselves. Looks like to me my baby sister has a crush on the pastor."

Tabitha blew her whistle at ten forty-five and all the kids made their way back to their parents. Baskets of dyed boiled eggs and chocolate bunnies were in the kids' hands as the sparks of glee filled their eyes from having so much fun. The teenagers were also full of smiles. As they entered back into the chapel, Tabitha stood at the main entrance and received endless compliments from all of them. Easter Sunday turned out to be a great blessing for the youth ministry, so all she can say is, "Thank you, Jesus, for everything being done in decency and in order."

David stepped to the podium when everyone was seated and greeted the church once again with a great Happy Easter. Amy was just about to sit in her usual seat when David called her to the pulpit to start the eleven o'clock service with a prayer from his wife.

Amy walks over and takes his hand for help onto the stage and then is handed a microphone from one of the ushers. The words that fell from her lips flowed from her spirit like the sweet water that came from the rock Moses struck in the wilderness for the children of Israel. Silenced engulfed the great structure as each word touched the depths of the congregation's souls. When she said "Amen," Pastor Grace hugged her and wiped the tears from her eyes with his handkerchief. An usher came and escorted her off the stage so that the pastor can bring the word in spirit and in truth.

"This morning, church, I would like not to bring to you the traditional Easter message of Jesus dying and rising from the dead for our sins; but instead speak about why Jesus died for us when in truth we didn't deserve it." Pastor Grace grips the side of the marble on top of his podium before opening his Bible to the New Testament. "Could the Temple of Christ please stand and turn your Bibles to Luke 23:39–43." David pauses for a brief moment and continues when hearing the fluttering of pages cease. "And the Scripture reads: 'One of the criminals who hung there hurled insults at him. "Aren't you the Messiah? Save yourself and us!" But the other rebuked the first man's selfish statement by saying, "Don't you fear God, since you are under the same sentence? We are being punished justly, for we are getting what our deeds deserve. But this man has done nothing wrong." Then he said, "Jesus, remember me when you come into your kingdom," Jesus answered him, "Truly I tell you, today you will be with me in Paradise. Amen and amen.""'

"Amen" came from all the rows of chairs in agreement to the Scriptures Pastor Grace read as they sat to hear today's Word from God. "I titled this message in the exact words of our Lord Jesus Christ. 'Truly I tell you, today you will be with me in Paradise.' See, church, today a lot of Christians are going to agree to disagree about the Word of God I'm about to preach this Easter morning. But then, on the other hand, some of us are going to let the word of God take root in our hearts and bear fruit recognizing exactly what Jesus the Son of Man and God did on Calvary that day. To be blunt, church, I honestly believe Jesus Christ didn't want to hang on that cross and die for the sins of the world. I say this because as the son of man, would you die for me if I didn't deserve it?"

The Temple of Christ shook their heads no when thinking about dying for someone who is sinful by nature. "We must also understand that if Jesus didn't ask the father not to die for us then laying down his life for the world would have been easy and therefore he wouldn't have endured one of his final temptations as man from Satan. Now let's move on to him being the Son of God. Jesus Christ the only begotten Son of God the Father, which makes him a God in the image of his daddy, could walk away from his death on the cross at anytime he had chosen too. I say this because if God the Father can do what he wants to do then God the Son can do the same. We must realize that there is no wrong but only right when it comes to being a God. One, Jesus was sinless from the beginning and his death was unjustly. And two, Jesus said out of his own mouth in John 10:17, 'The reason my Father loves me so much is because I lay down my life -only to take it up again.' He went on to say in verse 18, 'That no one takes it from him, but he lays it down on his own accord.'"

"The reason why I read the Scripture Luke 23:39–43 today is because I believe that it troubled Jesus's spirit that we the people of the world never accepted him for who he truly is. Which is Jesus, the Son of the living God. It all goes back to him being in the garden crying and sweating drops of blood begging his father three times to take the cup of death away from him. Please note, church, that this is the only recorded prayer in the Bible Jesus prayed for himself, and God chose not to answer him but remain silent. It was at this time I think Jesus looked back on his three years of ministry and seen only people who wanted to see, walk, hear, and be healed of incurable diseases. Some even asked him to raise the dead and the list goes on and on. 'Father, if you are willing, take this cup from me.'"

Pastor Grace falls to one knee as if he is Jesus while quoting the famous Scripture.

"Jesus was so anguished that night that the Father had to send his angels to strengthen his son in this time of grief, but still remained silent throughout each petition. 'But, Daddy, I can bless them with eternal life and so much more, and yet all they ever desire from me is to bless them with what will surely die.'" Pastor Grace is now on both his knees speaking into the air what he thinks Jesus was feeling at that time. Standing, he turns to the church and says, "'Never the less, not my will Father, but your will be done.' Once again I ask, 'Why did Jesus die for us when we clearly didn't deserve it?'"

Everyone in the church are sad from how the pastor revealed what Jesus may have been feeling at that present time. "In Luke 23:43, 'The man on the cross deserved all the punishment placed upon him that treacherous day for his crimes. It is this same man who could have asked Jesus for anything in faith and Jesus most likely would have granted it to him because he never shows partiality.' He could have said, 'Jesus, thy Son of God, please take me off this cross and I will sin no more.' No!" David exclaimed pointing into his Bible. "What he said was, 'Remember me when you come into your kingdom.' It is at this moment I believe Jesus grasped why his father remained silent when he prayed to him his heart out. Why you ask? Because if one person can see Jesus as the Son of God who can bless them with eternal life, then Pastor Grace, Deacon Cotton, Bro. Chuck, Tabitha, and the church to come can as well. This sinful man on the cross next to our Lord made Jesus Christ smile during a time of suffering. It is this same man who gave him that extra nudge to cry out loud in verse 46, 'Father, into your hands I commend my spirit.' The Bible goes on to say that after those words was spoken from Jesus mouth, he gave up the Holy Ghost taking him and the sinner on the cross with him to paradise. My prayer is that something was said here today in the Temple of Christ to help everyone understand why Jesus suffered, died, and rose from the dead on Easter Sunday. Amen, and Deacon Cotton will open up the doors of the church and dismiss all of you. Farewell, and please drive safe to wherever you're spending this glorious Easter day."

Everyone in the congregation stood and gave a round of applause as the pastor walked down the center aisle toward the main exit of the church. Men and women on both sides of the aisle reached out to shake his hand and commend him for dissecting the word of truth so that everyone can understand it. Amy is in the foyer when he came through the double doors. All she can say is, "David that was amazing," because she hadn't heard or seen him preached that way in a while. What's even more ironic is that he hasn't heard himself preach like that in a while either.

Amy and David stood next to each other greeting all the guests who were released first. A parting gift of a white bag with a pocket-sized Bible, a card, and some Hershey Kisses inside it is handed to each family as they exited the building. When everyone was gone, except for the cleanup crew, Amy pulled the pastor into her arms and said, "I love you, David Grace, and you never stop ceasing to amaze me." David kissed his wife as if it is the last kiss they would share together. "I love you too, Amy, always have and I always will."

Sunday's afternoon sunlight is waiting for the both of them when they stepped outside onto the sidewalk. Amy and David are parked in their assigned parking spots, so the two of them walked hand in hand with some pep in their steps to get out of the heat that's starting to make itself known. They both agreed to drive straight home because Amy has been waiting all day to give her husband the Easter dinner she had made earlier. Before leaving, David lets her know he will be a few minutes behind her so that she can get everything prepared just the way she wants too.

Amy takes off as soon as he shuts her car door. When she gets to the end of the parking lot, she toots her horn as she turns and quickly hurries to their home. David follows behind her but not as much as in a hurry and therefore loses Amy when she merges into traffic at the end of the corner.

He is enjoying everything about today while he takes the long way home through the small city of Beaumont. His windows are halfway down so the air is sending strands of his light brown hair over his Oakley shades. The digital clock on his dash tells him he's given his wife enough time to have dinner ready but to be safe he stops at a Speedy Stop for some gas.

"Her time is up," David said aloud while tightening his gas cap. The gas station he filled his car up at is on the side of the highway so he jumps inside his car and slams down on the gas pedal. His car is at 90 mph in the matter of seconds as he switched from lane to lane down I-10. "What good is it having a muscle car if you can't flex your muscle every now and then?" he asked, to his rearview mirror while letting off the gas pedal to slow down to the speed limit.

Lux is running around the front yard of their high-priced mansion with dirt all over his paws and grass in his jet-black hair when he gets home. The garage door is up so David pulls up next to her SUV wondering, *Why is everything in disarray?* When he opens his driver's door, Lux frantically jumps into his lap quivering as if he's been outside all day. "Where is your mother, Luxy, because Daddy has a bone to pick with her? Easter or no Easter."

David presses the garage remote on the wall and enters into his home with Lux wrapped in his arms. Before closing the door behind him he makes sure the garage door is operating properly. The short hallway from the garage is only a few feet long so he turns the corner ready to give Amy a piece of his mind.

"Amy!" David bellows when noticing that his wife is unconscious with her hands tied behind her back to a kitchen chair. Suddenly, a sharp pain ranged from the side of his head followed by a rainbow of stars and complete darkness covered him. David is out cold and to make matters worse, he should have seen it coming from all the signs.

"Wake up, Mr. Grace.," a voice said. "It's time for you to wake up." The voice waves a tube of ammonia underneath his nose to bring him into full consciousness.

David shakes his head in disbelief praying it is all a dream but the thought vanishes when he sees Amy still out like he found her earlier.

"What is this all about?" he asked still trying to gain his thoughts. "And what do you guys want from us?"

"Well, David, it's good that you asked those two questions." The man who has been doing all the talking so far said. "First thing's first, my name is John and my partner's name here is Doe. Together we are John Doe. Get the picture?" The other guy chuckled while standing with his gun to his side. "My partner Doe here is a very smart guy but he doesn't like doing a lot of talking. What that means is that any questions you have you will address only to me. Now the answer to your second question is, *your* money, Pastor Grace." John stressed the word your. "Your money, Pastor David Grace, is what we want from the two you," he repeats.

"Anything, I'll give you anything. Just please let us go Mr. John or whoever you are." David looks around for Lux who must've went and hid when he was knocked out.

"As you can see, David, we've done a lot of homework on you and Mrs. Grace because if we didn't we wouldn't be standing here in this highly secured mansion of yours. Right!" Mr. John gets in David's face and waits for an answer but doesn't get one. "Like I said earlier, Mr. Doe here is a very smart man and he has been monitoring all your e-mails and bank statements for the past six months. What brought you to our attention is that two months ago you had a pricey wall safe installed by Lock Safe in your office and shortly after $250,000 was withdrawn from one of your accounts. What's even more puzzling is that we couldn't find any other accounts, which includes your church, where it could have been deposited. So that led us to believe you have it here in that high-priced safe of yours." John snatches David by his arm and stands him to his feet. "And please don't try nothing stupid because we don't want anything to happen to that pretty little wife of yours."

David's mind is in a complete enigma right now, and for the first time since he could remember, he doesn't know what to do. The only three things he's figured out is: One, John is a Caucasian male with dark gray eyes and Doe is African American with dark brown eyes. Two, the two of them are smart and has done this numerous times before. And three, they both mean business so it's best to cooperate.

"Hurry up!" John yells pushing David in the back with the barrel of his pistol nearly knocking him to floor.

"Okay, okay! Just promise me when you get your money you'll be on your way."

John doesn't reply to his question, hoping his silence scares David enough to open his safe faster. For years, John and Doe has been monitoring the Internet while robbing people and not once had they had any casualties. Most of the time the victims realized they've been outsmarted and comply willingly wanting everything to be over with quickly. But then there's other times when they will have some dummy wanting to mess up a perfectly good plan. That's when Mr. John has to let his girl Nina Ross slap them around a few times with her steel hand and get everything back in order.

The picture of his deceased grandmother that covered the wall safe is already down when he steps inside his office. John pulls his bowie knife from his side and cuts the zip ties from David's hands. As he stands there with both weapons in his hands, he tells his victim to open the safe. John would have asked him for the combination to open it himself but David's thumbprint has to be applied first before you can punch in the numbers. While David is opening the safe, John puts his knife back into its sheath and pulls a black bag from his back pocket. "Good job, Pastor Grace, and I couldn't have done it better myself," John said, motioning for him to stand in the far corner.

"David!" Amy screams when she finally awakes from being hit over the head. "David! David! Where are you?"

The sound of Amy's panic-stricken voice causes Lux to start barking loud as he can from what seems to be a closet the perpetrators have put him in.

"Amy!" David yells back. "I'm here, baby. Please be quiet! It's almost over with, honey."

"David hel—!" A loud thud comes from the living room before Amy could finish her fearful cry for help.

Amy is out again and David knows it. Pushing off the wall, he lunges into Mr. John with all his strength. John drops the gun from being caught off guard but quickly recovers his footing. David is no pushover of a match because fear can sometimes bring out the best fighter in a person. The only problem is that fighting is what John lives to do. They both are an even match until David kicks John in the groin causing him to land on the nine millimeter that was out of sight. Right when David is in midair to pounce on top of him, John rolls over and pulls the trigger.

David doesn't feel the shot from the adrenaline flowing through every inch of his body. Finishing what he started, he continues to tussle with his assailant until he becomes weak from the bullet lodged into his abdomen. With what strength he had left, he ripped the ski mask from John's face. John pushes David up off him and realizes he has to do something he's never done before. As he stands to his feet, he looks David in the eyes and said, "Please forgive me, Pastor Grace," before firing two times into his chest.

John put his mask back on then he and Doe took the money and ran out the back door. After jumping numerous backyard fences, they finally ended up at their getaway car. Mr. Doe had to drive because John is still in shock that he had to kill the preacher for seeing his face. Nervously, he takes off his mask and tossed it to the backseat with his pistol.

Doe is the first to speak when they are almost on the other side of town. "I'm sorry, Robert, but I'm out."

"You're out. What do you mean you're out?" Robert exclaims still trying to understand what just happen.

"What I mean is that I didn't sign up to be killing people for money. Especially not no damn preacher!"

"So you really think I wanted to kill that man, Nate?"

"No. I mean I don't know!" Nate said evasively. "I guess what I'm trying to say is that I'm done with all this you dig. And you should be too after what happened today." Nate's response is cold but true so Robert takes his words seriously. "It's time for us to lay low and pray nobody heard those gunshots, or even worse, saw us leaving that house."

Meanwhile, David is crawling along the floor coughing up blood as he uses everything he have left in his tank to get to Amy. His stomach and his chest is like a paintbrush painting a picture of a red road along the floor, starting from his office and ending wherever his strength will take him. Finally, he reaches the one person who has always loved him unconditionally besides his grandmother and rolls her over onto her back. Tears of pain fall from his eyes as he looks at her head lying in a pool of blood. *I should have gotten here sooner. It's all my fault,* he thinks, replaying the last time they kissed in the foyer at church.

Using his weak arms, he pushes his upper body up and flops his head down upon the center of her breast. A heartbeat pounds heavily beneath her bloodstained blouse and causes him to smile because he knows that the love of his life is going to be all right. "I love you, Amy Grace. Always have and I always will," he mutters as the blackness of his pupils takes over his light gray eyes.

4

"**D**avid!" Amy ghastly screams from the bottom of her diaphragm. "David baby, please wake up!" Amy's hands are trembling but tied behind her back when she slides her slim body from underneath her husband's heavy head. Panting heavily from the tragic events earlier, she begins to gasp for air when she notices he is lying in blood that he has coughed out his mouth. Using her legs, she presses her back against the nearest wall and pushes with all her might until she's on her feet. "David love," Amy said softly still wheezy from the two blows to the back of her head. "David baby, please say something."

David stares into the blood-stench air when Amy squats to look into the abyss of his lifeless eyes. "God, no!" she screams running to the front door nearly slipping in his blood along the floor. With her hands still behind her back, she manages to turn the knob and open the door. A car's headlights are turning down her street so she races down the steps into the grass toward the vehicle slowing down.

The sun is going down and the moon that is almost above her give Amy a sense of what time it is. "Help! Please help me!" she yells over and over while her heart is pounding in her chest like a bass. The headlights stop directly in front of her, right before Amy's legs stopped supporting her weight.

"Amy, what's wrong and where's David?" her friend Tabitha said as Amy blacks out in her arms from shock.

"Where am I?" David asked into the darkness that surrounded him. "Amy!" David remembers his last thoughts and in haste he rolls off what seems to be a table trying to find his wife. His hands and knees breaks his fall, but for some reason he doesn't feel a jolt of pain.

Crawling along the floor in the pitch-black room, he finds a wall and stands placing his back against it. As he slides his feet further and further along the perpendicular seam, a small beam of light shines from around the corner. David doesn't know what the source of the light is, so he peeks quickly around the edge of the wall he's been following. What he finds is two circles shining bright through a pair of swinging double doors. *Amy!* he thinks as he runs through them as if they were not there.

David emerges in a hallway and the light that shined bright while he was in the darkness is not as bright as it was before. "Where in the hell am I?" David asked himself as he walked in a hall with a black-and-white checkered floor. "And where in the hell is Amy?"

The hallway he is walking on turns into a ramp with a small pitch ending at an elevator that reads basement. Before he can push the button on the elevator, a Caucasian nurse with a stethoscope hanging from her neck comes from out of nowhere and presses up. David remains silent because the lady is rude and acts as if he is not there. When the doors open, he is still a gentlemen and allows the woman to go in first.

The short elevator ride put a name to the place where he's been walking around clueless. As soon as he stepped inside the elevator, he read the control panel and it said Baptist Memorial Hospital. He didn't have to press a floor level because Nurse Heidi, at least that's what her name tag had on it, is going to the ground level. When the doors separated, he prayed he would find someone to help him get to the bottom of all this chaos.

People are everywhere when David stepped foot onto the shiny waxed floor. Doctors and nurses are trying to get to where they need to be while others are sitting waiting patiently to be attended to. For a brief moment, David forgets what his mission is, but quickly snaps back to reality when he sees a man letting his wife cry on his shoulder. The clerk's line has three people in it so he walks to the end of the line hoping it will be his turn to speak soon. "Two down and one to go," he said to himself in low voice.

Finally, the couple in front of him is giving instructions in what to do next so he steps to the desk but the clerk puts her head down and begins writing endlessly. "Excuse me, miss, but can you tell me if you have an Amy Grace here?" The nurses looks up only to scan the sitting area and starts to write again. *This hospital is rude,* he thinks recalling how Ms. Acu'na treated him when he visited Princess Jackson. "First, the nurse on the elevator and now the clerk."

Suddenly, David's eyes catches Bro. Chuck entering the elevator with some flowers at the end of the hall. "Bro. Chuck! It's me, Pastor Grace!" David yells trying to catch the elevator doors before they closed. Nothing is going his way today because he is two seconds too late.

Standing there dumbfounded, he guesses that the only person Bro. Chuck is coming to visit is his wife Amy because he is okay. The thought of her not being severely hurt made his nerves rest a little bit. Following the floors above the elevator doors, David becomes overwhelmed with joy when seeing the elevator stopped on level three. *Oh hell, I'll just take the stairs,* he thought turning around to find the staircase directly behind him.

Level three is quieter and a little less busy than the ground level he just left from. The stairs he speedily climbed should have left him out of breath but to his surprise his lungs and heart feels as if he's slowly walked them. Scanning the floor for a service desk, David looks at the names on the room doors to see if Amy Grace is on any of them. Walking a little faster, he motions with his hand to stop a nurse rolling a couple of IV bags. Before she can respond, Deacon Cotton catches his eye leaving a room halfway down the hall in front of him.

The deacon's head is low and his eyes are puffy like he's been crying all day. "Is Amy okay?" he asked approaching cautiously. Deacon Cotton only shakes his head from left to right while hugging his Bible as tight as he can.

Amy's door is left opened so he enters slowly hoping for the best. The first thing he notices are two members from his church sitting in the only two seats in the room. Bro. Chuck is on the left side of her hospital bed holding her hand praying for physical and spiritual healing for his wife. Tabitha is on the right side of Amy trying her hardest to hold back her faucet of tears so that she can be strong for her friend whenever one of Amy's outbursts of grief starts to set in. David becomes sad because it should be him consoling her and not their friends. Feeling out of place, he quietly walks to the window and takes a seat on the sill.

Where have I been all this time and why is nobody talking to me? David thinks while staring into the few stars of the black sky. *And why was I in the basement and not with my wife?* Staring at the lights on the ancient sundial below in the grass, David for the first time tries to add up Easter Sunday from the beginning.

He remembers Amy staying home this morning to make dinner and him preaching a message on why Jesus died on the cross for us. He then remembers Princess had a twin brother named Prince he never knew existed. His dog Lux pops in his head next running scared through the front yard when he got home. Thinking a little further, horror flashes through his mind when he sees the white man's dark gray eyes standing over him with a pistol.

"Excuse me, Mrs. Grace," a doctor in her scrubs said entering the room holding a box. "Sorry to bother you and your family at such a sad time but here are your husband's belongings." The doctor tries to hand the box to Amy but she leans her head onto Tabitha's shoulder and begins to cry. "If you can just sign right here." Bro. Chuck stops the doctor before she can finish her sentence and signs the property release forms. "Thanks and once again I'm sorry for your loss. If you would like to view your husband's body he will be in the hospital morgue in the basement. Please get with one of the nurses before going down there and they will have someone accompany you to where he is at."

"Amy baby!" David shouts while trying to grab his wife's hand but can't. "Amy, Tabitha, Bro. Chuck, I'm right here so how can I be dead?" David is trying his hardest to get anyone's attention but no one hears him or sees him. He stops his efforts and thinks, "I'm dead?" while rubbing his hand across his chest and face. "I don't feel like I'm dead," he said to the ears in the room that are not listening to him. Stepping back, David notices his fingertips from his hands are red from touching his shirt. Next, he looks into the window and tries to find his reflection only to see everybody in the room except for himself. "No Lord this can't be!" he screams, running over to Amy's bedside to try and hold her hand again. "Please God don't let this be for real," he said to the ceiling but reality tells him that his death is the only explanation to how nonchalant everyone is acting.

For the next hour, David paces the floor telling himself that he can't be dead because if he were he'll be in heaven with his grandmother. As members from his church came and went to pay their respects, he stood in front of each of them hoping someone would acknowledge his presence. When the members faded into only Bro. Chuck and Tabitha, Amy's tears dried up and what is surreal she now understands is real.

"Tabitha and Bro. Chuck," she said straightening her blond hair with her fingers.

"Yes, Sister Grace?" Bro. Chuck is the first to respond because he is the one who has been getting her what she needs while Tabitha's been staying by her side.

"First, I want to thank the both of you for putting up with me today. Especially you, Tabitha. I don't know how

I could have handled David's death if you wouldn't have showed up to my house when you did."

"That's what friends are for, Amy," Tabitha replied patting the back of Amy's hand.

"We love you and your husband, Mrs. Grace. Not only us but also the entire congregation of the Temple of Christ does also. From the day I signed up to be a servant of the Lord in our church I always was glad to be a part of something good in our community. I promise that you and your husband's work will continue to flourish into the pastors to come through the ages."

"Thank you, Bro. Chuck, because my spirit truly needed to hear that."

Amy closes her eyes and said a breath prayer to herself. When she said "amen," she never felt more ready to do what she didn't want to do. "I'm sorry but it's getting late and I want to see my husband before the morgue closes at ten thirty."

"Would you like one of us to go with you?"

"I'll be okay, Tabitha. Besides, you two have done more than enough already. Now go home and get some rest."

"Are you sure, Mrs. Grace?" Bro. Chuck stands and stretches his legs.

"Yes, I'm sure and thanks again for being so kind and patient with me."

Bro. Chuck and Tabitha catch the drift that Amy wants to be alone with her husband one last time. Before exiting, they both tell her to call them if she needs anything no matter what the hour may be.

"God bless you, Mrs. Grace," they both said as the room became silent when the door closed behind them.

Facing the music, Amy picks up the phone and dials the operator. David is standing next to her contemplating what he should do when he comes face to face with his body. Staying dead is not an option, so his plan is to do whatever it takes to get back into his body. *I know it's a long shot,* he thinks. *But if God wanted me dead, I wouldn't be standing here next to my wife,* he thought anxiously waiting for the nurse to escort Amy to the basement.

"Excuse me," a lady said entering Amy's room. "My name is Nurse Heidi, and I'm the head nurse over the basement's mortuary. To my knowledge, you're Mrs. Grace, and my assistant told me you wanted to see your husband before our department closed for the night."

"Nurse Heidi." David remembers how rude Nurse Heidi was earlier but realizes she wasn't being rude at all because he's dead.

"Yes, ma'am, that's true," Amy replied slipping a white T-shirt over her head that one of the women brought her from church.

"I'll be right outside the door whenever you're ready, Mrs. Grace." Nurse Heidi closes the door and waits patiently for her to come out.

In the mirror, Amy wipes her face with a soapy towel hoping to wipe away the redness from under her eyes and from around her nose. When seeing that her thoughts were absurd, her blue eyes began to water, but she uses every ounce of her strength to make sure that her eye glands remained closed. "Oh, David, why did you have to leave me so soon?" she said to the women in the mirror as she turns the lights off in the bathroom and goes to meet Nurse Heidi.

David walked the familiar walk to the elevators behind the two women wanting Amy to know that he hasn't left her alone during these dark hours of her life. Nurse Heidi is kind but her face is cold from the years of staring death in the face almost every day. He wished their friend Tabitha would have stayed as a crutch to lean on but Amy wanted to view his body by herself. All he can do now is pray that when whatever he is now meets the person he was before; the two of them come together and become one once again.

The elevator doors opened and the sign painted on the wall have a big black arrow pointing to the right with "morgue" stenciled above it. Nurse Heidi is only doing her job and David is invisible, so Amy is left preparing herself to experience what she thought she would never have to experience this soon in her life. The silence and stillness from the short elevator ride continued to flow around the three of them as they walked down the ramp stopping at a pair of swinging doors with two perfect circled windows inside them.

Nurse Heidi slides her badge through a keypad and the door's hinges are released so that they can swing freely. A motion detector senses movement and the lights turn on automatically. David's mind is starting to understand how this room's lights and locking mechanism works. Perceiving that the lights came on because of movement, he realizes that the doors he is now entering, are the same doors he ran completely through without bulging them at all.

Three bodies lay on three separate stainless steel tables. The only thing that are covering the bodies is a clear blanket of plastic. Nurse Heidi goes to the feet of the first body closest to them and checks the toe tag only to read that Charles Henderson is not the man she is looking for. Going on to the next table, Nurse Heidi raises the plastic, and before she can read the tag, Amy recognizes her husband's short pinky toe. "That's David, Ms. Heidi," she said sadly while closing her eyes and taking in a deep breath. The nurse checks the toe tag anyway to confirm Amy's strange identification tactics. Removing the plastic from his face, she gives Amy the clearance to see David one last time before his body becomes evidence in the ongoing police investigation.

"He's all yours, Mrs. Grace. I'm sorry for what all you endured today, and I pray that Jesus's peace be upon you during the days you miss being with your significant other. I know I'm no friend or relative but I'll be right here if you need my help to get through this."

Amy only nods her head to Nurse Heidi's friendly gesture. Stepping forward, her shoes feels like blocks of cement so she stops and tells herself that she can do this. David hasn't tried anything miraculous because he doesn't know where to begin coming back from the dead. Another reason for his delay in rising from the dead is because David is just as terrified as Amy at seeing himself upon the table. What's funny is that the only plan he's come up with is from the Walt Disney fairy tale, *Sleeping Beauty*. *If I can just get Amy to kiss me, maybe I will wake up and all this will be over with,* he thought looking into his pale white face.

"David," Amy said taking the final step in the longest shortest walk of her life. "I don't know what happened in our home today but what my heart is telling me is that the reason I'm standing here, my love, is because you would never let anyone hurt me. You were always so protective over me and for that I'm thankful. I'm sorry I couldn't have done more to help you because maybe we would both be alive if I did. You are my hero, David Grace, and I will go to my grave professing that until we meet face to face again. At least one thing good came out of this baby." Amy lifts the thick plastic and grabs his ice-cold hand while he is wondering what good can come out of him being dead. "Tell Grandma Grace and Jesus I said hi and according to the time in heaven, I'll be seeing all of you shortly."

Her words of love were like poetry out of the book, *Songs of Solomon.* Nurse Heidi stood in the background wiping her glossy eyes as she listened to Amy pour her heart out over the man she will never get to hold in her arms again. Almost nine years the fire in their lamp have been burning only for it to be blown out over a dollar that will be spent tomorrow. Nothing makes any sense as a tear rolls out the corner of her eye down to the top of her lips. "Good-bye, Pastor David Grace, I will never forget you and I will always love you," Amy said leaning over to give her husband one last kiss.

"Please God let this work." David shuts his eyes and prays as Amy's lips come within a half an inch to his corpse mouth.

"David!" A male's voice calls with authority from the hallway.

"Huh? Hello. Who is that just called my name?" David replies with joy. "Come out and make yourself known. I know you hear me because I heard you."

Everything is different when he opened his eyes. The lights are off and the only light shining is from the two circles in the swinging doors he entered. Only this light is not like the light when he woke up in the morgue. This light is ten times brighter and has fish scales of color floating through it.

Looking back at Amy, his eyes become wide when he sees she is frozen, hunched over his body with her lips pressed against his. Not only that but also the nurse is frozen too with her head bowed as if she is a praying doll. He doesn't know what has happened because time has completely stopped. The voice that called from the beautiful beacon of light is not answering him, so the only thing he can do is investigate its source. Besides, his Sleeping Beauty plan only worked for Prince Phillip in the cartoons.

Amy is stuck in time and David realizes that it's not fair for her to be that way because of him. He doesn't know if finding who or what is shining the mesmerizing light will put everything back to normal, but at least it's better than anything he's come up with thus far.

Leisurely walking to the edge of the fluorescent beams, he sticks his hand into the glitter of colors and concludes everything is safe. After removing his hand quickly, he sees that his arm feels tingly and it is glowing up to his elbow. "It's either now are never," he said looking back at his wife one last time before thrusting himself into the center of what looks to be sunlight.

Immediately, his body transfigured and he began to slowly move forward toward the swinging doors that once led to the hospital's hallway. As he stepped closer, the doors opened on their own letting him know the path in which he has chosen is the path in which he is supposed to take. When he placed his first foot inside the highly lit doorway, he thought about his church, money, cars, and even his dog Lux. When he placed his second foot inside the doorway, he thought about his love for Amy and how much he is going to miss her.

His eyes hadn't gotten a chance to adjust to his new sur-roundings when the doors slammed closed behind him and disappeared. After it was all over, David moved on into the next life and the clock on the wall in the morgue started ticking once again.

"I'm ready to leave now, Nurse Heidi. My time here is up. David is no longer with us anymore."

5

It took David's eyes longer than he had thought to see that the ground he is walking on is the shiniest piece of gold he's ever seen in his life. As he walked slowly, he drug his feet because a light fog hovered the surface around his legs. One foot ahead of him is all he can see and he hoped sincerely he isn't walking off the edge of a cliff or into danger. "David!" David keeps his mouth shut because the last time he asked the mysterious voice for a response he didn't receive an answer. Proceeding forward, the light in front of him became vastly brighter than the light surrounding him.

"David Grace!" David notices the authoritative voice sounding like rushing water is coming from the light that is becoming brighter as he walked. "It's me, Jesus Christ, the holy Lamb of God. Please step forward so that I, who am righteous, can judge you righteously!"

"Jesus!" David exclaims raising his hands while jumping for joy. "I made it! I made it to heaven!" He shouts falling to his knees and kissing the walkway of gold.

David stands, and out of nowhere a podium made of white marble with a ruby-red cross in the center of it is right in front of him. Jesus's eyes are like fire looking down on him and his face is like snow from all his glory shining off of his holy skin. The robe he is wearing is purple so that those standing before him can see him. A gold sash is hanging over his right shoulder and written on it in red letters are the twelve apostles' names who he taught while on earth. In his hands is a book and the title reads Grace. Jesus slams it down as if it is a gavel and turns the pages until he reaches the center of the book.

"Hello, Jesus," David said still overwhelmed with joy. "And thanks for accepting me into your kingdom." David's eyes have become fully adjusted to the endless cloudlike space around him, and he notices that Jesus is standing about twelve feet in front of pearly gates laced with gold.

"Hello, David Grace, your grandmother and mother never stop telling me about you."

My mother? David thinks looking to the entrance hoping to get a glimpse of her.

"Yes, your mother, David," Jesus said intuitively reading his mind.

David is a little embarrassed and becomes quiet when he realizes he has to watch what he is thinking. Jesus allows him to regain his composure before reading from the book with his last name on the cover of it.

"Today, David Grace, is the day my Father, who is the creator of heaven and earth, have called you to judgment concerning the things you've done under the sun with the gift of life he's blessed you with." Jesus thumbs through the pages and stops at a specific section in the book. "David, up until the time you received the name of your church you were on a path that made even the angels in heaven smile down upon you. It was on that day, five years ago in the summer, a seed was planted inside you that was not of me but of the wicked one. Everyone who has been keeping their eyes on you watched Satan plant the unrighteous seed in your heart but instead of you uprooting it, you did the exact opposite and allowed the seed to be watered."

"But, Jesus, I named my church the Temple of Christ after you." David tries to plead his case but is quickly stopped short.

"Be silent, David! Everything you want to tell me you should have told me before you stepped through those doors. And everything you could possibly think of I already know, so once again, be quiet, David!"

David retreats back into his shell when seeing Jesus's loving eyes become like a scorching fire.

"The Bible, which was written by the Holy Spirit through first the prophets and then the apostles, teaches you that my Father and I look at the heart. You, Pastor Grace, of all my Father's children should have known this better than anyone else. Now, a few minutes ago you interrupted me by professing how you named your church the Temple of Christ after me, but in truth you wanted to name your church the Temple of Grace after yourself. As a matter of fact, the only reason your church is called the Temple of Christ is because while you were at the courthouse the county clerk cringed when you told her the Temple of Grace followed by your last name. The small scrunching of her nose is what gave you the assurance that people may suspect your motives in becoming a pastor of my father's words. So you see, David, I know everything and nothing is hidden from me." Jesus flips a few more pages and continues. "Ah, Princess Jackson."

David's dimpled chin touches his chest when hearing Princess's name. Reason being, is because nothing is ever good when she is mentioned in anything that involves him.

"I know you know where I am going with this because your body language is screaming guilty as clear as day. But since what was in the dark is now coming into the light, I'll bring it verbally unto your attention anyway. If I'm not mistaken, I'll say about three years ago Princess Jackson was so-called "voted in" by the church as secretary to help you carry the load of all your pastoral paperwork. Is this correct, David?"

"Yes, Jesus, that is correct." David lifts his head to speak but lowers it again knowing where Jesus is going with this.

"If I may recall, Princess's name was not on any of the ballots, and Ms. Franklin won the vote by a landslide. So how is it, Pastor Grace, that the young Ms. Jackson won and not the elderly Ms. Joanna Franklin."

David doesn't say a word in hopes that Jesus will give him a pass on behalf of his silence.

"Could it be that you put her name in the election box and used your power as overseer of the church to place her into the position? Or could it be that the beauty of her physical appearance allowed who was unqualified to be superseded by the one who was well qualified? And we wonder why she was so infatuated with you from the beginning. As we can see, it is not by mere chance we are having this discussion so don't think for a second your cunningness can get you out of this one."

"But, Jesus!"

"Don't but Jesus me, Pastor! You knew from the book of 1 Timothy chapter 3 that as overseer of the church you must be beyond reproach, faithful to your wife, self-controlled, and not a lover of money or you may become conceited and fall under the same judgment as the devil. Also, in the book of Titus chapter 1, the Bible tells you as overseer you must love what is good, be upright, holy, and disciplined, holding firmly to the trustworthy message so that you can encourage others by sound doctrine while refuting those who oppose it. Need I say more?"

David shakes his head disappointed in how he mistreated the gospel since the day he took his position as the leader of the church.

"Let's not forget about your big Thanksgiving dinner that you supposedly gave for the poor and homeless in your community last year. Or better yet, your powerful Grace, One Prisoner At a Time ministry!" Jesus's voice changed from subtle to angry. "Lies, David! All of your good deeds were born in deceit and have now festered to the throne of truth!"

Jesus points his finger down upon David as his voice roared through the air ferociously. Reading a little further, Jesus said, "What about Mr. Freeman, David?" David shrinks at the sound of the mayor's name. "He is the man who blinded you and added to your demise since the day you met him. This is also the man who had you give and record the Thanksgiving dinner so that after being edited to his fancy he could use it to run for governor of Texas. And since you learned from the best you agreed to do it only if he agreed to sign the petition to get your Grace Ministries off the ground. After shaking of the hands, you promised him $50,000 a year until the grant expired and told him you'll be forever in his debt for his help in receiving the $250,000 from the state. What's so ironic to me is that only 15 percent of that money made it to the prisoners while the rest miraculously ended up in your accounts or your expensive wall safe."

"Lord Jesus, please have mercy on me! Did I not prophesy in your name, perform miracles in your name, and preach the gospel in your name?" David clasp his hands together in one solid fist praying Jesus will relent from the things he's done wrong and focus on what he's done that is good.

"David, you don't understand, I didn't write this book over your life. My father did and since we are one, he has granted me judge over it. He is truth just as I am truth so therefore whatever he writes I can only abide by it. Please understand that today is not the last day in which everyone will be judged according to if my father has written their names in the book of life. This judgment, David, is where you will spend your time of rest until that great day when the angels blows the mighty trumpets for the elect to be raptured into heaven." Jesus turns to the last page in the book and reads the words aloud God the father has written. "From everyone who has been given much, much will be required. And from the one who has been entrusted with much, much more will be asked. Depart from me, you workers of iniquity. I never knew you. The End!"

"What? No, this cannot be right, Jesus! Please, Jesus, talk to the father for me!" David falls prostrate with his forehead touching the ground. "Please, Lord, ask him to forgive me of my sins so that I can enter his rest!" David exclaims as his tears pour down upon his reflection in the gold.

"I'm sorry, David, but you had more than enough times to ask the father in my name for forgiveness," Jesus said with compassion. "When you died, it was me and the prayers of the righteous who gave you extra time to recognize your faults and amend them before the father. Instead, you decided to play God by trying to get back into your body. Your grandmother is the person who saw you wasn't comprehending what was going on, so therefore asked me to show you my glory. You, in turn, rejected what your eyes knew was true because your heart was still in the world with Amy."

"No, Lord Jesus! Please do not let this happen to me!"

"My Father's judgment is just and no one, not even his son can go against it." Jesus closes the book and said, "Please stand, because he who is righteous has judged righteously. My judgment is final."

David looked up from the small pool of tears over the golden surface and saw the podium that held his book is gone. Recognizing his fate, he stands wiping the tears from both his eyes. Naked is how he felt because there is no one there to hold him or say good-bye to before he goes to wherever his destiny holds for him. Staring at the glory before him, he looks past Jesus at all the different types of precious stones in the walls that surrounded heaven. The gate that stood directly in front of him read "Judah" in solid-gold letters. Between the pearl bars were two people in white robes who looked familiar, but Jesus's splendor is in front of them distorting his vision.

"David!" a young woman shouts with the sound of happiness in her voice. "Is that my son, David?" she asked reaching her arms through the space between each bar.

Jesus steps to the side and gestures with his hands that he may approach the holy city. "David, your mother and grandmother wants to see you before you move on to where light cannot commute with darkness. It is up to you if you desire to see them, but please know that they've been waiting earnestly to see your face again."

"Momma!" David runs to the gates and falls into his mother's opened arms. His grandmother is standing to the left of her daughter smiling because her prayers of them meeting each other have finally been answered. Nothing is said as they lovingly embrace one another only the way a mother and child can do.

His mother Ruth's eyes are sparkling with joy over the premature boy she gave birth to that has grown into a handsome man. She feels like she can be his daughter because her age had stopped at seventeen but her heart remembers the six months she carried him in her womb. Tears are on her cheeks from David's face pressing against hers as they hugged through the bars. Balling with disappointment, David notices that his mother or grandmother are not crying with him because he did not make it into heaven. Being a pastor, he then remembers Revelation 21:3–4. "They will be his people and God himself will be with them and be their God. He will wipe every tear from their eyes. There will be no more death or morning or crying or pain for the old order of things has passed away."

"David," his grandmother said, resting her right arm around his shoulders and left hand on the small of her daughter's back. "My dear grandson, David."

David begins to cry louder because his grandmother's words always could cut him to the bone whether they were good or bad. "Grandmother Grace, I'm sorry for letting you down and not being able to join you and mother in heaven. And I'm also sorry for using God's Word you taught me as a child for my own selfish gain."

"It's going to be all right, son. What's done is done," his grandmother said patting him on the back. "What you need to do now, Grandson, is have courage and never stop believing God is the author and finisher of all things of your past life or the life you are on your way to. I believe in you, David. I always believed in you, and I know that you are going to do the right thing when the appropriate time is presented to you."

"I believe in you too, Son, and I always loved you since the first time I felt your little feet kick me in my side." David's mother laughed softly while looking into her son's eyes.

Drying up his tears, he feels renewed because even though he's on his way to God knows where, he doesn't want to mess up his mother's and grandmother's happiness. Holding their hands, he cracks a smile on behalf that the two of them are safe in Jesus's warming brace. Staring into the holy city, a rainbow sits high in the sky crossing a river running down the center of it. On each side of the river are a line of trees full of fruit that his eyes have never seen before. Pastures of green grass with sidewalks of gold lead to different places along the roads heading into the city. Words can't describe its beauty or the divineness that he will never partake of.

In an instant, Jesus is standing with his loved ones and he comprehends that his time in heaven has come to an end. Not wanting to make a scene, he kisses both of his parents and steps back from out their arms. "I'm ready, Jesus, and thanks you for letting me say good-bye to my Grandmother Grace and my mother Ruth."

Suddenly, the light from Jesus Christ's holiness shot back like a lightning bolt trying to find a place to touch ground. When the light that shined before him came smaller and smaller until it reached the size of a faraway shiny dime, he felt alone again because God's glory is no longer in his presence. "Good-bye, momma," he said to himself as he looks around trying to find any sense of light in what has now become complete darkness.

The first thing he felt when the great Almighty turned the lights off is the unpleasant heat. "Where am I now?" he asked the blackness that he cautiously starts to walk through. Looking around, he sees nothing but the sky glowing like a dim pillar of fire giving him a small piece of hope to hold on to. Walking further, branches from trees break underneath his feet so he waves his hand from left to right trying to find the trees they broke off of. After minutes of what feels like fighting the dense air, the inside of his hands brush against a few tree trunks that are four feet in diameter. "What is this, a forest or something?" As the words came from his mouth, music of ancient tunes began to roam through the stillness of the air.

There in the absence of light, David slowly makes his way through the wilderness with his ears as his guide. The fire that spread across the sky allows him to see up close but not enough to walk at a steady pace. Attentive to his surroundings, he listens for any form of life but hears only notes from the playing of the lyre, harp, and flute growing more and more each step he took toward them. A cling from the clanging of a cymbal startles him when he notices the trees around him are only on each side of him now. He steps completely out of the wooded area and the dim light from above shines down on what appears to be a road. The music stops playing so he becomes as still as one of the trees until it starts playing again but in a different tune.

Continuing on to search for its source, he presses forward and finally finds an old cabin sitting to the side of the road. He stops in his tracks to contemplate if the cabin that he know is inhabited is safe or not to explore. Hotter and hotter he is getting so he waves his hands in front of his face, hoping for a gust of breeze to poke a hole in the bag of heat that is starting to suffocate him. Suspense and the wishful thinking of a fan, air-condition, or a cold glass of water makes him disregard the thoughts of danger, and causes his fist to knock rapidly on the wooden door.

"Come on. Come on, damn it. I know you are in there," he said shuffling his feet from side to side because his body is trying to conform to the unsettling heat. "Someone! Anyone please open the freaking door!" David shouts as his knocks become pounds to overshadow the music.

"Who goes there?" A deep voice asked from the other side of the thick door. The old hymns that graced the forest stopped and the male's voice shouts again. "I said who goes there? Who is it that is pounding on my door?"

At first, David's thoughts compel him to run for the hills but then he thought, *What hills?* Keeping his mouth shut, he ponders on how he should approach the first person he is going to meet in hell. "Should I stand my ground and speak up or should I hide and see if this man is my enemy." Before he can answer himself, the door swiftly opens.

"Who are you and why didn't you answer me when you knocked on my door? Please tell me that you are not deaf or dumb because you will not survive out here in Satan's jungle."

Caught off guard from the strange man's greeting, David puts together his next word carefully. "How do you do, Mister? My name's David."

"How do you do? Well, I's does just fine I guess!" the man said as his big belly begins to jump up and down in laughter before his face returned back to being serious. "Listen, boy. This is Hades and that friendly shit you're talking about ain't going to get you nothing around here but a quick ticket to the lake of fire."

David's eyes become wide when he sees the man is very serious in what he is saying. "What do you mean by the lake of fire? What, it gets worse than this?"

"You damn right it does." The man chuckles. "The name's KOG. It stands for keeper of the gate. Come in because my job is to give you some understanding about Sheol, also known as Hades."

6

Kog's cabin is creepy, and everywhere David looked a different medieval weapon hung on the wall. One wall had nothing but swords on it and another wall had only ancient spears positioned on stands on top of shelves. Walking along the boards that slightly shifted under his feet, David feels like a bull walking himself to be slaughtered.

"Now hold up, Kog." David stops and looks Kog in his bearded face. "What are all these weapons about? Are you about to hurt me or kill me?" he asked thinking to himself that was a dumb question because he is already dead.

Kog is beginning to become pissed off because here he is trying to help his foreign guest, and David's fearfulness may cause him to walk back out the door a sheep among wolves. It's been almost a century since he took his position as keeper of the gate, and during those years he's only had to send two people to the lake of fire. He remembered it like it was yesterday when they tried to ambush him on the very floor they are standing on. Replaying the standoff in his mind, Kog hopes this situation doesn't go sour because they too were frighten from being invited into his home after being sentenced to the pits of the graves. It was three altogether but one ran out the door when he seen Kog snap the necks of his buddies with his bare hands.

"First of all, David, let's get something straight. If I wanted to kill you, or shall I say send you to burn in the lake of fire, I would have done it a long time ago when your scary ass was banging on my door. Second, I know what you're feeling right now because believe it or not I too was found guilty and sentenced here to rot just like you. Yeah, yeah, you're probably thinking why me or better yet what did I do to deserve this? Well, David, that's not my problem and if you are as smart as you look, it shouldn't be yours either because like it or not we're stuck here until the last day when we will all be judged with the goody two-shoes in the sky. So sulk it up and get your shit together real fast like, or you're going to find yourself outside that door not knowing how to survive with all the assholes that are about to be gunning for your life!" Kog exclaims sticking his index finger in David's chest while getting into his face. "So what's it going to be, David? You can leave freely with no harm given or no harm taken. Or you can stay and listen to what I have to say to help you. I don't care what you decide but whatever you decide, do it quickly because my patience is growing smaller by the seconds with you."

David takes a few seconds to weigh his options and answers, "I'll stay," while rubbing the small dent in his chest from Kog's fat finger.

Motioning with his hand, Kog gives him the clearance to have a seat on his wooden couch. "I like you, David. Believe it or not, I really like you," Kog replied, before walking toward what looks to be a kitchen.

David takes a seat on the so-called "sofa" and feels a small pain from the hardness of the wood on his bottom. Shifting his butt for comfort doesn't help and he wonders if this is how Fred Flintstone felt when he came home from work every day. *Pain,* he thinks remembering how he couldn't feel a thing when he fell off the morgue's table.

Kog returned carrying an oval-shaped log about three feet long, two feet wide, and two feet thick. David could tell it had to weigh over 100 lbs by the way the black dust rose up off the floor as he dropped it down in front of him. Kog's 300 lb muscular but pudgy frame made the hand-made coffee table look like a bundle of twigs as he showed no strain when holding it as if it is nothing. Turning to go back toward the kitchen, David examined him more thoroughly to make sure Kog's speech wasn't just a hoax to get him to come inside so he can chop him to pieces with one of the swords on the wall. So far, everything's been kosher and besides being dead Kog seems to be an all right guy. At least from the outside looking in.

The first thing David noticed about Kog was his wool-like bushy hair that needed to be combed drastically and that his white face had speckles of black dirt around his forehead. *His clothes and walk is unique as well,* he thought, as he continued his observation while Kog dug through an iron chest tucked inside the bottom of a cabinet. Kog's shirt is a short-sleeved red flannel and his pants were solid black jeans that are clearly undersized.

His walk is swift but David couldn't comprehend how he can move at such a fast pace by only taking baby steps on his tippy-toes. A familiar face flashed in his mind as Kog walked back with a brown potato sack and a steel pitcher of what sounded like water swishing around inside of it. David couldn't hold his tongue any longer after Kog placed the bag and pitcher down and pulled a chair up to take a seat.

"Did you know you look like, walk like, and act like Mick Foley from WWE?"

"Mick Foley? WWE?" Kog repeats David's words trying to recall if he remembered the name when he was living. "Nope, can't say that I do."

"Come on. You never heard of Mick Foley aka Cactus Jack, aka Dude Love, aka Mankind?"

"Who was he? Or better yet, what was he if he had to keep to changing his name like that?" Kog opens the bag and pours the contents onto the massive log table.

"Anybody who's anybody knows who Mick Foley is." Nick pauses and says, "Where have you been all these years? In the Ice Age or something?"

"No, dick weed! If you haven't noticed, I've been in hot-ass hell for the past one hundred years wishing every day I was in the Ice Age." Kog lashes back to his idiotic comments.

"Sorry, sorry," David said raising his hands as if he's under arrest. "Just thought I'll bring some laughter up in this poorly lit place. And by the way, where did you get fire and kerosene from for your lanterns?"

"You want laughter? Well, ha-ha! Now there's your freaking laughter."

"Okay, okay I get it."

"I sure hope so because fun and games ended when God's light ran away like a train leaving you on the tracks in the middle of the night." Kog sifts through what looks like dark green fruits or vegetables and grabs two steel cups with no handles. Pouring two glasses of the clear substance from the pitcher, he said, "Drink up so we can get back to what you need to know about this godforsaken place."

"What is—?"

Kog raises his hand and stops him before he can finish speaking. "It's water, David. Nothing more and nothing less. Just plain old warm ass H20."

David senses that he's starting to get under Kog's skin and decides to keep his mouth shut for now before he overstays his welcome. Kog feels the change in David's demeanor and inwardly laughs because his angry lumberjack man from hell has broken yet another one who has entered Hades not ready for all the devils that are around every corner.

"Cheers," Kog blurts out into the silence.

"Cheers? Cheers to what?" David replied not wanting to say anything that might push Kog back over the deep end again.

"Cheers to a new life in complete darkness." Kog laughs loudly and his belly begins to shake reminding David of a jolly Santa Clause. "Come on, David. Raise your cup and have a drink with me."

At first, David thought cheering for being in the dark is stupid. But then he looked at Kog, the weapons on the wall, and the dingy cabin and realized that just as heaven is truth, hell, Hades, Sheol, or wherever he's at now is true also. It is at this very moment David adds everything up since he has left God's kingdom and understands what Kog has been trying to get through his thick skull since he stepped through his door. *I didn't make it into heaven, so therefore I must be strong and move forward,* he thought before raising his iron cup and saying, "Cheers to you too, Kog. Cheers to being in complete darkness." A loud thud sounded off the hardness of the steel cups as they both laughed together at the irony of the long road that lay ahead of him.

"David, I don't know what you did to get here and quite frankly I don't give a damn." David leans forward and listens wanting to know all the knowledge the keeper of the gate is about to give to him. "But believe me when I say, I do care if you make it down here or not. To tell you truth, you got lucky coming from God's glory by yourself because usually they're quite a few of you who come from heaven at the same time. When that happens, I just step outside my cabin and give them a crash course of what goes on around these neck of the woods. Why, you might ask, is because I trust no one after a few idiots tried to take me out for trying to help them, just like I am trying to help you."

"How can someone take you out if you are already dead?"

"Ah, I see you're starting to listen to me for a change and not just say anything that pops up in that peanut you have for a brain." Kog plucks the right side of his bushy head. "Remember earlier when I told you being friendly will get you a fast ticket to the lake of fire?"

"Yes."

Kog drinks another gulp of water and continues. "Well, David, down here we can't die because we are no longer in our mortal bodies anymore. The body you are in now is what I like to call a soul wrapped in skin that cannot die but can feel just as you felt when you were living in the world. The only difference is that you heal a whole lot faster and the pain doesn't last as long as it used too."

"So is that good or bad?" David asked wishing Jesus would relent on his decision and allow him to be with his mother were there is no pain or tears.

"Neither, because down here being hurt brings forth the worm of torment, which is Satan's most adored pet, to bring you to burn in the flames that are unquenchable and where there is weeping and gnashing of teeth."

"You mean the lake of fire that the Bible talks about continuously?"

"Yes, Mr. How do you do? My name is David," Kog replied sarcastically to let David hear how dumb he sounded earlier. "The lake of fire. That oversized crazed worm has everybody on their toes around here because Satan has programmed it to sense any soul that is blind and missing limbs that can hinder you from defending yourself. Hell, it evens shows up if you are a gimp. To make a long story short, be on your guard from this day on because Satan's desire is to play God and put us all in the fiery furnace a lot faster than the assigned day when we are supposed to be going there.

"So why doesn't everyone here come together as one and decide to live in peace so that the monster doesn't have a reason to display his presence?"

"Because it's not just the doomed souls you have to watch over your shoulders for, but also the demons, the mix breeds, night crawlers, those who sleep in the graves, and everything else Satan's unthinkable mind has in store for us. Not to mention the heat that rises and falls according to how much hate we stir up daily on his doorsteps."

"So what you're saying is that it's going to get hotter and that I have no choice but to fight or I will burn forever until my day of judgment again?"

"Hotter is an understatement to the temperatures that we get down here. Put it this way, what you're feeling right now is the coolest it's been in Hades for a long time. So you know what that tells me?"

"What?"

"That the fools outside these doors have been acting very badly lately and that your ass is as good as grass when you leave here."

"Leave. Why do I have to leave? Why can't I just stay here with you and keep you company?" David looks around the empty cabin and brings his eyes back to Kog. "If I'm not mistaken, it looks to me that you have enough room in here for one more."

Kog starts laughing and shakes all the weapons along the walls. His puffed-up chest rose abruptly nearly causing his wooden chair to tip over backward. "Now if that's not the smelliest piece of bullshit I have ever heard in my life." Kog straighten his posture and all four legs of the chair stood sturdily on the floor again. "You stay here with me," he continues to laugh. "Hmm, I wonder why I didn't think of that fifty years ago when a gang of girls who died on the beach in Paris showed up out of the blue!"

"Kog, I'm serious," David interrupts his time of glee hoping that Kog will let him stay with him until he's ready to be on his own.

"Kog, I'm serious," Kog repeats David's statements mocking him to the tee while continuing to laugh like there's no tomorrow.

"Kog, can you please stop laughing and answer me why is it that I can't stay here with you?"

Simmering down, Kog explains to him that being keeper of the gate is a solo job only. He couldn't answer why because he didn't know why. But what he did know is that no one is able to stay in his home pass a day after entering Hades. And two, tomorrow his cabin will vanish and end up somewhere else awaiting the next soul to come his way guided by his music from his 1800s phonograph.

"I'm sorry, old chap, but what you're asking is way out of my league." Kog waves his hands through the air as if he's reaching for the stars. "I wish it was that simple but it's not something that I can control. Like for instance this cabin."

"What about this cabin?"

"If you'll be quiet for a second I'll tell you what about this cabin." David presses his forefinger and thumb together and goes across his mouth with an imaginary zipper.

"This cabin is magical and only allows the keeper of the gate to abide in it. I don't know if Satan or God put it here but I do know that no one can come in here unless I invite them in and that it appears in different places throughout the outskirts of Hades whenever another soul is in need of knowledge concerning their new habitat."

"Is that how you are able to leave and get food or water without anyone breaking in?"

"Rightly said, and it also gives me time to keep my ears and eyes on things that is transpiring throughout the pits of Sheol."

Kog's conversation is intriguing to him because for the past few years of his life he hasn't had to listen to anyone who has had seniority over him. Or to anyone who was truly trying to help him. Listening intently, he sets his mind on not to miss any information on how to survive in a world where the number one rule is to hate your fellow brother instead of love your fellow brother. The latter is how his grandmother raised him, so hating someone for no reason is something he needed to learn quickly. If not, the worm of torment will soon be adding his soul with the rest of those doomed for turmoil.

"What is this?" David asks picking up one of the pieces of the dark green substance from the table. "Is it a fruit or a vegetable?"

"I guess you can say it's kind of both because it grows from a tree but nourishes our souls like a vegetable. Its source is called the tree of Zaqqum and it grows only along the boiling river of Raqueem. The natives called them zaqs for short."

"The boiling river of Raqueem?"

"Yes, you damn parrot. The boiling river of Raqueem. As a matter of fact, the water you're drinking right now comes from the river of Raqueem. Its temperatures are unspeakable and the only way you can draw from it is with an iron pitcher. Afterward, you must let the water cool down as much as possible in order to drink it. This water and this zaq are the keys to any obstacles you come to while out there among all these predators. This water and this here zaq can also heal your wounds faster than usual but only those that are not too traumatic or severe beyond repair. At the end of the day, it's like gold/money but at the same time a doctor when we are hurt. Not to mention eating from it regularly keeps us from aging."

"How is it that we age when we are considered dead?"

"Because this is hell, not heaven. You see, down here we don't get to eat from the tree of life which preserves our souls for eternity. Therefore, we age but not as we aged when we were living in our mortal bodies. Our aging process consists of one year for every ten years we are in Hades. That's why it's essential to eat from the tree of Zaqqum so that you can stay young and strong to defend yourself until that great day we are to be tossed into the fire. Now from what I've read in the dead scrolls the old keeper of the gate left behind for me to read, when we enter the lake of fire, whatever age you've taken on in Hades is reversed to the state you were in when Jesus sentenced you here from heaven."

"Wow," David said trying to devour Professor Kog's class of hell.

"Wow, is the correct word for all the steep walls you are about to be climbing starting tomorrow."

David winced when he heard the word tomorrow. Realizing that tomorrow will be soon be today, he stood to try another approach hoping that later he can convince Kog to stay a few extra days or perhaps forever.

"I've heard enough!" David stands and spread his legs while placing his hands on his hips as if he is Superman with his cape waving in the wind. "And I'm ready for whatever darts any evil thing down here can throw at me. I know this may be hard for you to believe, Mr. Kog, but I've won a fight or two back in my day. I also won the fencing tournament in my high school three years in a row." David walks over and grabs a dirk off the wall before going into his prized championship fencing stand.

"So all of sudden your name is Billy, middle name Bad, last name Ass," Kog said, turning his chair to face David standing behind him.

"Kog, can't you just hear me out on this and believe in me?"

"Believe in you! The only thing I'm believing in right now is that the heat has dropped to an all-time low. So what that means for you is that your fencing fighting championships better be as good as you say they are or—"

"I know, I know. My ass is grass."

Kog points his finger at him and smiles while acting like he's shooting a gun. David becomes a little sad because here he is pumping himself up to fight Satan's soldiers and all Kog can do is give him the wink and the gun instead of showing him some support. Sensing David's sadness, Kog explains to him that he can make it if he toughens up, keep his eyes and ears open, and never trust no one who says they are his friends.

"I tell you what I'm going to do, David," Kog said standing and placing his hand on his shoulder. "I see you've taken a fancy to that there dagger in your hand, so I'm going to give it to you. And since you were into fencing you can also have that chain mail hanging on the wall over the couch you were sitting on. I would give you my helmet, but it's too heavy for you to be carrying around and it will only slow you down if you need to make a quick exit from danger."

David walks over and pulls the chain mail off the wall and fastens it around his chest. Standing there in all his new war gear he looks down at himself in disbelief because just yesterday he was Pastor Grace and today he is David the dragon slayer. *If only I could go back in time,* he thought. *I promise I'll do everything different.*

"By the way, what is your name? Mine is Kenneth Dobbins."

"Grace. David Grace."

"Sorry for sending you mean vibes all day but you got to realize where we are and that the last time that only one person came from heaven the old keeper of the gate was beheaded defending him."

"So who became the new keeper of the gate?"

"You're looking at him."

"Oh, I didn't realize. I mean, I'm sorry for not putting it together when you told me the last keeper of the gate was beheaded."

"It's okay, I guess that's why I took a liking to you and made sure I didn't miss a thing in telling you anything that might help you on your journey."

"Thanks, Kog, and I'm sorry for not taking you seriously when you were only trying to help me with all that I'm about to endure."

Kog walks into the back room and return with an old jacket wrapped in a dirty T-shirt. Sitting it down at the arm of the couch, he squeezes it and pats it a few times and said, "This is the closest I got to a pillow in here, so get some rest because you are going to need it for tomorrow."

David takes a seat back on the hard piece of wood Kog called a couch and extends his hand for a handshake of thanks. Kog tells him to put his hand down and for him to remember the golden rule about no one in Hades is your friend. Lying his head on the T-shirt, David rests his long legs over the armrest, praying that in the morning he can convince Kog into letting him hang around a little longer. Yawning from being up for two days, he closes his eyes and asks Kog to blow out the lanterns shining in his face.

"Sorry, Mr. Grace, but I can't because they burn forever. It's fire from the volcanic geysers of Tanctum throughout Sheol.

"Volcanic geysers?"

Kog takes the lanterns off the wall and brings them in the room with him. "Get some rest, David, you have all eternity to learn everything you need to know that I haven't told you already about the devil's playground."

7

"Kog!" David screamed to the top of his lungs as he sat up on a bed of black gravel. Covering his mouth with his hands, he squints his eyes to look for predators through the abundance of tall trees that are surrounding him. Last night, he fell asleep on the most uncomfortable piece of furniture Bedrock has ever made, but today it is as if it was all a dream. Reason being, is because the T-shirt and dirty jacket he laid his head upon as a pillow has now turned into the dagger and the chain mail he thought he went to sleep in.

Staring into the forest, he stands and dusts himself off trying to figure out where in the world is the ancient cabin in the woods or the keeper of the gate he thought took a liken to him. Out of nowhere, before he can get his thoughts together, his left hand is engulfed with excruciating pain.

"Ooww!" he yelled. "Ooww!"

David grabs his left hand and raises it to his face to see what is making him feel like he is being branded like a cow. Gazing into his burning hand dubiously, a circular figure begins to become clearer as his hand starts to cool down. The word "Sharia" is what he makes out as he reads the letters inside a compass inside the palm of his hand.

"Sharia," he said wondering who or what has placed a working compass in the palm of his hand. "What am I supposed to do with a compass? I don't even know where I'm at?" Plucking it with his right middle finger he sees that the pin is spinning uncontrollably and said, "Or better yet a compass that doesn't even work."

Everything is amiss from what he had planned how he is going to approach today. Kog is gone without saying good-bye, nothing of familiarity is near him, and a broken compass has appeared in his hand for no apparent reason. Looking for signs of direction, David walks to the nearest tree to see if moss is growing on the north side of any of them. To his surprise he finds what he is looking for and rubs his fingers over the dark green life draping the base of the thick trunk. "Finally, something is going right," he said after silently thanking his grandmother for enlisting him into Boy Scouts during his younger years.

Returning to where he awoke so that he can retrieve the weapon and body armor, David notices on the ground, a few feet away from him, the brown potato sack Kog had on the log table. Rushing over, he picks it up and feels the bottom of the bag and realizes Kog has left him with some of the fruit vegetables. He opens it up and pulls out a thin piece of wood the size of a sheet of paper. After surveying the front and back, he begins to read the short note written in soot.

> Sorry, but you staying with me is something I can't control. Your life is your life and my life is my life. I don't know where you go from here but whatever you do, use all five of your senses because your soul depends on it. I hope these zaqs help you wherever your feet take you and that this iron cup helps you when you find your way to the boiling river of Raqueem. Remember that these zaqs are like money and also a doctor whenever you are badly injured. Sorry for my departure. Good luck and trust no one!

> Keeper of the gate,
> KOG

"Well, I guess that explains where Kog has went in a nutshell." Dropping the note, David pulls the chain mail over his chest and clips the sheath for the dirk to his side. "North is that way," he points with his finger. "So north is where I am going."

With his dagger in his hand, he walks under the shade of the trees that are beneath what looks to be moonlight. Small branches hang low that are blocking his path so he chops them like butter to test the sharpness of his double-edged blade. Looking for anything that can perhaps benefit him, he stops to see if the compass that miraculously appeared in his palm is working. Nothing has changed as he watches the pin continue to spin endlessly like he's in the Bermuda Triangle.

David becomes angry and places his left hand on a big round boulder nearby. He puts the point of his blade on the perimeter of the compass as if he is about to gouge it out. "What am I thinking? Cutting it out will be like cutting my damn hand off."

David retracts from his thoughts while glancing from side to side in hopes the worm of torment doesn't show up because he is thinking about hurting himself. Nothing is nearby or in the distance seems to have changed so he continues to move forward through the woods. An hour nearly passes by when he sees light shining down on a rocky road up ahead of him. Quickly, he picked up his pace toward the path amid in the wilderness until he reaches the edge of the forest.

He looks for danger before stepping from the massive trees into the brush running alongside the road. A sigh comes from his lungs because his mind can only imagine where the poorly lit path leads to. After fingering the guard of his dirk, his confidence builds to its potential, so he steps onto the pebbled paved road heading toward the direction the moss told him to go.

Walking under the clouds that have become gray smoke running throughout the sky, David wonders if this is Hades's daylight. When he arrived last night the sky was like a dim fire, and this morning it's like the moon is shining bright, but the charcoal smoke clouds sitting above him is hiding it. Whatever is giving him light he appreciates it, happy to be out of the woods and onto a road that will lead him to something.

The midnight light and the road makes him feel like he is in control of his life again. His feet no longer feels like weights so he moves more swiftly searching for what's next on his newfound path. Four hours later, a pole appears about a football field away at what looks to be a fork in the road. At first he doesn't believe what his eyes are showing him, and therefore slaps himself in the face to make sure what he is seeing is not a mirage. Speculatively, he blinks twice and then a third time for confirmation and his vision doesn't change from what he now knows is real.

Suddenly, before he can advance to investigate the crossing, a loud how comes from a copse of trees to the right of him. David frantically looks toward the area homing his ears for another unwanted sound. "Hoowww!" the cry from the unseen beast comes again, but this time a lot closer than before. Shaking in fear, David grabs everything he's got and takes off running for the intersection at the end of the road. Stride for stride he moved as fast as his legs will take him praying he's fled whatever is watching him from behind the trees.

That was a close call, he thought resting his shoulder on the wooden pole so that his body temperature can lower itself from the record breaking hundred-yard dash. After catching his breath, he looks up and sees the protruding pole in the ground is a three-way sign. To the left read Sodom, straight ahead read Gomorrah, and to the right read River of Raqueem.

Standing there under the unknown light from the sky, he tries to decide which way is less dangerous for him to continue on. He opens his sack of zaqs and remembers that Kog told him that the river of Raqueem is where they grow. Concluding that twelve zaqs should be good enough for now, he sets his mind on his last two options. "Sodom is considered in the Bible one of the most grotesque cities ever existed since time began. And Gomorrah was considered his twin sister but just a little less hideous." The words that came out of his mouth answered his own question, and therefore he decides Gomorrah is where he heading to next.

Taking in another deep breath, David turns to salute the woods from which he entered Hades's good-bye. As he raised his left hand to his eyes he noticed that the compass needle is no longer just spinning inside his palm but is now pointing north toward Gomorrah.

"So now you want to start working. What happened to you when I was pissing in the wind to see what direction I was going in?" David points his hand to the south, east, and west to see if it is truly showing him which way is north. No doubt the compass is working as the direction stays the same. "Well, maybe all the trees is what had it spinning stupidly. At least it's working now."

Before he can get himself together for the walk in front of him, the atmosphere changed from bad to worst. Hesitantly, David looks up to see what has the hairs all over his body in a frenzy. Stumbling backward, the pole breaks his fall and his eyes lock with the hidden beast in the forest he thought he had escaped. "Down, boy," he tries to say calmly as he stares at the biggest wolf his eyes has ever seen.

Darting his eyes around for cover, he sees there is nowhere to run and slides out his dagger slowly from its sheath. *Fight or run,* he thinks but quickly throws out the question because four legs are faster than his two any day. "Down, boy," he said again but more sternly. "Looky here, nice doggy, I have a treat for you." David slips his hand into the bag and pulls out a zaq. As he extended his hand for a peace offering, the great wolf charged at him with his head down as if he is a ram in battle.

The size of his head is huge as the force of its skull connected with the center of David's sternum. Flying across the humid air, he falls on his back and rolls three to four times. A cloud of black dust is covering him so he waves his hands trying to regain vision of his enemy. Just as the dust is clearing, the beast emerges out of the darkness in midflight with his mouth wide open full of sharp teeth.

David shifts his body in the nick of time and the ferocious wolf misses his head by inches. The dodging of the wolf's jaws opens his shoulder blade up to the beast's powerful bite. The stench of the animal's breath rises up to David's nostrils as he uses his strength to push the massive creature off him. Nothing is working because the wolf's weight is too great and its dark gray hairs have pointy tips like a porcupine. "Get off of me, damn it! Get the hell off of me!"

Anger grows within the beast's bite as he shakes his head trying to tear through the chain mail that is protecting his upper body. Lifting him off the ground as if he is a feather, the wolf tosses him as far as his jaws can throw him. Furious, the wolf snorts into the ground because of frustration. Creeping slowly, the beast from hell moves forward to try and finish what it has started. David, on the other hand, looks into his hands and sees that he has specks of lime-green ooze in his palms from where the needled tips of the wolfs hair penetrated his skin. *Is this what my blood looks like?* he thought wiping his hands on his pants leg.

The split seconds from being in the animal's jaws and being tossed through the air like a rag doll allows David to remember that the worm of torment senses fear, pain, and defenseless souls. Replaying Kog's kill-or-be-killed message in his head, he stands to his feet for the beast's next attack. "From this day on, I vow to fight for my soul or burn in the lake of fire trying," he said knowing that this is the first time in his life he had to defend himself or die.

Howling to the sky to mark his territory, the wolf displays the length of his fangs in a mouthful of drool hanging from its corners. Circling one another, David's knees are bent ready for the beast to charge him again. "Come on!" David yells beating his chest with his free hand. "Come on, you canine from hell, and watch me cut your ugly head off."

The wolf's eyes changes from solid black to red when seeing David isn't afraid of his presence. Metamorphosing its body, its claws grow an inch longer, its hair stands straight up, and its body grew bigger each new breath the creature took. David steps back to brace himself for whatever the beast is planning to do while raising his dirk to the side of his head as if he is holding a bat. "I'm ready whenever you are," he said hoping to sever a limb when he swings with everything he's got for the sake of his destiny.

Leaping off its hind legs, the wolf's sharp paws and teeth is all he can see coming at him under the poorly lit sky. Wanting his blow to be fatal, he recalls how Barry Bonds and Ken Griffey Jr. would put their hips into every hit for more power. As the beast's fangs become more visual throughout its furry flight, David slashes his dagger from east to west cutting open the wolf's breastplate like the branches that hung in the woods. Quickly, he ducks out of the way from the falling creature in the air.

As the wolf lies there, his chest rises up and down spitting out pools of neon-green blood over the ground. Slowly, David stood with his feet planted in the black dirt ready for another round in case the beast is playing possum. Squirming in pain, the injured creature tries to stand up on all fours but falls belly first into its own blood. David walks over and straddles the wolf's lower body while carefully keeping his legs away from its snapping mouth. "I'm sorry, Mr. Big Bad Wolf, but Little Red Riding Hood or the three little piggies are not in this story," he said raising his sword. "My name is David! And the name of this book is called Grace!" he shouted bringing the tip of his blade down between the ears of the back of its skull.

Victorious from his first kill in Sheol, David steps away from the predator triumphant wiping the blood from his blade on his shirt. The demonic worm pops up in his mind again so he moves away quickly from the lifeless body to be safe. Staring at the creature with all his condiments in his hands, he waits wanting to get a glimpse at what happens when you are defeated in battle. Since he pinned the wolf's head to the ground, nothing has changed so he concludes that the worm of torment is for human souls only.

Standing back at the pole, David looks at his Sharia compass to make sure that it is still displaying north in the direction of Gomorrah. The needle is working properly so he scans the area one last time for anymore surprises before proceeding forward. His mind feels more astute than it was before because he understands that at any given moment your soul can be taken from you. "Thank you, Jesus, for watching over me," he silently prayed not knowing why he is praying to a man who sent him to hell.

The coast is clear and there is no turning back now. With his mind set on Gomorrah, the only thing left to do is find the zaq he dropped before his fight with the mutant wolf. "Now where are you?" he asked the ground while retracing his steps back to the dead animal that is lying in the dirt. Dragging his feet along the surface of the ground, David's foot kicks the dark green zaq toward the creature that tried to shorten his time in Hades. "There you are."

David bends over to pick up the valuable fruit vegetable and hears a loud howl from the wolf. Drawing his sword, he notices a mist in the shape of the lifeless creature rising from its mouth and vanishes into thin air. When the mist disappeared, the wolf's body turned into a shell of ashes and fell into the black dirt.

"Whew, that was a close one, I think," he said running the back of his hand across his forehead. "For a second there I thought he had reincarnated himself."

Leaving the intersection, he doesn't look back as he walked toward the suspenseful town of Gomorrah. His movement is quick but cautious because the woods are still all around him. He didn't know if he should walk slower because he might be walking into danger or walk faster because danger might be closing in on him. One thing he could count on for sure is that a town no matter how bad it is will be better than being in no-man's-land the rest of his dreadful life in Hades.

Continuing on the path, werewolves, warlocks, and vampires start to run through his mind in more ways than one. Shivering from perhaps coming face to face with one of the creatures, David shakes the thoughts before they can take root and knock him off his victory horse. Focused back on what's ahead of him, the darkness of the woods makes him think of the headless horsemen waiting to chop the heads off anyone walking in his domain. "Why am I letting all those dumb myths get to me? If I am going to stay alive down here, I must stay positive or just give up now and fall on my sword."

His long walk from the crossing begin to change as the sky turned to the fiery glow it had the night before and the trees started to become fewer in number each step he took. Noticing that his path is now becoming an open field with a road going through it, David starts a light jog so that he can be out of the forest completely. His legs becomes a little lighter and his pace picks up when he notices rows of lights on high poles on each side of him.

The sight of the scenery changing makes him feel like he has unachieved the unachievable by making it out of the outskirts of Hades. Not only that but also a wooden sign that read Welcome to Gomorrah. "Yes, I did it! I'm finally out of that creepy wannabe *Sleepy Hollow*," he cheered. Just as he is about to finish his celebration dance his smiles turned into a frown when he realized that the letters on the wood were written in the same color of the afterlife's blood that came from he and the wolf. Staring into the sky as if he is looking for someone to save him, David draws his sword knowing that the road he is walking he must walk alone.

8

The road to Gomorrah leads to an actual town with buildings, people, dogs, and stray cats. From first glance you would think John Wayne the duke is going to ride up and say, "Howdy, partner." But after walking through the streets further, David noticed that some of the buildings were of the present day from when he was alive on Mother Earth.

Placing his dirk in its holster, he brushes off his Easter shirt and pants so that he doesn't look like a stranger looking for trouble. A woman walks past him with a stricken look in her eyes and stares at him in the face. "Good day, ma'am," he said, nodding his head to show her he is a gentlemen. The woman turns around and screams with an eerie shriek before pulling up the bustle of her old dress and running off barefooted.

"If that wasn't strange, I don't know what is."

The street that brought him into the underpopulated city lead to a saloon with black horses tied to a hitch rail all around it. Standing on the corner, music notes from a piano began to push themselves through the walls of the building as if a party is going on. Walking closer to the deck, two lampposts shined down on three wooden steps and up on a sign that read "Hell's Kitchen."

"Move out the way you piece of shit before I gut you like a pig," a guy said pushing David with his elbow so he and his two road dogs can get inside the saloon. "You're lucky the Pussy Cats are on tonight," he said, holding the door for his men. "Because if they weren't, me and my boys a give your green ass a key to the city you'll never forget."

David stayed out of there way but got a quick look inside before the swinging door slammed shut behind them. "Do I really look that obvious of just getting into Hades?" he asked himself looking over his attire. *It must be my clothes,* he thought. *I have to change from these church clothes quickly or I'm going to be the main target for anyone looking for a scuffle.*

Peeking through a windowpane, David sees why the streets of Gomorrah are so abandoned. He places his nose to the glass for a clearer look and sees rugged men sitting on barstools lined up at the bar while women waited on tables. Everyone inside are having a ball mingling with one another eagerly waiting for the main event that is about to come onstage. "Whoever these Pussy Cats are, they sure know how to pack a house."

"Hey, stranger," a waitress said in a decorated brazier and skirt with half of her body out of the door. "Hope I didn't scare you, but my manager said he doesn't appreciate you trying to get a free peep show on his girls."

"Oh, I'm sorry, I was trying to see if I was going to come in or not."

"So what's it going to be because here at Hell's Kitchen nothing's for free?" The waitress holds the door open with her foot so he walks in trying to look like he belongs. "Sorry, Mister, it's not me making you come in. It's my boss Demetrius," the woman said as the door slams shut causing him to flinch a little.

"Damn it, David. I hope nobody saw that," he mumbled under his breath.

Avoiding as much eye contact as possible, David scans the saloon for an empty table or chair to sit in. Making his way through the crowd, he takes his steps carefully so that no one is offended if he brushes up against them. People of all races are stacked on top of each other on the stairs all the way up to the upper deck. Seeing that there are no open seats available on the floor, he decides to lob around at the end of the bar.

"How do you do, Mister? I'm your bartender Artemis but my friends call me Diana."

"Hi, Artemis, I'm David," he replied bluntly so that she wouldn't think he is her friend or friendly.

"So what brings you into Hell's Kitchen tonight?"

David remembers that the Pussy Cats are appearing later and says, "Oh I thought I'll come see what all the fuss is about with the Pussy Cats that are about to perform."

"Well, you chose wisely because the Pussy Cat girls know how to put on a show that will knock your socks off."

"Oh yeah."

"Yes!" Artemis said with excitement. "If you think it's hot in here right now, wait until you see the Pussy Cats stroll up in here."

"You don't say." David stands up straight to show Artemis and whoever is looking his masculine frame.

"So what are you drinking, newcomer?"

"Can I get a water?"

"You can get whatever you want as long as you buy or tip me because Demetrius doesn't allow anyone at the bar unless they're paying or tipping."

David almost said something he didn't want to say when he heard the name Demetrius again. "What's the special?" he asked biting his tongue from his first thoughts.

"Tonight's special is the Loch Ness Monster and it only cost one zaq."

"What's in it?"

"One-month-fermented zaq and sap from the darkest trees of Sheol."

"I'll have a water," David said breaking a zaq in half and putting it in the tip jar with the other pieces.

Artemis leaves and pours a tall glass of Loch Ness Monster and places two black leaves on the side of the rim. "Here, David. If what you say is true about coming here to see the Pussy Cats, then you're going to need a drink when they come out. This one is on me and thanks for the tip." Artemis walked off to wait on someone else, but turned and winked before she reached her next customer.

Drinking is something he hasn't done since he was a teenager. Feeling more eyes on him than one, he tries to look cool as he takes a big manly gulp of the free drink. His mouth is immediately warmed when the Loch Ness Monster wets his tongue. Not knowing how the substance will make him feel, he decides to hold it in his mouth before swallowing.

"So how was it, boy?" a man said smacking him on the center of his back.

David puts his fist over his mouth and coughs. "Strong and spicy."

The man laughs. "Then that means I burped it on time while it was sitting and I mixed the sap in just right. By the way, I'm Demetrius the manager and I make it my business to know every new face that comes into Hell's Kitchen."

Demetrius is a six-foot, three-hundred-pound black guy and his arms are the size of the average man's legs. His body is round but solid and his baseball glove-sized hands looks like they can snap anything in two.

"The name is David, and the next time you sneak up on me, keep your damn hands to yourself."

"All right, Dave. I get the picture and I don't want any trouble." Demetrius chuckled. "Just remember one thing for me, big guy."

"What's that?"

"One, as long as you are in my bar, there's no fighting. And two, if there is any fighting, I am the guy going to be the one doing it!" Demetrius slams his big hand down on the counter while pulling a barstool to the backside of David.

When he walks off, David takes another gulp of his drink relieved that Demetrius didn't call his bluff. After taking another sip, he feels his brain is becoming light and his vision is a little blurry. "This Loch Ness Monster is making me tipsy. I need to slow down before I get drunk."

The spiciness in the drink makes beads of sweat form on his temple and behind his ears. A large propeller from a plane turned slowly above on a geared mechanism but cool air is something it did not produce. The heat inside his body and room temperature makes him unbutton his shirt down to four buttons under his chain mail. "How do these guys do this? You either have to get used to drinking these toxic drinks or be born in hell to sustain the hot affects it does to your body."

"Can I have your attention please?"

David stands on his toes to look over the heads of the men rushing to the male's voice onstage. What he sees is Demetrius speaking into a megaphone addressing the crowd. "Ladies and gentlemen, devils and demons. Murderers, rapists, and whatever other vile and hideous creatures hidden among us. Tonight, the moment we all have been waiting for has finally come."

"Demetrius, get your fat ass off the stage and bring out the Pussy Cats!" a man with a patch over his eye shouts hanging over the railing of the upper deck.

"Keep it up, Herod, and my fat ass is going to come throw your one-eyed ass outside on your good eye!" Demetrius shouts back jokingly pointing with his finger. "Now back to what I was saying before the last pirate of the Caribbean interrupted me." The crowd chants "We want the Pussy Cats" because they know what he is about to say. "Hell's Kitchen, I present to you the sexiest women in all Hades. The Pussy Cats!"

As soon as the manager finished speaking, the waitress covered the lamps according to Demetrius's signal. Like dominoes falling, the lights went out one by one until it is completely dark. Suddenly, a light appeared over the grand piano, and a busty black woman in a full-body cat suit begin playing the keys in a fast salsa tone.

Concentrating on the music is hard because of her thick thighs and circular breasts showing through the fishnet strings that held her clothes together. A cat mask covered her face so the audience's focus left her full curves and stared at her heart-shaped lips singing the song's hook, "Here goes my kitty cat."

The Pussy Cats came out on cue when their pianist drugged the *r*'s in purr during her last lyric. Everyone's attention are now on the curtains that are separated under the light that is over the stage. All of the men's eyes are wide open as five topless girls with fuzzy boas around their necks, cat ears on top of their heads, and curved tails pinned to their thongs rub on one another.

Two twins were Asian, two were Hispanic, and one is Caucasian. The Caucasian woman took front and center twirling and shaking her shimmy while the others followed her lead behind her. Each covering one-fifth of the stage. Picking up the song where the musician left off, all five girls took turns expressing their vocal cords when their part came up.

The sight of their perfect bodies had every man's tongues hanging out their mouths and some of the women in the audience were just as bad. When exiting the stage to work the crowd, David watched the men tug on the ladies' arms as they flaunted their figures and fiddled with those whom they chose to. The Caucasian women spotted the helpless minnow in the sea, and stopped in front of David giving him the okay to touch whatever he pleased to on her body.

"You see something you like?" she asked in his ear while sitting in his lap. Circling her hips, she rubs the back of David's head.

"Doesn't everybody?" David swallows the last of his drink and she wraps his hands around her waist making him feel the sweat that is rolling down her cleavage onto her stomach.

"You're not like the other guys in here," she replied noticing that every gesture made with his hands came from her initiating it. "Sorry, I can't stay longer but my job is calling me." Softly grabbing his ears, she pulls his face to hers and kisses him on the lips. "Good-bye, handsome, and the pleasure was all mine."

The dancer turned and smacked her backside before dancing off back to the stage. Joining the girls in their rehearsed performance, it is like she never missed a beat when she took her position. David is left gawking over what just happen but thankful that from the outside looking in it looked like tonight isn't his first rodeo in what goes on after death. A whistle from a man to the right of him shakes him out of his lustfulness. When the seductive song comes to an end, he looked around the bar and thought, *Why must dogs always chase the cat?*

Staggering to his feet, he watches the curtains close hoping to get another look at the topless white girl who aroused him. The pianist walks onstage shortly afterward and announces that the Pussy Cats will perform their hit single, "Purring All Night Long," after the break. Exiting through the curtains, the crowd's eyes stayed hypnotized to her bouncing butt until it disappeared beyond the draperies.

"So what did you think about Hell's Kitchen's Pussy Cat girls?" Artemis asked replacing his glass with another Loch Ness Monster.

"Huh? Oh, let's just say that there is no other name other than the Pussy Cats that will fit them."

Artemis laughs because she can hear in his voice that the aperitif is effecting his brain. "I knew you would like them, everybody does. That's why we have a full house tonight. Any other night it would be only me and my regulars in here."

David looked at the full glass of alcohol in front of him and ask, "Are you trying to get me drunk, Artemis?"

"Yes, but actually this one is not from me. It's from my play sister Cybele."

"Who is Cybele?"

"My roommate and the beautiful girl who gave you that free lap dance a while ago." Artemis touched the back of his hand and walks away giggling.

Hearing who sent him the drink caught him off guard and made him spit up what he recently sipped. Immediately, his mind remembers the passion in the kiss they shared and causes him to wonder if Cybele is eyeing him behind the scenes or not. The thought of it makes him straighten his posture and have a seat in the barstool behind him. *Cybele, hmm, now where have I heard that name before?* Disregarding his thought, he brings the glass to his lips and takes another sip, glad that he has survived thus far in Sheol.

The Pussy Cats returned on scheduled performing their hit single, "Purring All Night Long," and a few other songs. Flaunting their sexiness and Coke-bottle figures kept the packed crowd's attention, so violence became the last thing on anyone's mind. As the late-night hours drew to an end, men and women began to disperse back to the holes they crawled from. David, however, is stuck with a dilemma on where he is going to reside when the doors shut in Hell's Kitchen.

Still a little tipsy, he stands realizing that he is now one of six people hanging around the saloon to get a glimpse of any of the Pussy Cats that may be still on the premises. "What are you going to do, David?" he asked himself looking at his dirty face in the mirror behind the bar. Dipping his finger in the last of his drink, he rubs the blackness from his cheeks until his olive white skin returns to its regular color.

As he stood there, he watched the few people left diminish to two, including himself. Suddenly, burning lights along the walls began to be covered by the waitress leaving him with only one choice for the night. Having to exit, he drags his feet toward the swinging door that he entered with melancholy from what he is facing. His chest rises to his chin as he took the deepest breath he has ever took when he reaches the door. Thinking back to his day among the living, he remembers how he had everything figured out. Being in Hades is a different story because here he is homeless and does not have any place to stay.

"Hey, David!" David has one foot out the door when Artemis calls him. "Wait up!" she yelled, dropping her dishrag and hastily going over to meet him at the door. "I'm sorry but Demetrius had to leave early, and me and my sister don't have anybody to walk us home when I get off." Gazing into his eyes, she feels like a fan meeting her favorite superstar for the first time. "I was wondering…if… you…"

"What is it, Artemis? Spit it out." David already knew what she was trying to ask him but played the scenario as if he didn't.

"Oh, you men are so difficult!" Artemis slightly nudges his shoulder with her fist. "Can you walk me and my sister home tonight?"

Acting as if he is contemplating on his decision, he answers, "Yes, Artemis, I'll walk the two of you home."

"Great and thanks."

"You're welcome, and it's the least I can do for being so polite and making me feel welcome in Hell's Kitchen."

"You're so nice, David. Please have a seat while I let Cybele know you said yes. By the way, my sister said you were different and now I see why."

"How did she come up with that from dancing on my lap?"

Artemis laughed and walked behind the curtain to get Cybele. Before the curtains closed over her, she shouted across the floor, "Watch yourself, handsome, I think my roommate has a crush on you."

David sits at the table in the center of the floor under the propeller ceiling fan. During his wait, he taps his fingers to the beat of, "Here's Goes My Kitty Cat," on the table. *Is it Cybele who likes me or Artemis?* he thought with a smirk on his face. *I got to play this cool and let them know I'm not looking for a good time. When the time is right, I am going to be truthful and tell them I need a place to lay my head until tomorrow.*

Cybele emerged onstage first in some black tights and a loose T-shirt that had the word Meow across her breast. Artemis followed behind her in a pair of baggy pants and a sleeveless hoodie. The two of them are the exact opposite when it came to their appearance but David concluded that they shared the same taste in men because of how they both looked at him so deviously.

"We're ready whenever you are, David!" Artemis, who is the most vocal between the two said. "And thanks again for waiting."

David walks to the door and opens it for the ladies. Gesturing with his hand, the women step onto the outside deck smiling to one another.

"Oh, David, you're such a gentleman." Cybele's hip slightly brushes up against him going through the door and the girls giggle like teenagers to Cybele's comment.

Walking under the fire-night sky, the stillness of nothing moving through the streets gives him an opening to ask the girls some questions that have been puzzling him.

"I have a question, and if it offends you then you don't have to answer it." The question he wants to ask came up while he was waiting for the girls in the saloon.

"I don't mind you asking me any questions," Artemis replied. "Go ahead, shoot."

"I don't mind either, Mr. mysterious handsome guy who showed up in my life out of nowhere."

"Great." David stops walking and the girls stop too. "So, Artemis and Cybele…"

"Yes, David," they both said at the same time.

"Does everybody in Hades or whatever this place is go by fake names?"

"Fake names. Why do you say we are using fake names?"

"For starters, Cybele, your name means the goddess of fertility and ironically Artemis was her successor who was also a goddess. What's even crazier is that Artemis means Diana."

The girls were caught off guard at the knowledge David possessed concerning their names.

"David." Artemis pauses to think and then finishes what she is saying. "Me and my sister have been dead for over two hundred years and no one who has been here for only a couple of days has ever asked us that. Hell, no one that I have ever known has ever been able to put our names together."

"How do you know that?" Cybele blurted out. "Who are you, a professor or something?"

"No, Cybele, I am, I mean I *was* a pastor. And the reason why I know is because Artemis's name is in the Bible in the book of Acts. But I guess you two already knew that."

"Wow, a pastor!"

"Yes, Artemis, a pastor," he replied, recalling the days he preached the gospel. "But that was the past, and I'm done with that life because evidently pastors go to hell too."

"So that's what's different about you!" Cybele exclaimed. "From the moment I looked into those sexy gray eyes I knew you were not like the rest of those creeps up in Hell's Kitchen."

Interrupting, Artemis answered his question. "The answer to your question is yes and no."

"Yes and no everybody is going by other names, or yes and no only the two of you are going by aliases."

"Both, and we do it so that no one will know how long we've been in Sheol," Artemis quickly answered.

"So by me going by my real name is how everybody knows how I'm just getting here?"

"Yes and no."

"Why do you say that, Cybele?"

"Because no one wears those clothes you have on."

Artemis chuckled under her breath at Cybele's sarcasms. "I'm sorry, David, but you are a sitting duck for the hunters if you stay in those present-day clothes a day longer."

Taking a mental note of Artemis's statement, David thanks the girls as they approach the door of their late 1900s loft. Artemis and Cybele know he doesn't have a place to stay so instead of letting him sleep in the streets they asked him to come up for a few minutes.

"Hey, David, do you want to come up for a moment?" Cybele asked hoping he said yes. "Because I have some up-to-date men's clothing from my last boyfriend who stayed with us."

"Boyfriend."

"Relax, David. I promise you everything is safe. I haven't seen him in over fifty years."

David turns his back to the girls and looks at the fire above dimly lighting the street that may soon be his bed. Pondering on all that has been spoken tonight during their walk home, he turns around and sees that the ladies present him no harm. "I guess I can come up for an hour or two since you are inviting me in to help me with my fashion issues," he replied, obliged at the women's hospitality.

9

"What's that?"

"Huh?"

"In your hand, silly." Cybele squats down and puts her index finger in the center of the compass pointing north. "What's that circle thingy in your hand?"

David awakens to Cybele's crotch in his face. His eyes are quickly widen when what brings life into the world smiles at him through the see-through lace that covered her lips. Turning his face away from what is clearly inviting him to touch, he answers, "It's a compass, Cybele," as he pushes himself off the floor to stand to his feet.

"Oh boy!" Artemis walks downstairs in her boy shorts and catches David's rod of steel pointing at Cybele. "I'm sorry," she said placing her hand over her eyes while making a sideways V leaving an eye open. "I hope I'm not interrupting anything."

Cybele rises to her feet and runs her fingers through her hair. David can't help but to look at her nipples poking through her skimpy tan T-shirt. "No, Diana, you wasn't interrupting anything." Cybele smiles on the fact that her Jessica Rabbit shape never fails to raise a man's package. "But if you were interrupting us, Sis, please know that I wouldn't mind if you decided to join in."

Bashful, David becomes cherry red as he bends down to grab the sheet he slept on to cover himself. "Sorry, ladies, but us men have what we call morning wood every now and then."

"Yeah, I bet, Mr. mysterious handsome guy. If that is morning wood then I hate to see what late-night wood looks like," Cybele replies while walking off switching her butt from left to right up the stairs to their room.

Artemis laughs because she would hate to see what late-night wood looks like too. Dropping the sheet over his shoulders, he looks for his shirt that he took off last night. "While you were asleep, I put it on the back of the kitchen chair," Artemis said. Feeling that his earlier problem is starting to hang loosely, he drops the sheet and puts on his shirt leaving it unbutton.

"Thanks for putting a roof over my head last night, Diana." David is still a little sheepish from what he met face to face when he woke up this morning.

Artemis smiles because he called her Diana. "Normally, me and my sister will never invite anyone into our home but Cybele is a pretty good judge of character when it comes to meeting people. I guess you can call it a gift."

Cybele returns with a pair of blue jeans, a shepherd's checkered long-sleeve shirt and a size 11 cowboy boots. "Here, put these on. The boots are an eleven so they should fit you because you look like a ten, ten and a half."

"How'd you guess that?"

"Because like you said yesterday, I'm the goddess of fertility."

David understood the point Cybele is making when she mentions what her name means. As he looks her venomous figure over from head to toe, he realizes that she chose her name because she has been around the block a time or two during this life and the one before.

"Thanks, Cybele and Diana, for everything. I don't know what I would have done last night without the two of you." David remembers how he felt leaving the bar without a place to go. Last night worked out for the best but tonight will probably end with him sleeping on the ground with a hard rock for a pillow.

Artemis breaks the silence in the room. "Do you want to freshen up before you change?"

"Freshen up? How am I going to freshen up when there's no running water?"

"There's a well in the middle of town we can get pails of water from to clean ourselves with and wash our clothes. Of course you got to—"

"I thought all the water down here is steaming hot and comes from the boiling river of Raqueem?"

Artemis raises her hand as if to say stop. "Like I was saying before you cut me off, David. Of course you have to let it cool down to a tolerable temperature before you can use it."

"Sorry." David laughs because he did add his two cents in while she was explaining how obtaining water works.

"So, David."

"Yes, Cybele?"

"That compass lodged into your hand. What does it do, because I never met anybody who's ever had a moving compass inside of his palm?"

"I guess it gives directions but I think it has a mind of its own."

"Why do you say that?"

"Because it only directs me where it wants to direct me when it wants to direct me."

"That sucks." Artemis grabs his left hand and examines the compass. "Sharia, the path to the watery place."

"What was that you just said, Sis?"

"Yeah, what was that, Diana?"

"What was what?"

"You said that the compass in my hand means the path to the watery place."

"Yeah so. You didn't know that?"

"Uh no, not exactly. But what I do know is that it hurt like a bitch when whatever or whomever burned it into my hand."

Artemis began to tidy up their loft and picked up the sheets David slept on. Placing an end under her chin, she puts the corners together to assist her as she folded the sheet neatly. Cybele and David waited in suspense while she took her time to give them an explanation. Watching her clean and put loose items into the hall closet is like waiting on the tortoise to cross the finish line in a race against the hare. After surveying her handiwork and seeing that it is good, she went on to tell the story of the lady name Orpah, who had the same compass a few years back.

David's jaw dropped when hearing he isn't the first soul who has had a compass branded into their skin. Sliding the kitchen chair from under the table, he takes a seat and looks at Artemis with a "go on and finish your story" look on his face. Cybele is intrigued to know more also because she thought Diana and her shared everything that had some meaning in Hades. Sitting on the floor Indian style, she places her hands between her legs and gave Artemis the same look David is giving her.

"Now Orpah was a woman looking for an explanation of the puzzling grafted device like you, David. When she came into Hell's Kitchen it was a night when only my regulars were around the bar. As a matter of fact, I could count on one hand how many people were in the saloon."

"Okay, okay, Diana. We get that hardly nobody was in the place."

"Oh shut up, Cybele. You know how I can get when I'm telling a story." Emitting an exasperated sigh, Artemis skipped her profound detailed version and got straight to the point. "Orpah came into the bar with two warthog-looking men who from past history should not be the kind of guys a lady should be traveling with."

"Maybe she liked male company." David looked at Cybele with a shifty eye.

"I don't think so because they were acting friendly when that was never their MO."

"Come on sis, MO! Who are you, Sherlock Holmes now?"

"What she meant was persona or usual demeanor, Cybele." David raised his index finger to his lips and then pointed at Cybele. "We're sorry for intruding, Diana. Please go on."

"WTF? MO, persona, or whatever you want to call it. Who gives a damn? The bottom line is that they were faking to get something out of her."

"So what you're saying is that this compass in my hand is something good?"

"No. I mean, I don't know."

"So what are you saying, Sis?"

"What I'm saying is that some of the older souls who were in Hell's Kitchen that night told the woman the word *Sharia* means "the path to the watery place." There, now you have it. Now please don't ask me anymore questions about that dumb compass." Artemis stomped off upstairs to put on some clothes for the day.

Cybele stands to her feet and goes over to look at the compass more closely. Taking his hand, she rubs her fingertips over the directional device and reads aloud, "Sharia, the path to the watery place," as if wherever the mysterious place is was enchanted.

"Sorry, Cybele, but having this crappy compass in my hand ain't done nothing for me but cause me some pain.

"You got to admit, it does sound like it's worth exploring."

"Worth exploring." David scoffs. "Hell no, I'm not exploring some path to the watery place when I don't even know where I'm going to go to sleep at night. Let alone, if I'm going to make it to the next day." David pulls back his hand and buttons his shirt. "The only watery place I plan on going to is to the well in the middle of Gomorrah."

"Okay I get it, Pastor David."

"Please don't call me that."

Cybele said she is sorry and goes upstairs to check on Artemis. Standing at the top of the stairs she looks down and tells him, "You're special, David, and whether you like it or not, that compass is a part of you for a reason. Think about that, handsome, when you start to find your way in Sheol."

Artemis returned fifteen minutes later and apologized for storming out of the room like a big kid. Her choice of clothes made her look innocent as a fifth grader on the first day of school. David accepted her apology and apologized as well. Finding some common ground, they both laughed at Detective Diana's description of Orpah and the two strange perps.

The laughter is something they both needed and cleared the air for them to move forward into the day. Artemis goes to retrieve her cowgirl boots from by the door and hand ironed the pleats in her knee-high skirt after pushing her small feet inside of them. Next, she walks over to the mirror and blots the excess of her dark lipstick on the thin piece of skin between her thumb and forefinger.

"Voilà!" Artemis simpers. "I'm ready to go into town. What do you think?"

David shakes his head. "I think I was ready an hour ago."

"Shut up, silly. I'm a girl. Unlike men, we can't just get up and go."

Locking the door, the two of them left Cybele at the loft while they headed off to get some water. Being a gentleman, David carried the two five-gallon iron buckets for them because anything else would probably have melted under the intense heat of the boiling water.

"I found it!" Cybele ran out the front door barefooted with something metal in her hand. "Hold up, Diana. I got to give David something." David placed his hand on Artemis's shoulder so that she would hold up a moment. "I wonder what is that she has in her hand for me?"

"Probably nothing. She's just jealous we left her without telling her we were leaving."

David laughed to himself. "I think it's more than that, Diana."

Cybele catches up to them and hands David a medieval gauntlet. "Here, David, put this on."

"A glove. You stopped us to give him a glove?"

"It's not just any glove, Diana. It's a protective glove for my arm and hand." David takes the gauntlet when seeing that it is for a left hand.

"Try it on, David. You don't know what I had to dig through to find it for you."

David sets the buckets on the ground and puts his hand inside the opening while inching his fingers perfectly into the five slots designed for them. Working the metal down past his forearm, he wiggles his fingers in hopes that there won't be any resistance. To his surprise, his hand feels as if the gauntlet will not constrict his hand movements in any kind of way.

"Thanks, Cybele, but why the glove?"

"Because Diana said that those bad men were trying to figure out what the compass meant. And plus I thought it would make you look cool when you change into your clothes later."

"Is that it, Cybele? Because his escort into town is waiting."

Sensing Artemis's impatience, he says thank-you again to let Cybele know that she is holding them up. Cybele takes the hint gently and looks around to see if any faces are out and finds the streets are empty. In her eyes no one is looking so she lays her hands over her breasts and jets back to their home hoping that none of the citizens are in the windows watching her tackiness.

"Finally," Artemis said as the door to their home closed behind her roommate. Returning to their water mission, Artemis begin to explain other questions David have about purgatory. Such as, how fire in Hades comes from the volcanic lava flowing from the volcano of Tanctum. "It never goes out because it is fueled by the heat and not oxygen. Some rumored that it's fueled by Satan's presence himself but nothing supports those facts." She even went on to speak about how structures appear out of nowhere as if they've always been there throughout time. Sex and how souls in Hades cannot have bowel movements is another subject. "We don't eat anything solid enough to pass through our systems and zaqs are more like a vitamin to keep us healthy to the end. Urinating, on the other hand, is done frequently on behalf of all the water our souls drink when we find it. As far as sex, let's just say this is not heaven so anything goes when it comes to being a bad boy or girl."

David lets Artemis come on line about sex fly over his head as a morose look filled his countenance. "Dang, I can't believe I'm in hell."

"This is not hell, David!" she exclaimed seeing that he is not going to try and hit the curveball that she threw at him. "Trust me, this is not hell."

"So what do you call it then, Diana? You're here too just like me."

"I call it a resting place for those who didn't make it through the golden gates.

David becomes angry. "Hell, Hades, Sheol. When you add them all up, I'm not in heaven where everything is peaches and cream. Instead I'm down here eating zaqs and drinking hot ass water. After calming down a bit, he says, "At least it's not as bad as Kog made it out to be."

Edging the corner of a building, a large shadow covers them from above darkening the sky each time it passed by. Tracking its source, a loud squeal from a creature above followed by a battle horn brings both their eyes to the sky. The sound of a shofar blows again repeatedly, causing the locals to pour into the streets as if they know what the alarming sound is all about. Artemis's facial expression is like she has seen the devil himself as she stops David in his steps.

"Remember how you were just saying this place is not as bad as your friend Kog portrayed it to be?"

"Yes."

"Well, forget about that comment because you are about to experience a real day in Hades starting now!"

Artemis looks at Dagon flying through the air signaling for everyone in town to meet in town square. His winged prehistoric pet underneath him squawks and snaps his pointed beak at stragglers and those who are not moving fast enough.

"Diana, what's wrong, and why the sudden change in your mood?"

"Why?" Artemis grabs his gauntlet hand and hastily heads for town square. "Because the Devil's Advocates are back in the region of Golgotha and our few days of peace has just turned to chaos!"

10

Dagon lands his fierce pterodactyl in front of a bronze statue of an upside down cross. The weight of its webbed toes and lizard-like body causes dust to rise off the ground. People throughout Gomorrah stand one in front of the other listening attentively as Dagon captures the crowd's attention. He raises his hand for silence before sliding down from the saddle that is strapped to his pet's back. His eyes of death are the only section of his face you can see because a spiked bucket helmet set upon his broad shoulders. Artemis tells David that he is a demon under the spell of Queen Jezebel, because when he thrusts his lance according to her commands he does it without showing any feeling.

With distraught faces, the people didn't want to comprehend the darker force that Dagon is paving the way for. As he stands in front of the locals, Dagon explains why the

Devil's Advocates have been absent from their every day evil activities. Discipline and power is his reasons for his queen and king's disappearance. Not wanting any trouble, David concludes that it is best to stay out Dagon's radar as much as possible.

Artemis pushes him to the small space between the people and the building for extra cover. David doesn't like the way she is handing him, but her incumbent protectiveness lets him know that the Devil's Advocates doesn't have any sense of understanding. Abased because of her eagerness, he feels for his dagger that was left on the table back at the loft. Nothing is arm's reach to give him a leveled or upper hand so he submits to her thinking until their current predicament changes.

Black dust in the distance on the main road covers the sky as if a sandstorm is approaching. Pebbles and rocks on the ground began to jump like jumping beans from the vibration of whatever is trampling over the dirt surface. The sound of thunder that is ahead of the cloud halts behind Dagon, but the miasma of dust pounces down on Gomorrah like a Hawaiian wave on a gusty day.

"Silence!" Dagon's voice roars through the three slits that is in place of where the mouth slot should be. "Silence, you peasants, so the queen and king can speak!"

The sandstorm ceased leaving spectacles of its aftermath on any and everything that got in its way. When the dust cleared, five images including Dagon appeared from the shadows.

A great grizzly bear with a sea turtle helmet strapped to its head stands on his hind legs with his clawing paws to its side. Ahab is the king but he calls himself Azzazel. His bear's name is Smokey and their two minds are in sync so no leash is needed for taming the beast. After unraveling his whip, he strikes it at the feet of the people to show his authority. Pure evil is in the depths of his eyes as he strokes his fedora hat revealing a scar from the tip of his right ear, down his cheek, across his lips, and ending at the left side of his chin. The scar had to have happened before he died, because if it had happened in Hades it would have healed over time.

"Who he is supposed to be, Indiana Jones?"

"Shush, David. Be quiet before Dagon hears you and reports you to the queen."

Queen Jezebel steps down off her highly decorated chariot holding a scepter with a myriad of different-colored gems inlayed in its staff. In defiance of the shortness of light, her gold egg encrusted with precious stones becomes the queen's focal point each time she waved the scepter in display of her majesty.

A masked steed and yoke is what pulls her to wherever she desires. Anger is in every snort that the animal breaths as he nods his head and scratches its hoof along the ground ready to ride into battle. Queen Jezebel walks to the back of her chariot and places her high-heeled boot on one of three mummy-wrapped bodies squirming in pain from being drug so far. No one dares to free them out of fear of her murderous hands.

"Greetings, you ghouls!" she yelps maliciously stepping away from the figures lying on the ground. "Sorry we couldn't make it to everyone's favorite Pussy Cat show last night." Azzazel's grizzly bear falls to all fours so that the queen can ruffle the fur underneath his neck. "That's a good boy," she said, before returning to address the crowd. "I don't know what all you simpletons take me for but I could have sworn I gave you specific instructions on how everything should go on as usual as if the Devil's Advocates were still here."

"But queen." A women from up front steps out to plead the town's case.

"Silence and who told you to speak?" The queen snapped and with a straight face she shouts, "Dagon!" while pointing her scepter in the woman's direction.

Dagon grabs his lance from his pet's side and thrust it dead center into the woman's chest. The metallic tip of his jousting weaponry goes through her easily making her a human shish kebab. With his lance from his Hercules strength, he lifts her in the air and drives the handle down into the ground all the way down to the cone that butts up against his hand. Green blood oozes from her wound and mouth as she sits suspended in midair still alive awaiting for her profound fate.

"Anyone else would like to interrupt the queen?" Azzazel asks putting his hand to his ear as if to listen for anyone to answer his rhetorical question. "I didn't think so." Turning toward Jezebel, he bows at the waste with a joker's grin on his face. "Go ahead, my love. I'm sure you have the town's undivided attention now."

"Oh Gomorrah. Oh Gomorrah. I am truly disappointed in you!" Jezebel fans herself with her free hand before continuing to scold the locals. "A week ago from today, my king and I left all of you with strict orders to continue fighting, biting, hating, and killing or severe consequences will be taken on the city."

The townspeople put their heads down because the week of the Devil's Advocate departure they all agreed not to quarrel with one another unless they had to.

"Azzazel!"

"Yes, my queen."

"Do you feel how the temperature has changed since we've be gone?"

"Yes, my love. It feels like its six to eight degrees hotter than what it was before we left."

Jezebel points her scepter toward the crowd and explains how she has worked hard throughout the centuries to keep

Golgotha from burning up like the rest of the kingdoms in Sheol. She also goes on to profess how she thought she had some understanding with the people but evidently they have forgotten that this is not heaven so that makes Satan the sole ruler of the graves.

David stares in awe of the fear the three of them have in the eyes of the onlookers. He wants to be brave but the woman swimming twelve feet in the air retracts all his bravery. Besides, Artemis has pushed him further into the blind spot and begs for him not to do anything stupid or they both will wake up in the lake of fire.

Queen Jezebel shakes her head and swears that if Gomorrah's weakness and friendliness is not fixed quickly, Dagon, Azzazel, and their deranged pets will help them see where they are going wrong when it comes to being hateful. Her statements ends with her placing her scepter down on the chest of one of the squirming mummies and beckoning for Dagon to stand them up so that they may face the crowd. She doesn't have to ask him twice because he listens to her as if she is his maker.

Azzazel is the first to respond to the hobbled figure twisting their hips and shoulders in hopes of the bandages falling to the ground. Spinning around clockwise, he shows complete balance and dashing footwork as he makes his return on the number twelve in which he started. In the blink of an eye, he brings his whip speedily across his body striking all three men each time his hand raised and came down diagonally. Granite shards on the tip of his whip cuts them free and suddenly they all appear chained and gagged so that no one hears their cries of plea. With great humility, he doesn't say a word and steps aside recoiling the braided leather that can slice anything in half at the stroke of his hand.

The queen regains her position and continues to speak to her audience. "These three hideous men are the reasons why the Devil's Advocates were summoned to the far region of Ben Hinnom. One week from today, I received a telepathic vision from my leading prophetess revealing to me that our distant allies, the Sons of Darkness, were ruling their province in a puerile way." Jezebel grabs their leader Dathan by the lapels of his sleeveless garment and brings his bruised face inches away from hers. With a devilish smile, she puts her finger between his eyes and pushes his head away in disgust. "When the king and I arrived in Ben Hinnom, the heat was unbearable, nothing was in order, and the souls who were the leaders of disorder were running amok being best of friends with one another!"

Dagon moved closer to the three individuals when hearing the queen's tone change from angry to angrier. Looking toward the multitude, Jezebel goes on to say that today's meeting is an immolate to their lord Satan and an atonement for disgracing the land that he so graciously lets them remain before their day in hell succumbs them. Raising her scepter, she points it at the three men one by one and screams, "Off with their heads!"

David thought, *If only I was Alice in Wonderland, then none of this would be real because I'll wake up soon.*

Towering over the men, Dagon promptly raises his arms and bends his elbows behind his head. The words, "off with their heads," triggers his demonic brain to draw his battle-ax from the center of his back. Like a puppet on Jezebel's strings, he slices across the air one fatal blow causing all three heads to bounce on the ground at the queen's feet. The cut is clean but that doesn't stop blood from spitting out their necks. Jezebel's eyes never blink or her nerves never flinch at the sight of death that she has performed through Dagon's enforcing hands.

"Here you go, my queen." Azzazel pulls out a wrinkled handkerchief from under his silver-plated breastplate and gives it to Jezebel.

Using the tip of her boot, the queen rolls Dathan and his companion's heads from her path so that she can look at her reflection in King Azzazel's body armor. Despite the headless Sons of Darkness in front of her she still desires to display her royalty every time she's in the public's eye.

"Thank you, honey," she replied, wiping the blood splatter from her long neck while scanning her tightly stringed corset for any droplets. To straighten her hair, she uses her fingers like a comb on her ponytail that is propped up by what looks to be a half-inch gold coupling. When seeing all is well, she runs her hands down her hourglass hips before kissing the king and giving him back his handkerchief.

Tensity among the crowd grows by the seconds when the Devil's Advocates step forward from being judge, jury, and executioner. David doesn't know what exactly is going on but common sense tells him that when people start crawfishing backward that something very bad is about to happen. Feeling the change in the atmosphere, Artemis locks her arm around David's, keeping her eyes focused straight ahead. "Brace yourself."

David is about to say, "For what?" but the sentence doesn't get a chance to roll off his tongue because of the small tremors rumbling beneath his feet. The people to the left and right of him wobble back and forth like they have lost their equilibrium. Just as he is dividing two ladies with his hand to see, a fiery red object shoots out the ground and lands in between the lifeless stiffs who was beheaded.

"What in the hell is that?"

In a low voice, Artemis answers, "The worm of torment. Satan's number one pet."

With that said, all movement ceased. Even those who were crawfishing backward stopped at the sight of the worm's shark-like teeth. Fear, death, and the lack of not being able to defend yourself is what it feeds on. These are also the qualities that allows the blind creature to see. Running in fear is a quick way to become a passenger on the worm's perpetual tour to hell. When its sensor calls the predator forth, it's best to just stay out of its way from whomever it comes for.

Jezebel and the king raises their hands, palms up and chants, "Hail, lord Satan, the sovereign keeper of the grave." Slithering along the ground in a sine curve manner, the worm of torment seeks the stench of death that has summoned him. Its appetite is unending when devouring the soul's corpse and their heads as if they are nothing. Queen Jezebel explained their corrupt position in Golgotha beforehand so staring at the silhouettes of their bodies in the dirt does not affect anyone emotionally.

Louder and louder, the Devil's Advocates continued to chant because of the woman forked up on the pole is next to meet her demise. Artemis, David, and the town of Gomorrah waits with sullen faces hoping the worm will spare her. Fear plus pain plus frantic movement equals to being the next contestant to nosedive into the lake of fire. Being that her lungs are severely punctured, she can only scream so loud for her release.

The caboodle of people who knew her wanted to speak up in her defense but didn't because of Dagon's double-edged ax hanging from his hands. Suddenly, the death worm leaps straight into the air and lands on the end of

Dagon's lance deep-throating her until the end of its slimy tale disappears into the ground. The only thing left from its meal is the lance that went through the worm's body like a sewing needle going through a piece of cloth. In the past, the ancient souls told tales of how they've witness the worm of torment going through walls to get to souls that are doomed but nobody actually believed it. Today, all that has changed and the people are murmuring to one another about how hiding is practically useless.

Justice is served in the eyes of the queen. Raising her scepter, her steed pulls the chariot in front of her and stops. When she steps inside the chariot, she motions to Dagon and Azzazel that their time in Gomorrah has come to an end. Their pets know their masters, so the gigantic bear and pterodactyl walks to their sides. Azzazel is the first to jump on the back of his bear and Dagon follows after his flying friend lowers its head to let him on. The three of them line up one on side of the other with Azzazel in the middle. Stares of bewilderment are on their faces so the widespread of people remained silent waiting eagerly for them to leave.

King Azzazel speaks, "Today is a day our region Golgotha should extol the queen and I for governing our land the way Satan has commissioned us to. Just as the Sons of Darkness of the province of Ben Hinnom were dethroned for their disobedience to Sheol, the Devil's Advocates will someday be also if our land ever cries out for order. Tomorrow, we will be going throughout the region, starting with our capital Sodom, setting the towns straight that are not fulfilling Hades's expectations. You Gomorrah should be thankful you didn't have to fall into the hands of Dagon and I for lack of corruption while we were away." Azzazel strikes his whip to ground emphasizing the terror he would have placed on them. "Our queen, your queen, is, for one, tired from her travels. And two, out of respect for today's sacrifice to Satan, she has decided to give you a few days to have the town of Gomorrah back the same way she had left it."

Dagon's words are a few so he has nothing to add to the king's closing statements. Retrieving his lance from the ground, the people quickly move out of the way of the snapping jaws of the pterodactyl. Dagon holsters his weapon before kicking his heels in the flanks of his dinosaur pet. The flying beast's eighteen-foot wingspan spreads open and flaps taking him in the air instantly. Squeals and squawks are the sounds it makes as the creature soars in a circle like an eagle. Hades's daylight is starting to fade so each time it passes everything becomes dark until it makes another round in the sky.

Queen Jezebel shouts, "The king has spoken!" Narrowing her eyes, she lowers her scepter and said, "As you were, Gomorrah."

Azzazel pulls the hair on the back of the ferocious bear's neck, as if they are reins when he is ready to go. The queen rides off with Dagon ahead of her but he lags behind taking census of the faces that didn't appear to the sound of the queen's shofar. As the crowd dispersed, David is left standing with Artemis like a deer caught in the headlights. Artemis is well known from Hell's Kitchen and you will never catch her in public without Cybele. *Who is this guy with the iron glove?* he thought while wondering why Cybele directly disobeyed the queen's town meeting. At first he wanted to go and asked them both to explain themselves, but Queen Jezebel already leaving stops him. "Let's go, Smokey," he said, tugging on his hair again. "The queen is waiting." Smokey stands and then falls to all fours roaring to show the king's dominance over the people. Following his master's command, the bear turns to the left and speedily runs off to catch up with the rest of the pack.

Artemis is disappointed but content that the queen didn't wreak havoc on the citizens of Gomorrah. The lady who was sentenced to burn forever was her friend and always tried to keep conflict to a minimum. Seeing her leave still alive and aware of her fate hurt deeply. "It could have been me," she said to herself when the worm took her. However, David's innocence of never shedding blood in Hades shines some light of hope in her soul. As they talked, he gave her words of encouragement that helped stitch the scars inside her that she has been living with for a long time.

At the well, the locals that were one a few hours ago are now trying to figure out what the other person is thinking. The line for water is quiet because tomorrow they all must go back to fighting one another or else. People looked over their shoulders staying alert in case someone decides to start today. David feels he's out of place so he keeps his mouth shut while following Artemis's lead.

They gathered two pails of water from the well. While walking back to the loft, the only sound you can hear throughout the streets is hot water swishing underneath the handles. Standing under the clouds of fire that are slowly overcoming the light gray blanket that covered the sky, Artemis contemplates on how to tell David that he must leave in the morning. Cybele is all that she has in the afterlife and the two of them don't need any more trouble than what is already going to come their way.

David speaks as she is opening her mouth to break the news. "Artemis, do you mind if I stay another night? I promise I'll be gone in the morning."

"I don't mind and I'm pretty sure your number one fan Cybele doesn't mind either." Diana wipes her forehead, glad that she didn't have to be the one to tell him to go.

Continuing their walk, David thanks Artemis for showing him a different perspective of what being in Sheol is all about. He also goes on to tell her that whatever her reasons is for not making it into heaven wasn't because of being genuine or noble. Thanking her again, he said, "Diana, I must find my own way in Hades. And when the rooster crows in the morning it will be the beginning of me finding where I belong."

11

The board creeks under the boot of Dagon's heavy foot. Entering Cybele's and Artemis's room, his body armor squeaks each step he takes like it needs oil. Both of them lay on a mattress of cushions, unaware of what awaits them when they wake up in their safe haven. Azzazel is behind him and he motions with his finger for Dagon to stand on one side of the bed while he stands on the other. A beam above them dissects the room so Azzazel tosses his whip over it and takes the tail end in his hand. When his devious plan falls into place, he nods for his assistant to do what he does best.

Straddling the bed, Dagon bends down and grabs the two women by their throats. Opening their eyes to horror, their words are few because all their strength must go into trying to breath. Dagon is like a statue as he stands silent taking every fist and kick the girls give to get loose. Azzazel waits for their swings to lessen before wrapping the whip several times around Artemis's neck.

"Azzazel, no!" Artemis screams drooling in her words. "Please stop!"

"Good morning Artemis and everybody's favorite pussy cat." Azzazel chuckles. "Let me rephrase that because if this was a good morning then we wouldn't be here and the two of you would still be dreaming about white men coming to your rescue." Azzazel pulls on the handle of his whip and lifts Artemis to her toes. "By the way, where is your friend from yesterday?" Azzazel ask, looking toward the closet and to the corners.

David left a few hours ago while it was still dark. Last night he said his good-byes and decided to leave early to get a head start on the long day ahead of him. While Cybele's invitation to stay was very tempting, he decided to let her know that he is married and still in love with his wife Amy. The girls thought that was sweet of him and let Cupid continue to take its course. When he closed his eyes to go to sleep, he asked the two of them for a rain check just in case he changed his mind in the near future.

Artemis is choking. Pushing her feet into the mattress, she pulls herself up on the whip to keep from losing consciousness. Cybele scratches Dagon's arm but his body is like ice because he doesn't feel a thing. His grip tightens to show his superiority when her scratches turns to punches.

Both of their white faces look like mood rings as they change colors searching for air that their lungs cannot find.

Azzazel takes a step back to get more leverage on the pulley that is hoisting Artemis up like a log. The game of tug-of-war is on, and Azzazel is winning because he has caught her off guard. He can easily hang her but the fear of death in her eyes causes him to toy around with her life to make her think she may come out victorious.

"Artemis, this is fun but unfortunately I don't feel like playing anymore." Azzazel takes a step forward to allow the tip of her feet to rest on the bed. Tears fall from her eyes as she sucks up a big gulp of air. "Now, now, Artemis, there's no need to cry." Azzazel wipes a tear from her cheek with his dirty thumb. "Cheer up, today is your lucky day," he said, bringing his attention to Cybele while shaking his head. "I'm sorry, Ms. Goddess of fertility, but you have been sentenced to hell for disobeying the call of the queen's shofar yesterday."

Cybele's body is limp and her face is blue. If it wasn't for her eyes blinking in disbelief, one would think she is dead from the lack of oxygen.

"Azzazel, please don't!" Artemis screams for her friend's life.

"Or else what?" Azzazel pulls the whip to his chest, lifting Artemis to her toes again and then allows the tip of her feet to fall back to the floor. The tightening of the loops around her neck causes her eyes to nearly pop out her head. "Where is your knight in shining armor now, Artemis? Where is your friend with the iron glove?"

Artemis looks at Cybele's head hanging over Dagon's big hand. Her eyes are closed and her body is motionless because the grip around her neck has cut off all circulation to the brain. Cybele is her sister and if she was to die, life as she knows it will not be the same. Without thinking further, she screams, "Sharia!"

"Sharia?" Azzazel loosens his grip so that Artemis can speak without any hindrances. "What about Sharia, and how do you know about the path to the watery place?"

"Let her live and I'll tell you whatever you want to know."

"How about I let her breath, and if what you tell me is worth her life then I'll consider letting her live."

"Okay, whatever you want, Azzazel! Just please tell Dagon to stop before it's too late!" Artemis exclaimed.

"So be it. A deal is a deal. Dagon, let the disrespectful Pussy Cat go."

Dagon opened his vise-grip hand from around her neck. Red bruises are imprinted in her throat as she fell to the floor with the little life she has left in her. Artemis quickly falls to her aid, jerking the end of the whip from Azzazel's palms. Tears roll down her face onto Cybele's head that is in her lap. Lamenting for her friend to take a breath, she looks up and yells, "Damn it, Azzazel! Look what you have done!"

Cybele is lying still on the floor. One foot is in hell and the other is in the loft with Artemis. Rocking back and forth, Artemis whispers in her ear for her to please breathe. The sound of her sister's voice and the tears dripping upon her face causes her chest to rise slightly.

"Artemis, is that you, Sis?"

"Yes, but please don't speak. Just breathe. Breathe, Cybele. Just breathe." Artemis hears how weak her friend's voice is.

"I heard you, Sis." Cybele smiles." I heard you calling to me."

"Aw how sweet. Now tell me what you know about Sharia!"

Cybele sits up when hearing the word Sharia. "Diana, what did you do?"

"I'm sorry, Sis, but I had to tell them something or you would have died." Artemis looks down ashamed to look Cybele in the eye. "Sharia is what is written in the compass he has in his hand."

Azzazel remembers the gauntlet he wore in town square. "Is that why he wore that glove yesterday?"

"Diana, no. David is our friend," Cybele said, staring at Artemis who won't give her any eye contact.

Artemis looks up. "Cybele, you don't understand. I made an agreement with Azzazel and he kept his word so I must keep mine or we will both die."

"Answer the question, you cunt!" Azzazel yells to let them know he means business.

"Yes, okay! Is that what you want to hear? Yes!"

Her answer pulls the chain on the light bulb over his head. "Interesting."

Azzazel rubs his chin and paces the floor, thinking about the last compass that was in Hades. Stopping in his steps, he remembers how he sent two of his servants to follow up on a lead one of his spies told him concerning a woman with a working compass in her hand. Days he waited for them to return but when they didn't come back he concluded that they must have found something worth more than the wrath that he would have inflicted on them for their disobedience.

Jezebel was enraged and sent numerous of parties out to get to the bottom of the two disappearing. When those searching came back, they reported that the compass lead to a place called Sharia where cold water can be found. To this day, nothing could be proven concerning Sharia but the two servants who went AWOL were killed by the queen herself. As for the woman who had the compass, she was never found.

"Imbeciles." Azzazel pounds his fist into his hand. "I sent two complete idiots to find a small compass from a helpless woman and they couldn't do that. Imbeciles," he repeats. "What else?"

"What else? What do you mean what else?" Artemis asks.

"What I mean is what else are you not telling me?"

"That's it, Azzazel!" Cybele blurts out. "That's all we know."

Azzazel becomes angry when hearing her speak without being spoken to. "Dagon, could you please shut her up."

Dagon grabs Cybele by the arm and stands her to her feet. Artemis screams for him to let her go while swinging with all her might hoping that her punches may faze him. A sudden backhand from the heartless demon sends her flying halfway across the room. Cybele spits, kicks, and scratches trying to defend herself but nothing is to her avail as she is pinned back against the wall by the hand around her throat.

"Don't kill her, Dagon! I promise she will behave!" Azzazel reaches out his hand to help Artemis up but she slaps it away from her. "Azzazel, you are a monster!"

"I'll take that, if that's what you believe. Now where were we? Oh yeah, I remember what I wanted to know." Azzazel takes a knee to look Artemis in the eyes. "Which way was the compass pointing when you got a chance to look at it?"

Artemis closes her eyes and tries to remember but her mind becomes blank trying to recall yesterday morning. Cybele looks away because she remembers that the compass pointed toward the north when she asked David what was that circle in his hand.

"I'm sorry but I don't remember."

"You wouldn't lie to the king, would you?"

"You heard her, you creep! She said she doesn't remember!"

"Well, Cybele, unfortunately that's too bad for you. By orders of the queen, you are hereby sentenced to burn in the lake of fire until judgment day for not heeding to the queen's shofar to be present in town square yesterday."

"Dagon, no!" Artemis screams.

Dagon pops her neck to the right and steps back to watch her legs shrink from underneath her. Artemis becomes frozen because her mind is telling her what just had happened isn't real. Slowly the veil of disbelief is pull from over her eyes and her grieving heart causes her to crawl to her lifeless friend.

"Azzazel, what did you do?"

"A deal is a deal, and I believe I did pretty good at not breaking my word. I said I'll let her breath if you told me about the guy name David and Sharia."

"But you killed her!"

"No, you killed her. If I recall correctly, I said I'll let her live if what you told me was worth her life." Azzazel wraps his whip around his arm and taps Dagon on the shoulder. "Let's go, my most trusted servant. The queen and I have some towns to go terrorize and this is only the beginning of our day."

"You bastard!" Artemis shouts in tears. "I hope you burn in hell!"

Azzazel and Dagon walks to the entrance of the room. "You might have spoken some truth in saying that because we all know everyone's day in hell is coming. But until that day comes, I vow to hunt this David fellow down and send him there first." Azzazel pictures himself and the queen drinking a refreshing glass of cold water in their palace in Sodom. "Look at the bright side, when I do find him, Cybele will have someone to keep her company until you get there. By the way, thanks for telling me about Sharia. The queen will be please. Until next time." Azzazel takes two fingers and salutes Artemis. "Good-bye."

The foundation of the loft begins to shake like the building was sitting next to some train tracks. Small cracks in the sheetrock start to race through the walls, widening each time the room shifted. Artemis doesn't want to let go of her best friend but she must, or the creature that's coming for Cybele may take her too. Resting Cybele's head gently on the floor, Artemis closes her eyes and kisses her on the lips.

"Farewell, my friend. I'll never forget you," she said, as she exited the room to run down the stairs and out the front door.

12

"Oh David, I miss you, my love. I'm sorry that you left us unexpectantly but God is the author of all things, so who am I to doubt him in his reasons for taking you. All I ask of you is that you continue to be the man of God you were from the day I met you. Please, Lord, watch over my husband and use my beloved to minister to whomever you send his way in the afterlife. In your son Jesus's name, amen. I love you David Grace."

"Amy baby, is that you? I hear you, honey, but where are you? I don't see you!" David exclaims in a vertiginous state from the voice he realizes is in his head.

David is on a solitude road going east. The last person he has seen were two men riding horseback in the opposite direction he is going. It's been one week since he left the city of Demetria, following the directions of the compass and to his knowledge he is heading into the middle of nowhere.

Demetria was more upbeat than Gomorrah but hanging around longer than a couple nights is something he felt wasn't safe. Luckily, he had some zaqs to rent a room because sleeping outside among the people could have turned out to be treacherous. Since then, the ground has been his bed, and the rock he foreknew that was coming has been his pillow.

"Amy my love." David looks down the open road he's walking on and into the forest around him. "I heard you, my queen, and thanks for your prayers." David feels like he's lost his marbles because he's talking into thin air. "I don't know how I heard you but I did. I love you, baby, and when you get to heaven give both of my mothers a kiss for me," he sadly said falling to his knees and crying. "Sorry I didn't make it through the pearly gates, honey. I'm sorry I didn't make it."

Azzazel and Dagon are in Demetria, turning the city upside down looking for the man with the iron glove. The day the king found out another soul entered into Hades with a compass to Sharia, he decided to add to his regional overseeing to ask if anyone has seen a newcomer with a gauntlet on his hand. Finally, the answer to his question was received from an innkeeper who rented a room to an innocent face. After giving the innkeeper the third degree, the king was told that David had left heading toward the town's well.

At the well, Dagon enforced the throne's gavel on every citizen the king pointed out to bring to him. No one is able to honestly say that they saw or met the gloved man even though they wanted to so that the queen would be pleased. Slowly they sifted through the number of people like wheat until a single grain stepped forward in the form of a waif.

The destitute woman only slept at the main roads coming in and leaving the city. Nothing came or went without her seeing every detail on the individuals. Her lack of beauty is why she is homeless and her lack of strength makes any manual labor too hard for her to do. Not ashamed of her place in the afterlife, she bargains with Azzazel for a zaq to tell him all he wants to know.

Azzazel grazes the brim of his hat and laugh. "What is the name of the woman who desires to negotiate with the king and queen?"

"Queen Vashti," the woman replied with a deranged look on her face.

"Okay, Queen Vashti. I'll buy that, but only because Queen Jezebel is not present. Just don't let Dagon hear you repeat that too many times," he whispers. Azzazel walks over to Smokey's saddlebags and pulls out two zaqs. "So what is it that you have to tell the king that is so valuable, Ms. Vashti?" Azzazel places a zaq in front of her and when she reaches for it he quickly pulls it back. "Not so fast, missy. I know you must know something because crazy or not you wouldn't dare stand before me without information of use to me. If what you say can lead me to the man I seek then I'll give you two zaqs for your troubles."

Juice is running down the sides of Vashti's mouth from the first zaq he gave her to show he's going to stay true to what he says. Bite for bite she devours the fruit vegetable until it's all gone. The nutrients in the zaq settles in her stomach and quickly works its way down to her limbs giving her strength. Wanting more, she begins to speak about the Caucasian man leaving the city in the middle of the night.

"The man you are looking for is going east."

"What makes you so sure he's the man I'm looking for?"

"Because I saw him when he came into town and followed him hoping to steal the sack he had with him."

"And what direction might this mysterious man was coming from?" Azzazel takes his hat off and scratches his skull through his thick hair.

"I was at the south entrance tucked away in the woods when he walked into town."

"Was he wearing a glove?" Azzazel is all ears because the south entrance leads to Gomorrah.

"Not at first but he was when he left."

Azzazel hands Queen Vashti the other zaq and smiles as if he is her friend. "So, Vashti, how long ago did he leave the city of Demetria?"

"A week ago," Vashti replies while looking to the sky to make sure she remembered correctly. "If I'm not mistaken, I would say about a week ago."

"Is that it, Your Majesty?"

"Yes, Mister, that's it."

Azzazel calls for Smokey when he hears David has a seven-day jump on him. With Dagon scouting the area and Smokey's lighting speed, the two of them can catch David on foot by the end of the night. Pleasing the queen is all he desires as he quickly leapfrogs onto the back of his massive bear. Smokey roars because he senses his master is onto something that involves his jaws and claws shedding a lot of blood.

Dagon sees his king on his pet's back and signals for his pterodactyl to swoop down and pick him up. The king gives him strict orders to report back to Jezebel what they have learned and also the direction they are about to go to. When the king finished speaking, Dagon reaches out his arm and grabs the iron collar around the neck of his winged pet. The pterodactyl's feet never touches the ground as they both rose swiftly into the air.

"Hurry up and get back here! In order for my plan to work correctly, I'm going to need your eyes in the sky!" Azzazel shouts.

David is at a crossroad. His feet hurts but he must keep moving because he has utilized every minute of the gray clouds that are above him. A wooden pole is stuck deep in the ground and on it is a sign. Tilgath and Shiloh is to the left which is north. Rapha and Eglon is straight ahead, which is east. Field of Blood and the river of Raqueem is to the right, which is south. And west leads back to Demetria from which he came. Any of the directions besides south or west he would have gladly have chosen but his left hand is telling him to go toward the town that has the name blood at the end of it.

"This can't be for real," he said dropping his head. *Where in the hell are you taking me?* he thought shaking his hand vigorously. When his hands stops, he brings it to his face hoping that the direction has changed to the north or east. Sadly it hasn't and all he can say is, "Damn, now what are you going to do, David?"

The sound of a galloping horse in the distance causes him to leer to the north. At first he thought he had imagined what he had heard until the sound got closer. In a sudden dash he races for the trees doing what he has been accustomed to doing when travelers pass on the roads he's been walking along. Staring through the willows, he sees a figure wearing a hooded poncho stop near the spot he was just standing in and get off the horse.

A travois is strapped to a white palfrey carrying the hooded person's belongings. Taking a break from the horse ride, the figure pulls out a canteen and unscrews the top.

As the water goes down the mysterious person's throat, the hood falls from their head. Pure beauty is the only words that can describe the Indian woman standing before him. Stunned, he shuffles his feet snapping some twigs scattered along the ground.

"Please don't hurt me!" she screams. "I can hear you hiding behind those trees." David emerges from the forest with his dirk drawn just in case she is a wolf in sheep's clothing. "Please, sir, don't hurt me. I promise I am no harm to you. I came from the town of Heriopolis and I am on my way to Demetria. I have no zaqs and this is the last of my water."

"Relax, I mean you no harm either but please, ma'am, I must ask you to step away from your horse just to be on the safe side."

The woman raises her hands to David's drawn dirk and willfully complies. While standing on the side of the road, she stares at him closely as he pokes at her travois with the tip of his blade. Clothes for her journey is all he finds so he concludes that if she has a weapon it must be on her person.

"Ma'am."

"Yes," she said, hoping he would let her be on her way.

David realizes he never inquired the lady's name. "Sorry for not asking you earlier, but what is your name if you don't mind me asking?" He asks placing his dirk in its sheath to show her he's not one of the bad guys.

"Delilah," she replied lowering her hands. "And thanks for asking um—"

"David. David Grace." David is secretly in awe of her beauty and can see how the Delilah in the Bible could entice Samson to do almost anything she desired.

Delilah extends her hand. "Nice to meet you, David Grace." David steps away because he doesn't know if she's on the side of the fence that is manicured or the side of the fence that is full of weeds. "It's okay, David Grace, I understand."

"Please, just call me David."

"Okay, David. Whatever is best for you then that's what I'm going to call you."

"Once again, I'm sorry for putting you on the spot like this but do you have a weapon hidden on your person?"

"No I don't," she said with a smirk while raising her poncho to reveal she is only wearing panties and a bra. "You can frisk me if you like." Delilah turns around in a circle holding the corners of her poncho up keeping her seductive eyes locked on David.

"There's no need for frisking you, Ms. Delilah. I believe you."

"Are you sure, David, because I don't know who would enjoy it more, me or you."

"Yes I'm sure and thanks for the offer." David turns away and bites his knuckle. When he brings his attention back to Delilah, her poncho is down and she looks at him like "what kind of man are you?" David clears his throat and inwardly curses himself for his dedication to the vows he made to Amy. "I know this may sound weird but you are the first person who looked trustworthy for me to talk to since I left the city of Demetria."

"Demetria is pretty far, David," she said looking around. "Where is your horse or the animal you are riding on?"

David raises his boots one after the other. "You're looking at it."

Delilah covers her mouth and giggles at his sarcasm. "You mean to tell me that you've walked all the way from Demetria?" she asked pointing at his feet. "Sorry for laughing because it's not funny but Demetria is a very long way."

Conversing about their journey, David finds out that Delilah has been riding just as far from Heriopolis as he has been walking from Demetria. Her reasons for leaving is because her boyfriend was killed defending her and therefore left her vulnerable to the satanic souls running the streets of the small town. Everything she has she is traveling with to Demetria to start over with a friend that was sentenced to Hades shortly after her. Her only problem is that she doesn't have any zaqs to live on until she gets on her feet again.

David hands her one of the three zaqs he has in his sack in hopes that what he has given her can help her in some kind of way. When she ask what's his purpose for wandering on the outskirts between towns, he replies that he is on a quest to find Sharia. His only problem is that: one, he doesn't know if the place is real or not. And two, his unseen map is telling him to go toward the direction of the Field of Blood.

"I have an idea, David. Seeing that you have only a couple of zaqs left in your bag there and I am in dire need of money," she pauses. "How about we accompany one another to the river of Raqueem and along the way we can find the path to the watery place together. David doesn't catch that Delilah knew what Sharia meant without him telling her. Pondering on her request, the gentleman inside him doesn't want her to try and make the trip alone. His options becomes even narrower when a pain in the arch of his right foot begs him for some time off.

"So be it, Ms. Delilah, I'll join you. But only because you are correct in saying I am running low on zaqs. And I haven't had a drink of water in over a week."

Delilah smiles at David's accepting her invitation to join her in riding to the river of Raqueem. Grabbing hold of the saddle horn, she places her foot inside the stirrup and swings herself up into the saddle. David follows her steps by pulling himself up next and sits behind her on the horse's back. The horse neighs and whinnies at the shifting of his weight when he is settling in to be as comfortable as possible for the ride. "It's okay, Betsie." Delilah rubs her horse's mane. "David Grace is a nice guy."

Betsie trotted gracefully down the road pulling the travois while carrying the two of them to the Field of Blood. Delilah has never been there to give input on why they call it such a detestable name, but she has heard rumors that it is some sort of forbidden place. Meditating on the unknown ahead, he keeps his mind positive and prays that whoever branded him with the compass is on his side.

Riding from the crossroads passed some productive time. The closer they drew to the town, the clouds that were once charcoal gray now looked like the burnt orange clouds that shields the sun when it's setting on the beach.

The trees to the right and the trees to left began to grow in number as the scenery around them that was open pastures has returned to a dense forest. The long branches on each side of the graveled road combine to make an arch that soon takes away most of the glowing sky. Delilah has one hand on the reins and the other is clenched to David's arm around her waist. Step by step, Betsie's four legs rise and fall taking her master to what looks to be a terra incognita.

"I'm scared, David." Delilah speaks truthfully but the thought of finding Sharia doesn't allow her to ask to retreat from the tunnel nature has made.

"I admit I'm a little terrified myself. Just get us out of these woods and we'll figure out what's next later."

As they watched their surroundings closely, they listened for any sound of life that may be among them. Betsie's snorts and her hooves clacking bounces off the tree trunks send them mixed feelings on whether they are the only ones in the dark forest or not. David looks up occasionally to see if anything is waiting to pounce on them from above. The only thing that is on top of them is the dim sky glittering through the leaves like the white stars in the galaxies.

Delilah points to the end of the leafy tunnel. "Look, David. We are almost out of the woods."

"Yes, I can see. But then what?"

The Field of Blood is not a town or a city and it doesn't have a sign to acknowledge when one is there. Dead fields cover the terrace running up and down hills that stop at the river of Raqueem. Trotting along the meander, Delilah holds his arms wrapped around her even tighter when the stench of death rose from the dirt like dead animals that were unburied.

Delilah looks down and notices an infinite of circular mounds next to each other on the ground. David doesn't say anything about the mounds, but his instincts are sending a danger alarm through his brain. He keeps his mouth shut for the sake of not frightening his companion into veering off the course that for the moment is safe.

Focusing on the trees of zaqs that are at the end of the path, he whispers to Delilah to get as close to one of the trees as Betsie can take them. She listens without asking him why he is whispering in a place that seems uninhabited. Betsie senses the fear in Delilah and David but stays courageous throughout the ride despite the negative aroma rising off her back.

"Did you hear that, David?" Delilah brings her horse to a halt on side of one of the trees.

David looks around curiously while listening. "Hear what?"

"Shh, be quiet."

Sitting there in silence, David follows her eyes to the direction she heard the faint noise came from. The shivering of limbs and leaves in the trees begin to shake vigorously but nothing in eyesight seems to be the cause of the wind-like shutter. David quietly tells Delilah to move away from the trees and into the marsh near the river. As the travois is dragging across the last root from the tree they were sitting at, a bevy of cat-size agoutis races down the tree trunks and onto the path they were on. *That's no good*, he thought watching the rodents exiting the Field of Blood like it was on fire.

Delilah speaks wondering about the question mark written on his face. "What do you suppose that was all about?"

David doesn't know how to respond but his gut is telling him to follow suit behind the rat's first cousin. "I'm sorry, Delilah, but I think we should be going. Something is not right about this place so grab a few zaqs and let's go."

"What about?" Delilah tries to respond with a question.

"No!" David blurts out. "No, we are not going to Sharia. It was a mistake to think that it was real. Now pull Betsie up to that tree and then get us the hell out of here."

"But, David," Delilah pleads. "I think we can find it if we keep looking together."

David becomes angry and takes off his glove. While shoving his hand into her face he yells, "Don't you get it! Sharia is not real! And this compass has been bullshit from the day it appeared in my hand! Look!" David points to the S showing them to continue south. "The damn thing doesn't work! Right now it's telling us to get into the boiling river of Raqueem. Shit, maybe that's Sharia for all I know. Hell, anybody knows."

The tension in the air makes them both take their eyes off of their surroundings. Down below, a hand is slowly coming out the ground underneath the horse's belly. No one—not even the horse—is paying attention to the top of a skull pulling itself from up out the marsh. The swishing of the wet mud pushing against Betsie's hoof causes the horse to look between her front legs. Wildly startled, Betsie rears up and points her forelock and chest to the sky when the boney torso beneath her swings a sword at her fetlock. Delilah tightens her hands around the reins to try and get Betsie to put her hooves back to the ground but by then it's too late for the both of them.

David is first to do a backflip off the back of the horse. Falling onto the travois he smashes it instantly, pressing Delilah's clothes into the wet dirt. Delilah tries her hardest to hold on until Betsie jerks her head for her to let go. After a hard buck, she is tossed through the air about six feet beyond the trees, leaving Betsie with two wooden poles as the horse runs off to escape.

"Delilah, run!" David shouts before kicking the sunken face man in the chest, folding him in half like a piece of paper only for the skeleton with skin to return upright and push himself to his feet. "Get the hell out of here! I'll hold him off as long as I can. Just get back to the main road and don't look back!"

Suddenly, the same breed of men and women begin to emerge from the mounds throughout the Field of Blood. All of them have a weapon and shield in there skinny hands, armed to display why the Field of Blood has its name. Their body movement is slow and nothing can terminally hurt them. Pressing forward, the sunken face soldiers try to surround Delilah but she slips away from their grasp.

Without hesitation she runs for her life. When she is far enough out of danger she looks back to see if David escaped the creatures from the ground that came upon them. Her eyes are widen when her view of him is blocked by boney backs of men and women swarming around him like bees on honey. No sorrow comes from her heart because she was only along for the ride to be the first soul in Hades to discover the whereabouts of the mysterious Sharia. The path to the watery place.

13

There's nowhere to run. David feels like a football player about to be at the bottom of a pile on. Pushed back, he swings his dagger like a wild man but the cuts he inflicts on the malnourished citizens doesn't seem to hurt their abraded skin. David grows tired and weary as he defends himself against a species that can't be affected like the average soul in Hades. "Get back! Please get back!" he screams when the steam from the river begins to heat the metal in the chain mail around his upper body.

Backpedaling on the bank of the river of Raqueem, a man with a piece of his skin hanging off his face brings his sword fiercely down upon David. Before the blade can reach his shoulder blade, David raises his arm and blocks the blow with the iron gauntlet while pivoting out of the way. The pain surges in his forearm from the swords strike creasing the metal on the glove into his wrist.

Straining with all his might, he twists and turns the gauntlet until it falls to the ground. A ring of blood is smeared around his hand as he continues backward into the boiling water. Ripples from the heel of his boot trickles in the river starting at the point of entry he stepped and ending when the force behind the ripples weakens along the surface.

The water stirs again, but this time it's not from his boot. Lurking beneath the water, something the size of a school bus swims in the midst of the deep off the shore. Sitting still within the boiling river of Raqueem, the unknown eyes rise up out the water like a periscope.

David is tracing and traversing in his footsteps trying to fend off the soldiers that are extending their hands to nab him. Raising his sword to the fire burning in the sky, he yells, "Why!" and falls to his knees in the damp sand. His butt is on the back of his boots as he sits waving the white flag with his head hanging down.

"We are the Underlings and our master is the great Leviathan."

David pats his chest and rubs his face to make sure he is still alive. He doesn't know that the compass in his hand is glowing through the cracks of mud that is covering it. When he looks up, all but one of the Underlings have prostrated themselves to the ground.

The Underling who is standing speaks again. "Since the beginning of time our kind has retreated all those who has come in search of Sharia. Nothing can harm us because we were here the day Lucifer fell from heaven. Shortly after his fall, God created mankind in his image to rule over earth and everything that dwells in its atmosphere under the stars. Lucifer, who is now Satan, recognized that mankind was given a free will and could decide to disobey God if the opportunity was pleasing to their satisfaction. Satan waited centuries to get back at the father of creation and then his chance came in a woman. Mother Eve sinned first but the fall of mankind came through Adam. It is his giving into temptations that brought physical death upon your race of people. It is his sin that made Satan the ruler of Hades and hell. It is his spiritual death that gave Satan the power to create the worm of torment that defies God's son Jesus's judgment to Hades and instead throw you into the lake of fire. We, the Underlings, are destined for hell the day after judgment day. Therefore, out of reverence to the Creator and our master the Leviathan, we protect Sharia from those that are not sent. Many have come, few are chosen, but no one has ever succeeded in finding the path to the watery place."

"What do you mean that no one has succeeded in finding Sharia?" David asked angrily while timidly standing to his feet to face the stick figure in front of him."

"Because they had no compass, David," a soothing but powerful voice said from behind him. "And the souls that did have the compass such as you, either die from lack of survival skills in the afterlife or are robbed for their maps before they can successfully get on the path."

"Who said that?" David turns around quickly and a great shadow covers him as its source rises up out the water. Staring at the breathing tower before him, he drops his sword and thinks, "Oh well, I'm screwed for sure now."

"I am the great Leviathan in whom my soldiers speak of."

The Leviathan is a behemoth serpent with four small legs to move at a fast pace when on land. Its scales are greenish black and its long tongue is split at the end. Two fangs protrude out of the Leviathan's mouth when closed, and if needed its core spits out fire scorching anything in its path.

Tiny wings sit on the creature's back giving it extra leaping ability but its wings' size will not allow the beast to fly. Its body temperature is like that of a chameleon, when the lizard changes color to its surroundings. When it's cold, the Leviathan's body temperature will be hot and when it's hot, the monster's body temperature will be cold. This is another defense trait so that no matter where it decides to abode, the beast will remain unharmed throughout any catastrophic weather conditions.

"Leviathan? Whoa, whoa, whoa!" David exclaimed waving his hands in front of him as if to ward the massive creature off. "Please don't eat me, Mr. Leviathan! I am a family man and besides I don't taste good anyway."

David turns around to run but the Underlings spokesman is dead center in the only path among the prostrated soldiers. Frantically, he tries to push the scrawny man out of the way until he feels that the speaker is stronger than he looks.

"David."

"Please, Mr. nice sea monster in the boiling lake. Just let me go." David clasps his hand together as he bellows. "I promise I won't tell nobody about you or your Underlings."

"Pharaoh!" the Leviathan shouts to the soldier standing. "Let David Grace go!" Pharaoh responds by bowing his head and moving to the side.

David steps to the passage that is given to him not knowing that the mud covering the compass has hardened from the heat and fell to the marsh. A red beacon of light spreads over the prostrated people, causing the orange sky over the field to become violet. Nothing is making sense as he wonders why the compass has changed into a bright flashlight and how the Leviathan knows his name. Halfway down the man-made walkway, his heart tells him to stop and finish the mission he set out for when he left Gomorrah.

Disregarding his instincts to get as far away from the Field of Blood as possible, David returns to the bank of the river.

"Who are you and how do you know my name?" David inquired fearfully while raising his laminated palm above his head to get a good look at the talking serpent.

"I am the great Leviathan and I am the last of my kind. Unlike the Underlings I came here after the fall of Satan but before the fall of mankind. Therefore, this is my dwelling place until the day after judgment day as well. Satan, the Underlings, and the demons that fell with him from heaven are the only beings that know I exist. This is why I live in exile beneath the river in which no one can enter except Satan only. He is the supreme being of the graves and out of respect for the power he has obtained, I stay hidden so that the souls in Hades can revere him only. My desire is only to be the bridge to Sharia for those who the alpha and omega has blessed with the directions to receive cold water in Sheol. I found out that I had a connection to Sharia when the compass lodged in your hand as well as others begin to tell me all about the souls who had them. Very few has had the compass. Six to be exact. Four women and two men including you. All of them sought Sharia but none of them never found it. You, David Grace, is the first so therefore I am obliged to take you to what is rightfully yours."

"Take me. I'm sorry but my name is not Jonah and you sure don't look like a whale or whatever it was that took him to Nineveh." David shutters when he remembers how the Bible said Jonah was in the huge fish's belly for three days until he was vomited up onto dry land.

The Leviathan laughs. "There's no need for you to think so harshly of me," he said lowering his head and laying it in front of David. "My purpose is to take you across the river to Gehenna and from there you must continue following the compass until you find what you have been looking for.

Meanwhile, Delilah is on the road that leads back to the four-way crossing, panting from running for her life for the last three hours. The adrenaline that pumped through her veins has now ceased leaving her extremely exhausted. Her feet are still moving, just not as quick. Two long trails lay in spurts in the gravel from where she couldn't pick up her legs. Stopping periodically for rest, Hades's night sky hovers above her, giving her only seconds to rest.

Walking alone at night, she feels like open game for any of Satan's creatures waiting to maul her until the worm of torment comes for her body. *Where's Betsie when I need her?* she thought, after the mayhem that can be afflicted upon her settled into her thoughts and wouldn't leave no matter how hard she tried to shake them from her mind.

Dagon is flying high in the sky hiding behind the mist of clouds being watchful for anything that doesn't fit in the terrain below. His demonic eyesight is like that of an eagle, so whether night or day, he can see the hairs on the back of a person's neck if he focuses hard enough. His pterodactyl eyes are the same, therefore the search for the man with the iron glove has become extremely in Azzazel's favor.

The pterodactyl is the first to spot Delilah jog walking in the dead grass on the side of the road. If it wasn't for her unsteady movement, the flying beast probably would've overlooked her because her Indian skin blended in with the ground quite well. Squawking like a hawk, the ptero-dactyl points its beak toward the direction she is walking. Dagon quickly takes heed to what his pet has preyed upon and kicks his heels in the beast's side to go down for a closer look.

Open fields are on this part of the road. The trees are about two miles up ahead but even if she ran as fast as she can she couldn't beat the eighteen-foot wingspan that is swooping down on her. The loud squeal from above is what brought Dagon's presence to her attention. Her legs that were once weights are now light as a feather. Survival races through every inch of her body when the wind in her lungs causes her muscles to loosen up.

The trees down the road are far but the word hope makes them look closer. "Run, Delilah," she said aloud as she runs for the woods in the letter Z. Delilah covers about a half of a mile before being snatched into the air by Dagon's pet's webbed toes around her shoulders. She tries to shake loose but the strength in its claws will not allow her to move. All she can do is be still and wait because the ground is too far to fall to.

Azzazel is deep in the forest using his hunting skills to dissect everything that is not in its place. He knows he's on the right path because David's footprints led to broken branches and broken branches led to a bed of leaves with a rock in place for a pillow. Time after time, he's found these man-made structures in the woods on side of the road from Demetria. The last one was found a couple of miles ago so he doubts he'd find another one as Smokey brought him back to the road near the four-way crossing.

Dagon came with Delilah as he is kneeling down to examine the coming and going travois's markings in the gravel. Delilah is standing helpless before Azzazel wanting to run but the pterodactyl rows of triangular teeth makes her think twice about running.

At first, Azzazel doesn't acknowledge her because his train of thought is trying to figure out who would want to travel to the forbidden Field of Blood. "Ah, David, could it be you who hitched a ride or perhaps stolen someone's horse to find food near the river of Raqueem?" he thought turning to the woman his demonic friend has brought to him.

Azzazel devilishly smiles at the woman's beauty. "And who might you be, Ms. lady in the night?"

"Delilah," she answers but only because Dagon is breathing down her back.

Azzazel looks down at her worn-out boots covered in mud around the soles. "Let me guess. You are the owner of the horse pulling the travois to the Field of Blood and the river of Raqueem."

"How do you know that? There was no one around when we left this crossing."

Azzazel takes his hat off and holds it in front of him. "Let's just say I have a sixth sense for knowing certain things."

Delilah smarts off to his comment. "Sixth sense. Huh, I'll say it's more like you were spying on us from the woods."

Azzazel suddenly becomes stern and his voice changes to a man who has no patience. "Enough! He roars causing her to flinch. "Do you know who I am?"

Delilah replies quickly hoping that the man in front of her will return to the man who was kneeling on the ground a few minutes ago. "No, I'm sorry for—"

"Silence!" Azzazel steps forward and grabs her by her chin. "I am King Azzazel and the ground you are standing on is in my kingdom. Evidently you must be from another region because had you had been from here you would have known who I am. Now that our acquaintances are out of the way, I would like to know who is this *we* that you were just talking about before you rudely took my kindness for weakness."

Delilah's knees are shaking. Her palms are sweaty and her brown eyes are the size of an owl. The mentioning of King Azzazel brought fear in her soul instantly because that makes his spouse Queen Jezebel and the man behind her the treacherous Dagon. Everyone in her province Bin Hinnom has heard of the hideous trio within this land and how they rule over their kingdom on a zero-tolerance basis. It was in her region that the Sons of Darkness was dethroned for the lack of not ruling in the utmost of hatefulness. Delilah wasn't there to witness the dethronement but those who were present said that Dathan and his followers were drug off by their feet on the back of Jezebel's chariot.

"The guy who was riding with me is David." Delilah stands as still as she can because her face is still in the grasp of Azzazel's hands.

"And where might this David be now?" he ask tightening his grip while looking into her eyes.

"Dead. Last time I saw him he was surrounded by creatures coming out of the ground with swords in their hands. He was on the bank of the river of Raqueem with nowhere to run. The only reason I am alive is because he brought all the creatures' attention toward himself so that I can get away."

"Aw, so touching." Azzazel releases her face. "But enough of the damsel in distress stories." Azzazel looks past her. "Dagon, fly over the Field of Blood and see if what Ms. Delilah is telling us is true." Azzazel returns to his devilish charming self. "And as for Delilah and I, we will be shortly behind you."

Dagon climbs on the back of his pet and flies off in the direction the king ordered him to go. Delilah tries to talk her way out of returning to the Field of Blood, but Azzazel picks her up by the waist and sits her down on Smokey's saddle. Leaping onto his trusted companion, he pulls the hairs on the back of the bear's neck. Smokey dashes off in lightning speed hungry for the action he knows that soon will be coming his way.

Nighttime is what every evil being looks forward to. In Hades, it's always dark but those living in this realm consider the charcoal gray clouds day and the burnt orange clouds night. It's something about the night that brings out the worst in people. You can steal in the night. You can hide in the night. You can hunt in the night. And you can sneak up on your opponent and overcome them during the night. All this and more you can do throughout the night. This is why Azzazel is going to get to the bottom of the myth of Sharia tonight. Delilah said David is dead but she also told him that the compass led him to the river of Raqueem. Dead or not, Azzazel knows that no one is dumb enough to enter the Field of Blood unless they were onto something worth risking their life for.

Approaching the Field of Blood, Delilah sees Dagon standing next to his flying friend on the meander that leads to the river. Azzazel rides up next to him and asks did he see the man they are looking for. Dagon shakes his head no but then presents David's gauntlet. Azzazel doesn't like the fact that David isn't wearing it. And he especially doesn't like the fact that Delilah's story may be true because the glove is dented severely. After carefully examining the open area, he tells Dagon to show him where he found it.

"I'm sorry, King Azzazel, but this is where I get off." Delilah jumps down before Azzazel can stop her from getting off Smokey. "I know you probably will kill me for not going on further but I figure I would rather die by you than whatever those things is down by the river."

The man Azzazel is looking for is in the vicinity and the hunter in him can feel it. Two weeks he's been tracking this David fellow and finally he has him under his nose. Delilah's disobedience makes him want to chop her head off with the sword he has in his scabbard. The only reason he doesn't is because her screams may warn whoever's out there that he and Dagon is coming.

"You've done well, Ms. Delilah, but don't ever defy my authority by telling me what you are going to do. Is that understood?" Azzazel asked with blood in his eyes.

"Sorry, my king," she respectfully replied knowing that she was seconds away from dancing with the devil in hell.

"You're free to go, Ms. Delilah, and enjoy your walk back to town." Azzazel tips his hat and pulls Smokey's hair. "Let's ride, Dagon. I can't wait to meet the citizens of this blood-stench field that Ms. Delilah is so afraid of."

14

A light fog sat over the face of Gehenna. Before descending into the depths of the river, the Leviathan told David to let the compass guide him and to stay cautious of the lava geysers from the volcano of Tanctum. The fog only goes so far from the shore so David has his flashlight palm to the ground to see if he can spot any eruptions before they happen. Each step he steps he steps carefully praying that God sees him through nature's land mine field.

Gehenna is a desolate place and nothing lives there because the ground won't allow it. Lava flows underneath the surface of all Hades, but it is here that multiple geysers occur throughout the lifeless town. Also, the tree of Zaqueem doesn't grow on this side of the river; therefore, making it impossible to sustain life for anyone crazy enough to want to live there. Past and present structures still appear out of nowhere but with no one around to take care of them, they sit untouched like the underwater city of Atlantis.

Finally, the troublesome fog is behind him and the ground he is walking on appears to be charred from the hot lava continuously flowing upon it. Everything before him is visible because the fluorescent glow within his hand covers a widespread of the terrace. Strings of mist pushed themselves from big and small geysers giving David an added awareness of where and where not to step. He tries to avoid them completely but the best he can do is walk in between them.

The ground under his boots starts to shake causing him to pause and give a closer look to the burnt dirt around him. "Please God don't let that be that damn worm of torment coming for me," he mumbles remembering how the oversized worm showed no mercy to Artemis's friend. Suddenly, the movement abruptly stopped and the sound of a train's air brakes releasing before taking off comes from the left of David's foot. Hot steam pushed from out of the black crust from what he thought was a safe geyser to walk by. The pressured mist missed his face by inches but the unbearable heat turned his white cheeks to crispy red.

What followed is what keeps life from exploring this side of the river. David knew something was wrong when the ground shifted like a category 3 earthquake. Quickly diving to his right, the geyser that cooked his face burst into molten lava reaching the height of a two-story building. David rolls two to three times dodging the burning globs of drops showering down upon him. Groveling to his feet, he clears enough ground to only escape with tiny bead holes burnt into his pants.

After a wipe to his forehead and a sigh of relief, he courageously raises his compass and continues south. All five of his senses are as keen as ever as he uses each one of them to try to diagnose where the next geyser will erupt. To his right, a ways down, another geyser spouts to the sky, but David is far enough from the lava to stay focused on the guidance of the compass. As he passes a few old and new buildings, he wonders, *How can I be on the path that leads to cold water when the only thing around me is a boiling river and hot lava?* Taking a steadfast approach at dealing with the task at hand, he decides not to allow his thoughts to deter him from where his heart is resolutely telling him to go.

Weary from his long day of trials, his legs are starting to become harder for him to pick up. The geysers that once were everywhere have reduced tremendously, so therefore resting is something that his mind is telling him to do. Trying his hardest not to stop, his hamstrings and calves screams for some time of relief. A wooden bench is in front of a rundown adobe structure up ahead so with the help of willpower he trudged forward for what he has concluded to be his resting place.

The bench is old but looks to be sturdy enough to hold his body weight. Just before he is about to sit down, the red light in his hand changed to aqua blue. David looks into the compass for understanding and sees that north, south, east, and west is gone and the word SHARIA is in all caps. "Am I here?" he asks himself trying to identify anything that has to do with water. Holding his hand in front of him, he slowly swings it from side to side hoping it will show him what to do next. The closest buildings are fifty to sixty feet away from where he is standing so that left the adobe structure is what caused the compass to change colors.

Reaching for the doorknob, David's hands start to blink on and off. Hesitantly he turns the knob because of the unknowingness of what is on the other side of the door. Before he opens it, he looks back and realizes how far he has come to get there. Overcoming the mutant wolf, Jezebel, the Underlings, Leviathan, and the scorching lava geysers gives him the extra push he needs to cross the finish line that he has finally made it to. "It's either now or never, David," he said as he watches the door open and stop with a thud when it reaches the clay wall behind it. When he crosses the threshold, the aqua-blue light turns off and the compass disappears like it was never in his hand from the beginning.

The rectangular structure is empty. Four walls of adobe brick supports the wooden beams that once supported the absent roof. Black dirt carpeted the floor and a solid gold door stood suspended upright in the center of the building. David thought, *How can a door stand on its own?* as he stepped forward to investigate the answer to his question. Engraved in the header of the door is the word Sharia. Amazed at the beauty before him, David walks around the doorframe to see if what he is looking at is an illusion or a gimmick. After walking in a 360 degree circle he finds himself scratching his head saying, "Now what?"

A brilliant-but-peculiar light is in the crevice of the golden door and frame. *Where is that light coming from, if nothing is on the other side of the door?* he thought while running his fingertips along the seam down to the gigantic pearl in place of the doorknob. Ardent, he pulls the door slightly ajar and the brilliant light engulfs the small room causing him to place his hands over his eyes before he loses his eyesight.

Slowly, he lowers his hands until his eyes adjusted to the light. Opening the door further, David finds himself mesmerized at the beauty of what's behind the door. Men, women, and children in shining white robes lie in the grass next to a stream playing with lions, zebras, and other wildlife animals. Angels fly around them in circles laughing and smiling with praying hands. He wants to enter the door but two cherubim stand guard on each side of the entrance.

One of the angels, enjoying the company of the people, noticed that the door to Hades is open. Separating herself from the crowd she flies over to the stream and dips an aqua-blue sphere against the flow of the gurgling crystal water. Hovering only a few feet over the green grass, the angel lands between the silent cherubim.

"Glad to see you made it, Pastor Grace," she said holding the sphere in both hands as her arms crosses the threshold. "This is for you."

David takes the sphere in awe of the glory and peacefulness of heaven. Before he can say thank-you the door slams shut and folds in half, and in half again, and in half again until the folding of the door turns into a spectacle and vanishes. Finally he gathers his thoughts and he feels like the rich man in Hades when he saw Lazarus across the great gulf fix in Father Abraham's bosom.

Across the seething river of Raqueem, Azzazel is examining David's staggering footprints in the dark sand at the end of the shore. Tracing in his footsteps he sees the defense David tried to put up against whatever attacked him unexpectedly. Delilah's story is true up until when the frantic footprints changed to a more steady movement.

Carefully picturing the so-called "battle" that took place where he is standing, he tries to sum up David's demise. Something is missing, because the fighting for survival David seemed to now be a man given the opportunity to leave freely. The footprints in the marsh shows David's boots stopping near the meander and returning to the very spot he tried to fight off whatever was attacking him.

Azzazel is perplexed as he and Dagon stare into the direction David's boots were facing when his trail stops. "Where are you, my friend?" he asked looking over the boiling river. "For surely you are not dead like the Indian cunt professed."

The river is hot but trying to find the missing piece to David's puzzle is more important than the heat upon both of their faces. Silence lingered in the air as they stood unaware of the hands making their way from out of the ground. Smokey is on the meander when the first body appeared from a mound near him. Quickly reacting, he blusters at the many torsos separating him from his master. The call of his furry friend breaks his thoughts and causes him to turn around in haste.

"Aha!" Azzazel elbows Dagon to get his attention. "There are the skeleton creatures that has the answers to all my questions!" he yells unraveling his whip and striking it to the feet of the Underlings so that they can maintain their distance.

Pharaoh raises his sword so that none of his soldiers will move unless he commands them to. "We are the Underlings and our master is the great Leviathan. Since the beginning of time we have protected this land from all those who walk upon these grounds who are not welcome."

Azzazel becomes infuriated when he hears not welcomed. "Not welcomed, he says," he said staring into Pharaoh's sunken eyes. "How can I not be welcome in my own land?"

"I am Pharaoh and our master Leviathan is the ruler of the ground you are standing on. Whoever you or whatever you seek is not here so therefore my master desires for you to leave before troubles finds you."

"Before trouble finds me?" Azzazel scoffs. "My name is King Azzazel and I am the ruler of this region which makes me the ruler of the ground I am standing on as well. Therefore, you Pharaoh must submit to the throne of Queen Jezebel and not to whatever this Leviathan is. I'm sorry but leaving is not an option and please don't mention trouble to me again because I am trouble. Now where is the man who was wearing this damn glove?" Azzazel shouts throwing the iron gauntlet into the mud.

Dagon pulls his battle-ax from the center of his back when he hears the sound of war in his king's voice. Smokey pushes off the ground with his front paws and stands erect on his hind legs. His long claws are to his side as a loud roar comes from the back of his purple tongue and pushes through his sharp teeth and black gums. Soaring high in the sky, the pterodactyl squawks at Azzazel and Dagon preparing to do battle down below. Landing beside Smokey, the dinosaur tucks his wing to its side and waits for the signal to destroy the Underlings.

All odds are against the Devil's Advocates but they have faced worse odds than these before and came out triumphant. Their pets are behind the Underlings and they are in the front of them so at least they have them surrounded.

Azzazel becomes tiresome of the silence. "So where is David, and out of respect for who I am, I refuse to ask you a third time!"

Pharaoh drops his sword. "Underlings attack!" he shouts furious of the king's disobedience to the Leviathan's request.

Azzazel is the first to react to the charging soldiers. With the skill of his whip, he strikes with accuracy and coils it around the forearm of a woman with a raised dagger. The quickness of his hand pulls her arm causing the sword to soar through the air toward him. In less than a blink of an eye, the woman is left with only a shield as he reaches out and retrieves the weapon from the air by its hilt. Dropping his whip, he unscabs his double-edged sword from his back while taking his stance in the wet sand. Shoulder to shoulder, him and Dagon readies themselves for the opposition they provoked without hesitation.

Pharaoh leads just as a leader is supposed to. Stepping forward, he locks swords with Azzazel while blocking a hard blow with his shield from the dagger. The impact of the two blades colliding sounds off over the battlefield as sparks glinted from their technique blows and dissipate.

Azzazel is not more skilled with the sword than Pharaoh but he is a lot faster. Sensing the advantage over his opponent, he blocks a blow over the top and spins around to the back of the Underlings' commander. The king's speed is too quick to defend and leaves Pharaoh helpless to what awaits him. Azzazel dashingly slices his blade parallel to the ground severing Pharaoh's hairless head down his right shoulder.

With both swords in his hands, he feels the thrill of victory as he stands waiting for the corpse to follow the skull to the ground. Seconds goes by and Pharaoh's body is still standing. Azzazel tries to fathom why but before he can, the headless corpse turns around and drives the pommel of its sword down onto the top of his head. Azzazel falls down in a daze as the headless Pharaoh bends down and places his head back on his shoulders. All Azzazel can do is retake his stance because he knows he may have bitten off more than he can chew.

Dagon is on a rampage fending off the skeleton-like soldiers from among his king's battle. Slicing fiercely, he cuts off arms, legs, hands, and heads as if the perfection of his swing is robotic. Even he is amazed at how no blood is shed at all the limbs he has severed. Before he would kill and wait for the worm of torment to come for the scraps, but the Underlings don't die like the souls he has encountered. Every part he cuts away from one of them they put back on and return fighting only for the limb to be cut off again. It doesn't matter how hard the challenge is to him because war is what he lives for and if it came down to it, it will be what he would die for as well. As for the moment, Dagon's body armor will keep him fighting until the latter befalls him.

Smokey and the pterodactyl are doing their part on the battlefield for whose land each party is on. Unlike Dagon who sometimes think for himself, the only command their pets know is cease and destroy. From the time Azzazel crossed blades with Pharaoh, Smokey and the winged beast have been ripping apart the Underlings, making their maimed body parts longer to be put back to their full state of being.

Charging forward, Smokey lowers his big head and battle rams ten to twelve soldiers with his sea turtle helmet. Frail bodies twirl through the air landing on top of the skin-and-bone soldiers. Standing back erect, he uses his long claws to slice and dice anyone at paw's reach.

The pterodactyl grabs three of the Underlings after mauling a half dozen in its pointed teeth. A soldier is clamped in each of its webbed toes and another is in its beak. Spreading his wings across the Field of Blood, the muscles in its legs pushes off the ground sending the ancient bird above the layers of orange in the sky. When the flying beast returned to sight, the soldiers were gone, and in an instance, the pterodactyl is gone again with three more Underlings.

A blow to the helmet caused Dagon's head to turn toward the water. His eyesight is superb as he watches David approach the shore of the river. The sight of David helps him regain his footing and thereafter he snatches the sword from the man that hit him. Dagon drives the blade into the soldier's chest down to the guard.

"Master!" Azzazel's hands are full when Dagon calls to him.

"What is it, Dagon?" he asked over the constant clinging of the blades. "Can't you see I'm busy?"

Dagon punches an Underling approaching him from his blindside. "The man you seek is on the other side of the river."

"What? How? Where?"

Azzazel comes down hard on Pharaoh's wrist and knocks the sword from his hand. Narrowing his eyes, he sees a figure on the bank of the other side of the river. The steam from the heated water distorts his vision into being fuzzy, but he is still able to see movement through the mist smoke sitting above the bubbly surface. And besides, Dagon wouldn't dare lie to him out of respect for the queen.

Pharaoh picks up his sword and returns the blow. Azzazel falls to one knee and crosses his blade to defend himself. The sword's sharp edge falls into the center of the blades X and stops the force of Pharaoh's power. Quickly pushing himself from the ground, Azzazel leaps through the air and chops Pharaoh's head off a second time. The beheading before taught him a lesson so this time he cuts off Pharaoh's arms to slow down his elasticity. With Pharaoh not able to put himself back together so quickly, Azzazel is able to buy some time to get out of the warzone.

"Well, Pharaoh, it's been an honor fighting soldiers of your caliber." Azzazel stands over Pharaoh's competent head as Dagon holds off his followers. "Please forgive me for not staying but we have found the man we have been tracking across the boiling river of Raqueem. Time is of the essence because I refuse to let him slip from my sight again. If I desired to, I could drive the tip of my sword through your skull just to see what would happened. But if I did that and you were to die then we would no longer have the opportunity to meet on the battlefield to see which soldiers are the greatest. As for now, I must retreat to handle my queen's business. Until we meet again, Pharaoh, tell your master, the Leviathan, this is my land and I'll see him in hell fighting for it!" Azzazel kicks Pharaoh's torso and legs to the ground and pins his body to the black sand with the dagger he took from the woman. "Dagon!" he shouts before whistling for Smokey. "Get us out of here!"

David is on the shore of the other side of the river, tapping the toe of his boot in the water so that the Leviathan can bring him back to the Field of Blood. He thought he was to retrieve the sphere and stir the water when he obtained the prize, but evidently the plan he discussed with the Leviathan has been changed. Geysers are erupting in the distance around him and his patience is running low because of the fear of being barbecued where he is standing.

The fog on the ground is making things worse, because his sense of sight has been taken away from him. All he has left to rely on spotting an eruption is hoping to hear or feel and outburst before it happens. If he does not calculate the eruption correctly, his fate in Hades will end with him holding the sphere of Sharia waiting for a talking sea monster.

"David." The Leviathan raises his rays of dawn eyes barely above the water. "Run and hide. Two men have been tracking you and have lifted their eyes and saw you in the land of Gehenna. One claims to be a king and the other is a great warrior. My army, the Underlings, have fought well with the men and their beast, but their persistence in not retreating have brought your presence to their attention. These men are very skilled at killing and their ferocious pets take heed to their commandments. One of their beasts has massive wings and, as we speak, they are taking flight to seize you. I cannot interfere with your destiny in the afterlife. My purpose I fulfilled when I brought you to this forbidden land. Now go and hide, my friend. And if you are the man your compass tells me you are, I'll see you again shortly to return you to your faith-filled journey."

The Leviathan disappeared just as fast as he reappeared. Running as fast as he can, David runs through the fog disregarding the volcanic geysers. Searching for a place to hide among the uninhabited structures, his mind begins to wonder why King Azzazel and Dagon are after him. He comes to realize that the sphere in his hands is the only answer probable, and therefore his friends, Artemis and Cybele, had to have told them.

A tall brick building with lancet-arched windows is to his left so if anyone was looking for a hiding place that would no doubt be the best place to hide. Detouring to his left, he opens the oak doors to the building and uses his hands to feel around in the dark to find a place of refuge. A wooden structure about five feet tall is all he can quickly find in the limited time he has before the hounds catch wind of his scent.

David slides what feels to be a velvet drapery and balls up as small as he can to tuck himself inside the alcove. The last words in Kog's letter is all he can think of when sliding the drapery to conceal his awkward position. *Look what trusting people has gotten me,* he thought in anger being silent as a church house mouse. "Now what am I going to do?"

Azzazel is leading the way using only his intuition. The fog and geysers have covered David's tracks so the hunter in him must rely on putting himself in the hunted shoes. Surveying the land, all the buildings would be great hiding places, but only one stood out above the rest for one who is trying to hide in fear for their life. Of course the hunt would've been a lot easier if Dagon's pet could have carried Smokey's weight. But Azzazel loves the sport of predator and prey, so therefore Smokey's enhanced sense of smell would have taken the fun from out of the game.

Entering the building, Dagon covers one side of the cluttered space while Azzazel covers the other. Row for row they search under the wooden benches not leaving a seat unsearched. The absence of light is not helping so they remain quiet listening for anything that may lead them in the right direction. Azzazel tells Dagon to search the back while he continues to work his way around the four corners of the brick walls. He can practically smell the sweat dripping from David's body but rationally thinking he may be wrong.

"My king!"

Azzazel runs to Dagon's voice at the back of the enormous building. "What is it, Dagon? Did you find him?"

Dagon is standing in the back door. The door is wide open but no clues support that the man they are looking for exited that way. Azzazel gazes into the sky and stares at the dark gray clouds chasing the orange clouds to wherever they come from. Closing his eyes, he tries to put himself in the prey's shoes again. Everything he knows about hunting men leads to David being in this building, but maybe the long day of fighting may have misconstrued his perceptiveness. While waiting patiently to what the king's next move is going to be, Dagon notices Azzazel's hand is under his armpit applying pressure to a wound he had received during battle.

"My king." Dagon hoisters his ax at the sight of green blood oozing down the side of Azzazel's silver breastplate. "You're hurt."

"Yes, Dagon, I shall say that I am." Azzazel recalls how Pharaoh shielded a blow which left his striking arm defenseless to Pharaoh's sharp sword. "And what's even worse I think we may have lost our rabbit." Azzazel wince as he pauses to think again. "Come, Dagon, for I may have made a mistake. Out of zealousness to capture our white friend, I forgot to take into consideration three important facts."

"What's that, my king?"

"That one, he is very astute just I am astute. Two, that someone had to have helped him get to this side of the river. And three, that same someone may have already taken him back."

15

The sphere's glow is what broke David's cramped slumber. When Azzazel was searching for him, he tucked the ball underneath his shirt so that the fluorescent light wouldn't seep through the sides of the draperies. He meant to have come out when the coast was clear, but Azzazel's tracking abilities were too good to trust that he had left so easily.

Accidentally, he fell asleep and accidentally the chain mail shifting at his movements in his sleep revealed the treasure he is hiding. When his eyes opened, he fumbled a bit trying to recover the sphere, but the silence of the building made him feel confident that his long hours of solitude had paid off.

One leg straightens out the velvet curtain. His second leg came out and planked on side of the other. Pointing his toes, he stretches his lower body until his knees pop. With both of his hands, he pull on the base of the wooden structure until his butt is sitting on the floor. "Oh!" he screams to the sensation of the blood circulating in his stiff limbs as he stands pleased with himself for surviving one more night in Sheol.

The aqua-blue sphere in his hands looks like earth if one is standing on the moon. Rubbing his hands along the circumference, his fingers brushes against a small handle. When he tries to pull on it nothing happens until he figures out he must turn the handle first before pulling. A small spout rises and without thinking he tilts his head back to drink the sparkling water he saw the angel put inside there.

Ounce for ounce, the refreshing liquid went down his dry throat giving him energy he hasn't felt since he stood on the streets made of gold. The water is so good that he tries to drink it all at once but the more he poured the more came out. Suddenly, he realized that the substance will never cease and that the compass truly led him to the path to the watery place.

"I have to get out of here before the Leviathan thinks Azzazel found me," David said in a low tone, still being careful in case anyone ears are open he cannot see. As he turns to leave, he remembers he lost the brown sack Kog gave him when he back flipped off of Betsie. "The target and reward on my head is too great," he said looking down at the sphere. "I have to find something to put you in or the first person I meet will kill me before I have a chance to explain myself."

David looks for anything to put the sphere in with the limited light the gray clouds are straining to give through the arched windows. Stopping, he blinks a few times so that his eyes can adjust to the shimmer of light he has for guidance. "What kind of windows don't allow light to go through them?" he asked himself looking over to the arch cutaway in the brick. Like a lightbulb turning on in his head, he sees why. "Where am I?" he asked aloud but from his past life he thinks he knows the answer. After staring into the blue-and-purple stain glass, he looks around with more scrutiny to confirm his assumptions.

"A church!" David gasped when he came face to face with a marble statue of Mary holding her son Jesus after they took him down from the cross. "What is a church doing in Hades?" His question is quickly disregarded when he chuckles to the fact that he is a pastor and he is in Hades too.

The scene of Jesus's death is definably real. Whoever sculpted it had to have been a master of their craft because of the depiction of the sorrow upon Mary's face. Her eyes are low and her head is down. Her firstborn is gone and you can feel her pain as to why she can't look up at the people who did this to her son she lost her virginity to when he was born. A single cross looms behind her to display the injustice of the Jews and Roman Empire.

Jesus's head is wrapped in thorns and his arms are sprawled limp over the strength of his mother's. A single hole is in each one of his hands and feet from where the long nails pinned him to a cross. His ribs have slashes in them leading around to his frail back. David remembers how in those days you could only be flogged forty times, so instead they counted to thirty-nine in case of a miscount. His heart saddens at the thought of how Jesus felt during the unlawful beating, because to him it had to have felt like one hundred or maybe a thousand times the whip struck him.

The hole in his side from a spear was uncalled for. The mocking soldiers could have went about other means to reveal if God's only son was truly dead. David wondered if Mary screamed in agony or fainted when blood and water gushed from under Jesus's bruised ribs onto the dirt in front of her. "INRI," David said looking to the sign above the cross Jesus hung on which stands for, "This is the king of the Jews."

Mary and her son Jesus Christ brought a tidal wave of grief upon him. As a pastor, he preached the gospel to be exalted and to fill his pockets beyond measures. He studied the Bible, knew the Bible but never has he placed himself in the shoes of the men and women in the Bible. If he had had as he have done today, he would've had a more in-depth understanding of what Jesus did on the cross for the world on Calvary. "How did I miss that?" he questions himself thinking about all the sermons he preached. "Or maybe the Holy Spirit was trying to show it to me, and I was too caught up in the cares of my bank accounts to see it." A tear of contrition forms in his eye as the first sign of those to come afterward.

Weeping softly, David feels broken and ashamed. Broken because of the pain Jesus endured so that we can have fellowship with God. And ashamed because of not accepting the father and son's gift wholeheartedly so that we can always be in their presence. His eyes are watery as he drags his feet to the wooden structure he spent the night in. Placing his hands on top of it for support, he finds himself standing behind a rugged podium. The tears in his eyes fall more heavily when he sees an open Bible sitting on top of it with highlighted Scriptures.

The highlighted Scriptures were Psalms 139. It read:

> You have searched me, Lord, and you know me. You know when I sit and when I rise; you perceive my thoughts from afar. You discern my going out and my lying down; you are familiar with all my ways. Before a word is on my tongue you, Lord, know it completely. Such knowledge is too wonderful for

me, too lofty for me to attain. Where can I go from your Spirit? Where can I flee from your presence? If I go up to the Heavens, you are there; if I make my bed in Hell, you are there. If I say, "Surely the darkness will hide me and the light become night around me," even the darkness will not be dark to you; the night will shine like day, for darkness is as light to you. I will praise you for I am fearfully and wonderfully made; Marvelous are your works. Your eyes saw my unformed body; all the days ordained for me were written in your book before one of them came to be. How precious to me are your thoughts, God! Where I to count them, they would outnumber the grains of sand; when I awake, I am still with you. Search me, God, and know my heart; test me and know my anxious thoughts. See if there is any offensive way in me, and lead me in the way everlasting.

Reading the Scriptures for a second time, David puts himself in the author's shoes. Psalms 139 was written by King David, the slayer of Goliath the giant. Throughout the Word of God, King David committed some of the worst sins in the Bible, and yet in Acts 13:22, the Apostle Paul says that he was a man after God's own heart.

What great of a compliment any man can receive especially after disobeying God's strict commandments. While guiding his fingers down the highlighted words, he stops at Scriptures that jumped out to him more than others. Meditating on the Word of God, a revelation is revealed to him concerning the answer he never sought to look for on why Paul and God said what they said about King David in Acts 13:22.

"Lord, I always knew King David knew how to repent and when to repent but everyone who grows in a relationship with Christ comes to that realization. If what I believe you are showing me is correct, King David received such accolades because he revered you as being omnipotent, omniscient, and omnipresent in and over his life. This is why King David wrote, 'You have searched me Lord, and you know me. You perceive my thoughts from afar. Where can I go from your Spirit?' His reasons, Lord, was because he knew he was a sinner and he knew how to repent, but even if his repentance wasn't good enough and he was sent to hell for them, he still would acknowledge you for the Almighty Lord you are. That's why he concluded by writing: 'Search me, God, and know my heart. See if there is any offensive way in me, and lead me in the way of everlasting.'"

David stood relishing on the revelation. Standing behind the podium brought back memories of his times in the pulpit. Amy would be on the front pew smiling and agreeing to every word that came out of his mouth. The pureness in her worship made souls who were lost flock to her for what must they do to be saved and go to heaven. Prayers of repentance would shortly follow as one behind the other repeat Romans 10:9, "If you confess with your mouth, that Jesus is Lord, and believe in your heart that God raised him from the dead, you will be saved."

Jesus sentencing him to Hades fell on him like a boulder from the sky. Remembering the fire in Jesus's eyes to how he mistreated the gospel, David recalls how he has not once since he stood before the throne of truth repented for his sins with his mouth and with his heart.

"Lord Almighty, your judgment is just. If it's not too late, please forgive me of my sins. I love you and thank you for the revelation I received today. I now realize just as the great King David did that confessing my sins and repenting from my heart are the keys to continuous fellowship with you. As I look around, I see that no matter where I'm at you are with me just as King David wrote in Psalms 139. Thank you, Jesus, for entrusting me with your word, and I ask that you be with me as I step out on faith to do what I should have done when I was called to preach in the natural world. Lord, no longer will I wonder about like a shooting star who has no ending. Today, when I leave this confines, I leave as Pastor David Grace who has a purpose to fulfill for the Lord in Sheol. And as long as I have breath in my lungs, my soul will never stop professing that Jesus Christ is Lord. Amen." David wipes his tears and closes the Bible to take with him on his new journey.

Sharia's sphere is on the floor next to his foot. The aqua glow from below reminds him that he needs to find something to put it in. His pupils have fully adjusted to the shortness of light so the hidden spots he didn't see before he now sees a lot better. Beneath a window near the entrance is a knight's shield and armor on a stand. From first glance, it looks like someone is wearing it because the helmet is down. David approaches it admiring the protective shaped metal for a man in the early days trying to display their nobility.

A leather satchel is around the vacant knight's gorget, and David can clearly see that the dates of the bag and armor are from two different eras. The satchel is old but the armor is much older. Finding what he has been looking for, he slides the leather strap from around the nickel-plated helmet. As he holds it in his hand, the cut on his wrist that is rapidly healing reminds him that his hand would have been cut off if it wasn't for the gauntlet. One is on each of the knight's hands so he takes the left one since that was the hand that needed it when Pharaoh struck at him.

"Why thank you, my dear boy. Don't mind if I do," he said sarcastically in his old English voice while putting his new findings on. Before going to retrieve the sphere, he grabs the dilapidated shield and puts it on his back.

David wondered if the shield had once been in a real battle because the mustard-colored cross that is on the face of it had a few dents in it.

"The Leviathan!" David snaps to how much time he's been in the chapel. Racing to the door, he looks back at the marble statue one last time before pushing the thick piece of wood to exit.

David Grace steps out of the church quoting Proverbs 3:5–6, "Trust in the Lord with all your heart and lean not on your own understanding; in all your ways submit to him, and he will direct your paths."

Picking up the pace, he makes his way through Gehenna heading to the shore of Raqueem. The fog is lifted and only a few strings of steam are vaporizing out of the geysers. David stays clear of them and runs to the river looking for any sight of the creature that has helped him in more ways than one. With the tip of his boots, he stirs the water watching the ripples travel through the waters boil. *I'm too late*, he thought. *The Leviathan is gone.* After stirring the water some more, he gives up and goes closer inland in reverence to the hot lava that might shoot up unexpectedly.

"Hello, David. Glad to see you again, my friend."

David hears the powerful Leviathan's voice and joyfully makes his way back to the water. "I thought you gave up on me when I didn't return this morning."

"How can I give up on a shepherd of God?"

"So you knew all along that I am a pastor?"

"Yes, Pastor Grace, and also other things that I'm not accountable to tell you because your destiny still lies before you. Let's just say that we all have a purpose in life and in death but some people's purpose are more important than others."

David has an idea of what the Leviathan is talking about, but for some reason he wonders if it's more to it than what he thinks it is. A geyser erupting far behind him made him put his questions to the side until he reaches safety.

The Leviathan lowers his enormous head. "Get on, David. Let's get you out of here."

On the other side of the river, David hops off the Leviathan into the morass clenching the sphere and Bible so that it won't pop out of the satchel. "Thanks for the ferry ride, you big brute," he said, laughing as he high-steps through the dank sand toward the dead grass.

The Leviathan becomes silent because he's never heard of a ferry. "What's a ferry, David?" he asked trying to remember if he heard the term in his ancient days.

David looks at the prehistoric monster pondering on the term and shakes his head because he forgot the beast's age. "It's something or, in your case, someone that takes you across a wide span of water."

Placing the term into his memory bank, the Leviathan and David share a few laughs before their time together comes to an end. David thanks him for warning him about Azzazel's intentions to capture him and for helping him find Sharia. The Leviathan encourages him to stay true to himself and the road he walks on will continue to be laid out for him. He also said to never give up on his beliefs because what he believes in is the only thing this evil world cannot take from him. David took the words of wisdom ready to face whoever or whatever comes in his way from the task he has set his mind to do—which is preach the gospel to the lost souls in Sheol.

"Well, my big friend, I guess I'll be going." David waves good-bye and turns to leave.

"Hold up, David. I almost forgot to give you something."

"Forgot what?"

"Why do you think I brought you to this end of the Field of Blood and not to where you initially crossed?"

"I don't know. I thought you forgot where you picked me up from I guess."

The Leviathan laughs. "No, David, I didn't forget where I picked you up from," he said, pausing to let David's mind wonder. "I brought you here because I have a gift for you. Well, it's more like I found a gift for you."

David doesn't have a clue what his behemoth friend is talking about. Looking around he sees nothing and thinks the Leviathan is pulling his leg. "So where is it? I don't see anything."

The Leviathan nods his head past David to the trees. "It's beyond the foliage of those trees over there about a few feet in. I had Pharaoh tie her up for you when I found her eating zaqs along the ground."

David is still clueless as he goes to the area his friend said for him to go. Before he gets there he hears a whinny to his right behind the leaves. Using his hands, he moves branches from his path and finds Delilah's horse Betsie. The horse remembers him when he smells his hand to take the reins.

"Calm down, girl." David rubs the side of her neck because her blissfulness to see a familiar face is making her a little skittish. "Let's get you out of here." Leading her to the open grass, he stops to untie the poles from the crupper and saddle that held the travois. "That a girl," he said. "I bet it feels good to have that burden off you." After giving her some cold water from the sphere, he swings into the saddle. Betsie is refreshed as she heeds his commands to bring him back to the river.

David tries to thank the Leviathan again but before he can get his words out of his mouth, the Leviathan said, "No need to thank me again, David, for I know that's what you are desiring to do. Farewell, good shepherd, and it brings me great joy to have met a man with so much faith. Just beyond those trees, a little past where you found the horse, is a path only the Underlings and myself knows about. I don't know where it leads to but at least you will be safe from the hands of the king until you get to wherever the path takes you."

As soon as the Leviathan said that, he leaps into the air to show David his thirty-foot serpent-like body. When he dives into the water, not a splash is made as he submerged into the river of Raqueem to await the next soul in search for Sharia.

"Come on, Betsie, let's go. We have some work to do for the Lord," he said, kneeing Betsie to enter the forest, confident that he has found his place in the afterlife.

16

Dark trees are all around David. The path he's on is only a few feet wide so whoever made it had to be going in one direction. When Betsie first stepped onto the path, David didn't know which way to go so he let the reins go limp so that she can decide for him. Something drew her to the right so to the right is where they went. He doesn't know why he trusted the horse's judgment but what did he have to lose in the middle of nature's abyss.

Trotting down the secret trail, David misses the compass that he grew accustomed to being part of his hand. Even though the compass didn't disclose to him the directions he wanted to go, it did however let him see which direction was which way. Blind to where he is going, he fixes his eyes on the firmament above and smiles because whatever happens from that day on, God will have the last word in his will in heaven.

Time is going by slowly but surely. An hour and a half has passed and he is becoming bored from staring at the back of Betsie's bobbing head. The high trees on both sides of him are close together and the murky gray clouds are limiting his vision beyond them. All he can see is to the front of him and to the back of him and either way looks to have no end. "I hope this hidden path leads to something soon or I'm going to change into a monkey and climb to the top of one of these trees," he jokes, patting Betsie's mane.

Betsie stops without warning, but begins walking again. David's mind is in left field when she does it and therefore he doesn't catch the hesitation in her trot. Without warning she stops a second time and instead of advancing as she did before, she neighs and snorts to the cluster of trees on the right side of the walkway. David swings down from the saddle and leaves Betsie while he explores the trees his horse nodded in the direction of. As he moved toward the trees, the spacing between the trunks widens and he is able to see deeper into the woods behind the wooded barrier.

Walking further, he sifts through the low branches until he finds himself about ten feet away from a small meadow with a cabin sitting in the center of it. His mind is instantly boggled at who might reside in the out-of-sight dwelling. Deducting his alternatives, he decides to go back and get Betsie and dauntlessly knock on the cabin's door. It's been over two hours he's been riding and he needs reassurance that the path he's on is not leading him into harm's way.

David takes a step back and his foot presses down on something with resistance. As he lifts his leg to see what it is, a noose tightens around his ankle while a boulder falls to the ground not too far from where he is standing. The two motions are simultaneous and heaved him upside down into the air. Back and forward he swings unaware of how he missed the trap when he walked over it the first time.

A cowbell toned in the distance. Twisting and turning, David tries to find the exact direction of the sonorous sound. The ear-splitting dings make him jump rapidly and cause the satchel to slip from around his neck. The side pocket with the Bible stayed buckled but the sphere pushes the flap opened that concealed it when the bag plunged to the ground. As he looks with disgust at the sphere peering at him from underneath the flap, he hears the bell is barely ringing. David surmised that the bell is tied into the trap that he is caught in because the alarm only makes noise when he is moving.

Feeling sinister to how today's events have played out, gravity starts to pull all of his blood to his head. His vision begins to become cloudy so he bends at the waist to clear his mind. Reaching for his dirk to cut the rope from his leg, the muscles in his lower back gives out and his long body straightens out again. He quickly puts his head upward to bring some light to the red darkness that is flooding his brain. Before he knows it, a hard thud stops his efforts short and he blacks out to the solid blow to the side of his head.

"Get his bag, Michal, and then help me cut him down so we can get him to the house."

❧

David is sitting in a chair in a land that he knows for sure he's never been to before. Two female angels are arguing about a demanding matter that they can't seem to come to an agreement on. He attempts to listen in on the conversation but they are beyond the range of his ears. All of sudden, out of nowhere, a throne made of sapphire stone lowers down in between the angels. Upon the throne is a figure like that of a man. Abashed to not being in agreement with one another, the two of them fall prostrate to the ground and cover their heads with their exquisite wings.

From the waist up, he looked like glowing metal, as if full of fire. And from the waist down he looked like fire with the appearance of lambent light surrounding him. His radiance is unspeakable so David turns his head in regards to the majestic power in front of him.

The man on the throne said to David, "Son of man, stand up on your feet and I will speak to you." As he spoke, the spirit came into David and raised him to his feet, and he began speaking again. "Son of man, I am sending you to a rebellious people that have rebelled against me. They and their ancestors have been in a revolt against me to this very day. The people to whom I am sending you are obstinate and stubborn. Say to them, 'This is what the sovereign Lord says.' And whether they listen or fail to listen—for they are a rebellious people—they will know that a man of God has been among them. And you, son of man, do not be afraid of them or their words. Do not be afraid of what they say or be terrified by them, though they are a rebellious people. You must speak my words to them, whether they listen or fail to listen, for they are rebellious. But you, son of man, listen to what I say to you. Do not rebel like the rebellious people, open your mouth and eat what I give you."

Then David looked, and he saw a hand stretched out to him. In it was a scroll, which the man unrolled before him. On both sides of it were written words of lament, mourning, and woe. And he said to David, "Son of man, eat what is before you. Eat this scroll then go and speak to the people." So David opened his mouth and he gave him the scroll to eat. Then he said to David, "Son of man, eat this scroll I am giving you and fill your stomach with it." So David ate it, and it tasted as sweet as honey in his mouth. He then said to David, "Son of man, go now to the people and speak words to them. For I, the Lord, takes no pleasure in the death of anyone, declares the sovereign Lord." In the twinkle of an eye, the angels and the man was gone and David is back seated in the chair that the Spirit lifted him from.

⌁

"What are we going to do with him, Michal?"

"I don't know, we never had this problem before."

"We have to think of something soon because we can't keep him here forever," a woman's voice replied. "Not to mention this funny-colored ball looks valuable and I'm sure somebody will come looking for him because of it."

"So what are you implying we should do?" Michal asked.

"I say we get rid of him and go back to our solitary lives of peace."

Everything is blurry and the knot on the side of David's head is the size of a small mountain. Regaining his consciousness, the taste of honey is in his mouth. David tries to rub his head but his hands and feet are chained to the floor. The restraints around his wrists and ankles have no play in them so instead of attempting to get free, he decides to play possum and wait for his capturers to make a mistake.

Last time he was in this sad plight he died from three gunshots from trying to be a hero when he should have stayed calm and cooperated. This time, he understands that one of his lives is already gone because of his heedlessness and the one he is living now will be gone also if he slips up again.

"Get rid of him! And just how are we going to do that, Orpah? I hope you're not saying what I think you're saying," Michal retorts.

"I'm sorry, Michal, but we have to kill him because he knows where we live, and if he's found this place once, I'm sure he can find it again."

Michal looks at Orpah with a grim look on her face and shakes her head no. "Why, Orpah? Why do we have to kill him? We don't know the first thing about killing nobody!"

"I know that he is not leaving this place alive. And I know that we agreed to protect our home and one another by any means necessary." Orpah grabs an iron pole leaning against the wall. "I'm sorry, Michal, but it's either him or us."

Michal stands in the way so that she cannot get a good swing at the man sitting in the chair. David's eyes are closed but he is listening to everything that the two women are talking about. He rolls his head and acts like he is finally coming into consciousness.

"What happen to my head?" David ask opening his eyes. "Who are you and why am I tied up?"

Orpah hollers for Michal to move out of her way. "Don't worry about who we are, Mr. sneaking around private property." Orpah tries to move Michal but Michal doesn't budge.

"Damn it, Michal, move! He already knows too much and now he's seen our faces."

"Orpah, no! We can at least ask him what business he has on the outskirts of Hades."

The name Orpah sounds familiar but the knot on his head is causing his memory to only go back to when he left the Field of Blood.

"For what? So he can just lie to us like everybody else up to no good in this godless place."

Michal grabs her hand with the pole in it. "You didn't lie to me when I found you lying on the side of the road with your hand nearly cut off." Michal looks her in the eyes to show her that she's not with killing a helpless man.

"Don't give me that sob story, Michal, about how I was mistreated and left for dead by those two idiots who carved that compass out of my hand only to have it crumble when it was taken from me. Or, how you nursed me back to health so that the worm of torment wouldn't come for my weak soul. Every day I thank you for your help, Michal, but this is a man and not a woman so therefore I am not giving him the opportunity to come back here and harm us."

David's thoughts are coming back to him and he remembers Artemis telling him the story about Orpah coming into Hell's Kitchen with two men. "Orpah, I know you." David interrupts the women arguing over his life. "I mean I don't know you exactly, but I have heard of you. If I'm not mistaken, you had a compass to Sharia in your hand and you were looking for the path to the watery place with two strange men."

"And how do you know that? I've never met you before."

"A lady by the name of Artemis told me when she saw the same compass in my hand two weeks ago."

"You're lying, Mister. We looked at your hands when we put chains on you remember and we didn't see a compass in either of them." Orpah narrows her eyes at Michal because Michal knows what she is saying is true.

"Yes, you're right in saying I don't have a compass in my hand, but you're wrong in thinking I've never had one."

Michal speaks. "And why is that?"

"Because it disappeared when I found Sharia."

"So you mean to tell us that we are to believe that you found the mysterious Sharia and the compass vanished when you got there?"

"Yes, that's exactly what I'm telling you to believe, Orpah." David stops and remembers that the Leviathan said that the compass was a blessing from God.

"What are you thinking about now? And it better not be no funny business."

"Orpah, this is not you," David said, looking her directly in the face.

"What do you mean this is not me?"

"What I mean is that you are a good person at heart because that compass came from God, and I feel he wouldn't have just given it to anybody."

"He's right, Orpah. This is not you," Michal said mildly while taking the pole and leaning it back against the wall. I remember how you told me you received the compass after giving your last zaq and cup of water to someone who was very ill. I also remembered that you said that you lived a life of bitterness when you left your sister-in-law, Ruth, and your mother-in-law, Naomi, to return home. You said things for you was never the same and you began to serve the god, Chemosh, with your people. In death, you vowed to do unto others as you would want done unto you, and therefore you helped those in need when you were able to. I admit, Orpah, I didn't believe you about some of the things you had told me before, but hearing this unknown man speak today, I ask you to please forgive me."

"So what are we going to do, Michal? We can't trust this man well enough to set him free." Orpah's voice changes from earnest to stern. "Say for instance we do let him go. What if he doubles back and come and kill us in the middle of the night while we are asleep?"

David hears enough slanders and decides to speak up on his behalf. "Now hold on, Orpah, before you go into more falsifications about me." David sits up as straight as he can.

"My name is Pastor David Grace and I am a man of God who veered off the path of righteousness and ended up here just like you. I know you may find this hard to believe, heck, I myself find it hard to believe, but I think I've read about you in the Bible. If I'm not mistaken, I believe you are from Moab and your husband who died was name Mahlor or Kilion."

"How could you know that, Mister?"

"David."

"Right, David. I've never told anybody that before. Not even Michal. Are you a prophet?"

"Sadly I'm not, but I am a shepherd of the Word of God. Like I said before, I read about you in my Bible. As a matter of fact, I can show you if you like me too." David pours over the room to see if he can spot his satchel. "Did, you ladies, by any chance pick up a leather bag when you snagged me from the woods?"

Michal picks up the satchel from behind David. "Are you speaking of this bag, David?"

"Yes that's it." David notices the sphere is gone. "Did you by chance find a ball inside of it when you found it?"

"Yes we did, Pastor, but that is not important." Orpah's snaps thinking he might be trying to pull a fast one. "What's important is you proving to us that you are sincere in what you are saying so that we can decide what we are going to do with you."

"My apologies. And I fully understand why you two have to be so cautious when meeting strangers. Michal, could you please dig in that front pocket and pull out that black book for me."

Michal unbuckles the metal latch and pulls out the Bible. "Got it."

"If you would be so kind, could you find the page that says Ruth."

Michal opens the book but the words are just black marks on white paper to her. "I'm sorry, David, but I can't read this."

David is stunned to hear her response. "How is it that you can't read English when you can speak it so fluently?"

"Because our language is not written this way. And two, being in Hades over a millennium of years we've learned to speak a lot of languages. But English is the one that is the most prominent to speak so the majority of everybody in Hades speaks that one the most."

"Wow. I can't believe you two are over a thousand years old," David said, surprised at what he's hearing. "Well, Michal, it looks like you're going to have to be my hands and flip through the pages for me until I say stop."

"Okay, I think I can do that for you."

David guides Michal to the book of Ruth. After she finds it, he has her hold the Bible in front of him so he can read the story about Orpah's sister-in-law, Ruth, and her faithfulness to her mother-in-law, Naomi. From beginning to end he read and he could sense that Orpah never knew how Ruth overcame adversity and ended up obtaining a name of great valor in history.

Tears of joy of how Ruth remarried a remarkable man vanquished her tears of sadness on how she left Naomi after her husband died and returned to her people. When David finished Ruth's story, he let her know that if he had been in her shoes after such a traumatic loss of her main support passing away, he would have probably returned home too. Michal hugged her friend and reassured her that she loved her very much for sticking by her side during her tough times. Taking a set of keys from a silver ring on the wall, Orpah unlocks the locks and David hears the chains fall to the floor.

"Thank you, Orpah. Thank you for trusting me enough to release me."

Michal and Orpah are still a little timorous to David being unshackled in their home. As he stands, they both take a step back anticipating if they made the right decision. David discerns their body language and assures them that he is who he says he is. It took a few minutes for them to let their guards down but what else can they do. What's done is done. After massaging his wrists, he extends his hand for a proper greeting. Both women gladly accepted his handshake when they observed the guileless in his eyes.

"Nice to meet you, Michal and Orpah."

"It's nice to meet you too, David." Michal replies with a grin on her face.

"What are you so perky about, Michal?" Orpah asked.

"Oh it's nothing. It's just that my husband's name was David and he too was a man of God."

"You don't say," David said, picking up his Bible from the table. "Well if it makes you feel awkward calling me by my first name, I don't mind if you called me Pastor Grace."

"It doesn't make me feel awkward at all, David, but I would prefer to call you Pastor Grace anyway."

"Why is that, Michal?" he asked.

"Because it has a godlier ring to it and Orpah and I need as much God as possible right now. You know, being two women in Hades and all."

"You can say that again, Michal." Orpah agreed.

"So your husband was a godly man, huh?"

"Yes, David. As a matter of fact, he was the godliest man I've ever known. And he was a great king."

"A king?" David said astonished.

"Yes, a king! He was born a sheepherder, the son of Jesse. Grew up to be a shepherd. Gained victory over any army that rose before him. And ruled over Israel as a man devoted solely to God."

"This is unbelievable. So you mean to tell me you are Michal the daughter of King Saul who was given to David for killing Goliath and two hundred Philistine soldiers?"

Michal is just as surprised as David when hearing him speak on behalf of her late husband's doings to please her father to wed her. Her mouth is closed but her facial expressions spoke louder than words.

David reopens the Bible and begin to read how her husband became king. Michal stood nodding her head to the words that are coming out of the baffling black book. As King David's story turned toward how she despised her husband in her heart for celebrating unto the Lord concerning the ark of God, she began to shed tears on Orpah's shoulders. Her wailing became louder when the Bible said that she was unable to bear children because of her foolish hatred.

"Stop, please stop, Pastor Grace," Michal said recalling her last days on her deathbed without a descendent to leave behind.

"I apologize, Michal, I must have gotten beside myself. I didn't take into consideration that my reading the Bible may pierce your soul."

"It's okay, man of God, because your words were true and I needed to hear them."

Orpah cuts in and speak. "Pastor Grace, what is that book that you call the Bible?"

"God's Word to us, from the beginning of mankind to the death of his son Jesus Christ the savior of the world."

"I remember this Jesus Christ entering Hades but death couldn't hold him because he never sinned. At least that is what he said when he was preaching about believing him so that we can be saved."

"Yes, now I remember, Orpah. If I recall correctly, Satan deceived the majority of us by saying the man named Jesus was lying and the place he called the New Jerusalem was no better than Hades. Satan also said he was going to change some things in Sheol for the good if we decided to stay. But as usual, that was a lie because things got worse when Jesus rose through the clouds with a great number of people who trusted in him as the only Son of God."

"So that Jesus fellow was actually the Son of God and telling the truth after all, Pastor Grace?"

"Not only was he telling the truth, Orpah, but also since the day you saw him leave Hades many have believed and joined him in heaven."

"Wow, just think, Orpah, we had a chance to leave this place and be with God if we only believed in his son Jesus."

Both women are contrite for not receiving their golden ticket to heaven. David is bewildered on what he should do to encourage them to continue in doing good but then remembers the vision of the glorious man sending him to speak to the people in Hades.

"Listen." David sets the Bible down on the table. "It seems to me that we are all in the same boat when it comes to being regretful of the poor decisions we made in the past to get us in Hades. I don't know about you but I'm saddened that I didn't take Jesus seriously and instead did what I thought was best for me at the present time. I know it's impossible to go back in life and fix our wrongs, but I believe that it's still possible to secure our future. Yesterday, God blessed me with finding this Bible by accident and in finding this Bible my eyes were open to seeing my purpose. My purpose in Sheol is what I'm doing right now standing with the two of you. My purpose is to tell all those willing to listen that Jesus Christ is the Lord of all things, and if they believed in this that they will be saved in the last days. Do you believe this, Orpah and Michal?"

Orpah and Michal looked at each other in tears and then brought their attention back to David. "Yes, David, I believe," they both said keenly.

"Bow your heads and repeat after me. Lord, please forgive me of my sins and for rejecting your precious gift to me so that I may be saved." David pauses after each sentence so that they can repeat the prayer. "On the day your son died, Jesus came to the lost sheep in Sheol and preached what I must do to be saved. Today, Lord, I've heard that same message once again and now understand that I missed out on being with you and your son in heaven. I'm sorry, Jesus, for rejecting the gospel and I thank you for dying for my sins. I ask you to come into my heart so that I can serve you wholeheartedly from this day on. I love you, Lord, amen."

After they were finished praying, David gave them a big hug and told them that the Bible says, that the angels in heaven are rejoicing because they gave their lives to Christ. Stepping back, he lets them know that there's one more thing left for them to do to complete their salvation. When they asked what it was, he told them that they needed to be baptized for the remission of their sins.

"I don't know what this baptize is," Michal said, rubbing her arms. "But I feel like I'm free and a big weight has been lifted off my shoulders."

"Me too, Michal," Orpah said smiling.

David explained to the ladies the fullness of accepting Christ as their savior. "Baptism is an outward appearance to the world that Christians are children of God and that the church should always do it whenever water is present."

"But we don't have any water present, David, and surely you don't desire for us to be baptize in the boiling river of Raqueem."

David laughs. "No, Orpah, I don't desire for you to be baptize in the boiling river of Raqueem."

"Then what, David?" Michal asked.

"Could one of you bring me that blue ball you found because this is the day that the Lord has made. And when I finish baptizing you two in the name of the Father, Son, and Holy Spirit, we will rejoice and be glad in it. Amen."

"Amen," Orpah replied walking off to retrieve the sphere.

17

Michal and Orpah woke up with prayer and thanksgiving for being in fellowship with God and his holy son Jesus Christ. Last night, both ladies were amazed as David educated them about the history of the man named Jesus they accepted into their hearts. Michal was most fascinated when she found out that Jesus's genealogy came from her former husband King David. What caught Orpah's eyes and ears was when David spoke about a man called Apostle Paul who gave up a life of comfort to preach salvation to the world. When exiting the cabin to continue their early day, Orpah has an idea and prays David/Michal will support her.

Around back, is a corral with three horses including Betsie. Unlatching the wooden gate, Michal walks inside and breaks two zaqs in half and feeds the horses a snack. After the horses come to Michal, Orpah ties their reins to a hitch rail on the back of the cabin and unbuckles their cinch to unsaddle them.

"That's a good girl," Michal said, rubbing Betsie's neck for not being afraid to come to her. All three horses are right where Orpah wants them to be so she uses the sphere to pour water inside a nearby bucket to give them a bath. Before proceeding to bathe the animals, she gives them some refreshing water to wet their dry tongues.

Orpah washes the horses with her friend and feels this is the best time to bring up the idea she had earlier this morning. "Michal." She stops for a minute from washing Michal's sorrel to try and find the correct words to say but nothing special comes to mind. "I've been thinking."

"About what, Orpah?" Michal replies while scrubbing Betsie's barrel with a brush.

"About the message Pastor Grace preached to us about God's love for us and his son Jesus."

"I know!" Michal exclaimed. "Isn't it awesome how God gave us his only begotten son that death will not have the last word over our souls?"

"That's what I've been thinking about too but a little deeper than that."

Michal refrains from washing Betsie because she can see something is really on her friend's mind. "What is it, Orpah, spit it out. Obviously it's important to you and if it's important to you then it's important to me also."

Orpah drops the dead leaves she is drying the horses off with. "You're such a good friend and I figured you would say that." Orpah turns and faces Michal. "Last night, Michal, as Pastor Grace was reading about the great people in the Bible, I noticed something all of them had in common, including Jesus."

"And what was that?" Michal asked trying to figure out what her friend is about to say before she can say it."

"That in faith of what was promised in Jesus, the majority of them endured terrible pain and suffering to bring forth the message of God's love for us so that everyone can have a chance to obtain salvation. Yet none of them before Jesus's death on the cross received the promise, but because of their faith and hard work for the promise they were credited saved. Not to mention the apostles and those who accepted the promise what suffering they had to bear to the let the world know that the promise professed in the Old Testament was real. And not only real but also can be received if only they believe that Jesus Christ is Lord and continue on with the message of Christ to all who are lost."

Michal is overjoyed in her soul on how her friend was enlightened by the words of truth David ministered unto them throughout the night. She received the same message but not as broad as Orpah did. But what is shocking to her is that Orpah spoke the word of God in a simpler and more understanding way. As Michal resumed to listened, Orpah finally got around to what she is feeling in her heart to do for the Lord.

"Michal?"

"Yes, Orpah."

"What are we doing out here in the middle of nowhere?"

"I don't know. I guess we're staying safe from all the evil people in Hades."

"So we are going to stay out here until judgment day hiding from everybody in Sheol?"

"It's been working for us this long, why won't it continue to work for us?"

"One, because it's not safe. And two, we are now born again through the blood of Jesus, therefore, we have taken on an obligation to tell someone else how to be saved just like those men and women in the Bible."

"Not safe!" Michal exclaimed looking around at the life they've built for themselves. "How are we not safe, Orpah?"

Orpah puts her hand on Michal's shoulders. "Because Pastor Grace found us, Michal. This is how we are not safe."

"Pastor Grace is not going to tell anybody about us. He's our friend and a man of God."

"He doesn't have to tell anybody, Michal. Just as he found us by accident somebody else can find us also. The only difference will be is that maybe that somebody will not be so nice in letting us live."

Orpah's words punched Michal dead in the face because her friend is right. Taking a few steps to ponder the undeniable truth, she turns around and says, "So what do you suppose we do?"

"I say we do what the Bible is calling every soul to do when they are saved by grace."

"I don't understand, Orpah."

"Michal, I think the time has come for us to leave this place and help Pastor Grace tell the lost souls in Hades what must they do to be saved."

"Oh, Orpah, isn't that going to be dangerous or worst, a death wish?"

"I should say so, but we are covered by the blood of Jesus, and even if we die and burn in the lake of fire, we will be with God in heaven when Jesus raises us up on the last day."

Michal's eyes sparkle when she hears that her faith in God's son has already given her a seat in heaven. "Well if you put it that way, Orpah, I say yes I'll go and preach the gospel with you and Pastor Grace. Besides, I couldn't manage this place by myself anyway." Michal smiles and gives her friend a hug to seal their agreement."

"I guess it's settled then," Orpah replies, jubilant to be considered as one of the great people in the Bible. "We'll tell David our decision as soon as he wakes up."

"Come, Orpah. Let us finish washing the horses so that we can begin our morning target practice."

"Sounds like a good idea to me, Michal, because God or no God we must defend ourselves if the situation calls for it," Orpah said, foreseeing the precarious road up ahead of them. "I'm willing to burn in hell for the sake of the gospel, but if I do or when I do, I'm not trying to do it anytime soon."

"You and me both," Michal replied knowing that when they start this new journey they may never return to their cabin in the woods again.

A quarter of the day is gone when David sits up and stretches on the couch he passed out on. The door is closed so the heat could not vent from the lanterns. If the door would have been opened or cracked, he most likely would have slept all day. Especially since the night before he slept crouched inside of a podium and the night before that on the ground deep in the woods. Hot from the lack of ventilation, he walks to the door and opens it because the cabin's air is stuffy. As he looks into the sunless nature around him, he quotes 1 Thessalonians 5:18. "Rejoice always, pray continually, and give thanks in all circumstances; for this is God's will for you in Christ Jesus."

David slips his boots on and calls for Michal and Orpah. The only answer he gets is the placidness of the wooden walls on every side of him. His satchel is still on the table where he left it but the sphere is nowhere to be found. The thought of cold water quenching his thirst leads to him becoming fully awake so that he can take the first steps in his day. "Let's go, David," he said to himself standing in the doorway. "It's time for you to go greet your new sisters in Christ."

Edging the corner of the front of the cabin, David hears the horses and the women talking around back. The entry-way to the corral is open so he walks inside to see the ladies shooting arrows at a couple of targets about fifty yards out. Betsie, a sorrel, and a roan are hitched to a rail drinking water from three separate buckets. His sphere is on a ledge off to the side so the horses won't knock it down or trample over it.

"Good morning, ladies." David picks up the sphere and imbibes a gulp of water. "Ah," he exclaimed wiping the overflow from the corners of his mouth. "I know I said this a thousand times last night but thanks for letting me rest my head here last night. I really needed a sound sleep with-out any worries so I can gather myself for this never-ending mission I'm on."

"No, thank you, Pastor, for opening our eyes to the love God has for us," Michal said, pulling an arrow from her quiver. "You know what's strange, Pastor Grace?"

David simpers to hearing himself being called Pastor Grace again. "And what's that?"

"Today I feel better than I've ever felt in my entire lifetime when I was alive on Mother Earth. Isn't that strange, Pastor, being that I'm in Hades?"

"No, it's not strange, Michal. It's not strange because when you two accepted Christ into your hearts, the new creation you've become came forward and the old you has gone away."

"Wow! So that means I'm not the same person I was yesterday, Pastor?"

David winks and points his finger. "Now you're getting it, Michal."

"Orpah too?"

"Yes, Michal, Orpah too." David smirks at Michal's infant innocence to her newfound faith.

Michal sets an arrow in her bow and pulls the string back as far as she can. After taking a quick aim, she releases the arrow sending it flying through the air toward a target hanging from a branch. David can't see exactly where she hits the target but he know she did because it reeled from the power of her shot.

"Bull's-eye!" Michal whooped as if she knows she hit the target square in the center.

"Great shot, Michal," Orpah said. "Now it's my turn."

Orpah repeated the same steps and let her arrow glide through the air. Just as before when Michal took the shot, the target swung back and forward on the branch.

"You girls, are good when it comes to that bow and arrow."

"I'm okay but Michal is a pro when it comes to archery."

"Don't shoot yourself in the foot, Orpah. You're better than okay. After I taught you the basics you were striking those targets just as good as me."

"Where did you learn how to shoot so good, Michal? If you don't mind me asking."

"My father, King Saul, taught me and my brother Jonathan how to shoot the arrow and use a sword. He said, he wasn't going to be around forever so we had to learn to defend ourselves if need be."

David thought about those ancient days of war and wondered if he would have survived in an era where it was kill or be killed. "You ladies don't stop ceasing to amaze me." He chuckles. "And I feel sorry for whoever steps on this property not welcome."

"We're not worried about this property anymore, Pastor," Orpah said shooting another arrow but this time at the target on the trunk of the tree.

"Orpah's right, Pastor Grace. We're not worried about this cabin anymore." Michal shoots another arrow at the same target Orpah shot at.

"Oh, and why not, might I ask?"

"Because we're coming with you," they both said in unison.

"What? This is not necessary. I don't want anything to happen to, you ladies. I mean, are you serious?"

"We can handle ourselves, Pastor Grace," Michal said shooting a third arrow at the target causing it to wobble again on the branch. "And yes we are very serious."

"But this path I've chosen has a wicked king and queen seeking my life for God-only-knows-what reason. I suspect it's for the sphere of Sharia but it may be out of pure cruelty."

"Pastor Grace, you forget we've been here longer than you have so we know all about the Devil's Advocates. King Ahab or shall I say, King Azzazel and Queen Jezebel's sole purpose in the afterlife is to please their lord Satan." Orpah puts her bow around her shoulder. "I think it's time for them to hear our purpose in the afterlife and who we live to please. Jesus Christ our Lord and savior over heaven, earth, and now Hades."

"Amen to that, Orpah," Michal said putting her bow over her shoulder. "So what do you say, Pastor, because we are not taking no for an answer. Just as Jesus and all the great people in the Bible sacrificed themselves for what they believed in, we are also willing to sacrifice ourselves for our beliefs."

"And what are your beliefs, Michal?" David inquired to see if they really understood what they were getting themselves into.

"That when you accept Jesus as your personal savior, you must from that day on minister to all those who are lost so that they can have the same opportunity you had when you accepted him in your life."

David couldn't believe that they received the full gospel in such a short period of time. Before Jesus ascended into heaven he told his disciples and those present to go and preach his name to all nations beginning at Jerusalem. The road to redemption was going to be rocky for Jesus's followers because he was sending them out as sheep among wolves. Michal and Orpah heard and knew what they had to endure to be considered a child of God so therefore, who is he to tell them that they can't fulfill their salvation the way all Christians are called to do?

David raises his hand in front of the ladies and makes an imaginary cross in the air. "I thank you, Father, Lord of heaven and earth, that you have hidden these things from the wise and prudent and revealed them to babes. The Word of God says, 'The harvest truly is great, but the laborers are few, therefore I must pray the Lord of the harvest to send out laborers into the harvest field.' Today, Lord, I pray for more labors for the harvest in Hades and thank you for answering my prayer in my sisters in Christ, Michal and Orpah, amen." David hugs each one of the women while letting them know that he gladly accepts their offer to join him in preaching love and peace in Sheol.

"Thank you, Pastor Grace, for allowing us to accompany you. I assure you Michal and I will not get in your way of your ministry and that we will assist you the best way we know how."

"God Bless you, Orpah, for your zealousness. And God bless the eyes which will see the things you see. for I tell you that many prophets and kings have desired to see what you have seen concerning Jesus Christ and have not seen it. And to hear what you've heard and heard it."

"So what now, Pastor?" Michal asks.

David looks toward the horses. "We saddle the horses, pack our bedrolls, and mount up. Come, we need to get going before it gets dark. History has shown that it is better to walk in the light before darkness overtakes you. Because whosoever walks in the dark does not know where they are going."

Walking to the horses, Michal asks, "David, you said Jesus is light when you read to us the story of the Apostle John, right?"

David laughs softly. "I see you girls don't miss a thing. And yes, Jesus is light, Michal. So let us continue to believe in the light while we have the light and in doing so we will become children of light."

Orpah saddles her roan while Michal saddles her sorrel. As Michal is getting her steed ready to ride, Betsie nudges the back of her shoulder with her nose.

"What is it, girl?" Michal asks patting the side of Betsie's face.

"Her owner was a woman," David answers for Betsie while buckling her saddle to her side. "I guess she misses a woman's touch."

Michal rubs her nose with Betsie's nose. "What's her name, Pastor Grace?"

"Betsie, and she is the sweetest thing you'll ever meet."

Orpah speaks up when seeing Michal has already fallen in love with the white palfrey. Also, she's knows Michal's horse Jax is a rough ride at times when he's acting up. "How about you ask Pastor Grace to let you ride Betsie for a little while and he can ride Jax?"

"I couldn't ask the pastor that, Orpah."

"Why I think that will be a great idea," David said, rubbing Betsie's nose.

"Really, Pastor, I can ride her?"

"Yes you may ride her, Michal, if you don't mind me riding old Jaxy boy over there. I like his tan coat and big chest."

"That's because Jax is a battle horse. He's not scared of anything," Michal said.

"Then it's settled. Michal, you'll ride Betsie and I'll ride big Jax over there." David walks up to Jax. "You hear that, Jaxy boy. It's me and you from here on out." Jax snorts as David is staring into his fearless black eyes.

David shepherds the horses around front of the cabin while the women went inside to gather all their belongings that they are going to take with them on their expedition. The two ladies fetch their swords, shields, and small daggers from their underground stash. They also collect every zaqs in the house. Placing their weapons into the proper sheaths, Orpah picks up the sack of zaqs while Michal does one last check for anything they may have missed.

"I think that's it, Orpah. I don't see anything else we need."

Orpah inspects the room from where she is standing. David's satchel is on the table and the Bible is inside of its side pocket. She motions with her finger and tells Michal not to forget David's small luggage. Michal places the leather strap around her neck and meets her at the door. Usually when they left the cabin they would lock the door behind them but this time they didn't because they didn't plan on coming back.

Sentiment to what they are leaving behind, they reminisce on the blood, sweat, and tears they had to undergo to build the cabin. It started with the two of them visioning a safe and secure physical home and now they are departing for a safe and secure spiritual home. Wiping the watery gloss from their eyes, both ladies pray that whoever finds the cabin are blessed just as they were blessed when they finished building it.

"Are you ladies all right?"

"Yes, David, we're okay. It's just that we've stayed here practically forever and the place kind of grew on us," Michal replies handing David his satchel.

"I completely understand and thanks for getting my bag." David puts the sphere inside the satchel and closes the flap. "Please take your time, I'm ready whenever you are."

"We are ready now, Pastor Grace," Orpah said giving David the bedroll she packed for him. "Like you said earlier, we must walk in the light while we have the light."

David smiles and deposits the satchel in Jax's saddlebags. His dirk is sheathed on his side and his shield is straddled across his back. Swinging into the saddle, he pulls Jax's reins to the left with his gauntlet hand leading him to turn in a full circle. Dust is quickly picked up as Jax's strong leg presses his hooves into the dirt. "That a boy, Jax," he said feeling the power in between his thighs. "From this day on, you will only go into battle for the Lord."

Orpah and Michal mount up when they see David is in the saddle ready to ride out. The two horses follows their master's commands and walks up on side of Jax and halts. David gives the women a nod and they nod back.

"This day I tell you, my dear sisters, that you will be blessed beyond measures. For Jesus said out of his own mouth that when he sits on his glorious throne next to his father, those who have followed him will also sit with him in heaven. And everyone who left houses, brothers, sisters, fathers, mothers, wife, or children for his namesake will receive a hundred times as much when they inherit eternal life."

Michal hears all the blessings that are coming her way and becomes excited. Looking at her new brother and sister in Christ, she said, "Giddyap, Betsie! Let's ride!"

18

B lackbird is a raven and the chief messenger for Queen Jezebel. Whenever the queen has a message to convey throughout the land of Golgotha, Blackbird's feathers make sure the towns under her power receives the queen's edicts. Sitting in a windowsill inside the king and queen's palace, Blackbird waits for the queen to finish writing Areopagus in Kidron.

King Anubis and his successor, Athaliah, have arrived bringing gold, scented oils, royal cloths, and zaqs. Their appreciation comes from the queen giving Anubis her gaveling hand of supremacy to become king over Ben Hinnom after she dethroned Dathan. The annual Soul Reapers Conquest gladiator match is a month away but Anubis's gifts have lifted her spirits into moving it up to next week. Pushing herself from behind her cedar desk, Queen Jezebel rolls up her note and puts it in a cylinder strapped to

Blackbird's leg. After tightening the cap on the plastic tube, she picks the raven up with the palms of her hands and says, "Fly, Blackbird. Go and find you trainer, Areopagus."

Blackbird drops from the arched window and immediately his wings spread to support his weight in the air. Flying swiftly over the region of Golgotha, he soars beneath the clouds without any hindrance. No obstacles is in his way as he flaps his feathers over Sodom, Demetria, Tilgath, and then over the high cliffs of Kidron. Descending into the rocky walls, Blackbird circles over Areopagus's house like a vulture circling over a carcass.

Areopagus is a soothsayer and he trains wild animals to understand and listen to their master's commands. Smokey, Dagon's pterodactyl, the queen's fierce steed and his flying friend, Blackbird, are only a few among his prized handiworks. His wife, Asherah, is a witch and an expert in underworld healing. After his battle with the Underlings, King Azzazel retired to Kidron to be healed by one of her many remedies.

Two days have passed since she has put a bandage of soaked dead leaves on the gash inside his armpit. Asherah wished she had more time to do her work, but Azzazel feels he must return to his search for David before the trail gets cold. Areopagus stands to examine the wound when his wife is peeling the last leaf off. Right as he is about to divulge to the king his diagnoses. Blackbird flies through the window and alights on his assigned perch.

"Blackbird, you're home!" Areopagus ignores King Azzazel's wound to see what message the queen has sent to him. Unscrewing the cap to the tube, he pulls out the letter and pets Blackbird because it's been over a month since he's seen his winged friend. King Azzazel stretches his arm and stands when Areopagus is unrolling the letter to read.

Queen Jezebel message reads:

> My dear servant, Areopagus. I know the day is growing shorter by the minutes but I am putting forth a new ordinance on behalf of the annual Soul Reapers Conquest gladiator match that is to be held in the coliseum. King Anubis, whom my king and I put into power over Ben Hinnom, is visiting our region and I thought it best to entertain him and his guest while they are in Golgotha. The Soul Reapers Conquest match is scheduled for next month, but Anubis's presence has lifted my spirits to moving it up to one week from today. My dear, Areopagus, I am counting on you to let Kidron know that this is a mandatory present edict from the throne of Queen Jezebel. If you are to see my king, I ask that you bring to his attention my wishes and to let him know that he is needed back in Sodom. I, the queen, write these words in my own hand so therefore it

will be to your best interest for you to honor what I have written in this letter.

Jezebel

Azzazel smiles when his wife's letter comes to a close. Asherah is rubbing various oils on his cut that is now only a hairline scar. The soaked dead leaves, oils, and her witchery has completely healed the king, but since she was rushed in making him well, Asherah lets him know the pain will go away as if it was to heal normally. King Azzazel laughs as he puts on his breastplate because the pain under his arm is nothing compared to the pain he inflicts on the souls who disobeys the laws of the land. Areopagus hands the king his hat after he places his sword in its scabbard and his whip along his side.

"Areopagus," Azzazel said, tucking his handkerchief under his breastplate.

"Yes my king."

"Please send a message to the queen stating that I will be in Sodom at dusk tomorrow. Also let her know that among my expeditious return, I will deliver her edicts to Demetria and Gomorrah."

"And when do you want me to send this message, my king, for I can see that Blackbird is tired from his travels?"

"Very well then," he said rubbing his chin. "It can be delivered at first daylight."

Azzazel agreed to Areopagus's request because his wife Asherah restored his arm back into full fighting condition. This reason and this reason alone is the reason he agreed to his request because any other time he would've punished Areopagus for playing him for a fool. Everyday he's watched Blackbird fly to the ends of Hades for the queen only to return and do it all over again. Blackbird was Areopagus's first pet until the queen realized the raven capabilities and ordered the bird to remain in her palace. When it's all said and done, Areopagus misses the company of his feathery friend and is too afraid to let anyone know it.

Azzazel takes a seat at the table and asks Areopagus to use his gifts to help him find David who has eluded him for the past two weeks. Areopagus sits across from him and gestures to his wife to bring him the cards in the rickety jar on the shelf. "How about we consult the cards, my king?" he asks. Asherah opens the jar and brings her husband a deck of tarot cards. He takes them and looks deep into Azzazel's eyes. "Now be still, my king," he said touching the deck to Azzazel's forehead. Shuffling the cards, Areopagus tells the king that he can only see what the cards will show him. "Three cards, my king. In three cards we will know about the man who has been a thorn in your flesh."

The first card flipped over and a man in a loose garment with a piece of rope for a belt is standing next to a sheep sitting at his feet. In the man's hand is a shepherd's crook and in his other hand is a black book with a cross on it. Areopagus's eyes widen because this card has never surfaced in all his reading in Hades. "The man you seek is alive and has a purpose far greater than any man you've encountered in the afterlife," he said, shuffling the cards a second time to make sure his reading is correct.

Areopagus sets the deck down and instead of pulling one from the top, he spreads them out and picks one randomly. The card that flips over has the man from the first card in it so that tells him that the cards are revealing to him the truth. The difference is that in this card the sheep is dead and the man is blocking a blow with his shepherd's crook from a knight with a crown on his head. Areopagus looks up at Azzazel and says, "The knight in the card is you, my king, and you will meet the man you are searching for on the battlefield." Azzazel likes this card and can't wait for it to come to pass.

Areopagus shuffles the cards a third time and asks Azzazel to pull any card and flip it over because the last card represents his fate. Azzazel does as he is told and flips the card right side up for Areopagus to see. Almost immediately, Asherah gasps at what the card is showing pertaining to Azzazel's future. The card displayed the knight with the crown on his head kneeling before the man with the black book and shepherd's crook.

"What does this card mean?" Azzazel demanded.

Areopagus stammers as he is reading. "It means that you will someway or somehow humble yourself unto David and respect his purpose and allow him to be the man he is called to be."

"Never!" Azzazel slams his hand on the table and slides the tarot cards on the floor. "I'll die first before these knees bow to some peasant who threatens the throne of my queen!" he yells, causing the chair legs to screech as they slide across the floor while he's getting up.

Dagon rushes through the door when he hears the state of confusion coming from inside the house. Areopagus and his wife are huddled in a corner terrified that the king may become violent and kill them. Asherah speaks up before Dagon can react to Azzazel's anger.

"King Azzazel," she said boldly while releasing her husband to step forward. "Areopagus's gifts of fortune telling are only a helpful tool for those seeking to know their future."

Areopagus remains silent hoping that his wife's deceiving methods gets them pass the bloodbath that he knows the king and Dagon are capable of inflicting on them. Never, not once, has the tarot cards been wrong when he gave a reading. Carefully cogitating his thoughts, he decides to follow in line with Asherah and tell the king what he wants to hear.

"My king," he said, stepping on side of his wife. "Asherah is right when she says my gifts are only a gift. Now that your fate has been brought to your attention, you can rewrite your destiny."

"How can this be when it was me who picked the last card and not you?"

Asherah apprehends that their words has calmed him down enough for her to seal the deal on keeping her and her husband alive. Gathering the cards from off the floor, she places them back inside the old jar. "Because, my king, it is you and only you who can walk in your shoes," she said, facing Azzazel. "And as you walk your chosen path, my king, the stars in the sky will line up according to your steps."

Azzazel looks at the paleness in the faces of the husband and wife and returns to his tranquil self. The witch and the soothsayer are known to be con artists to get what they want but con or not he takes in what they are saying. "I look forward to the day I kneel to this David fellow. And if that day shall come I look forward to driving my sword into his chest and watching him fall to his knees in death before me." He turns the doorknob and faces Areopagus who is still leery because he is so unpredictable. "As you were, Areopagus, and I expect my queen to have my message at first daylight in the morning," he said, opening the door. Stepping aside, he gives Dagon space to leave Areopagus's quarters. "Dagon, it seems our hunt for David will have to wait until a later day. Come, let us go into Kidron and relay my queen's ordinances firsthand to the people."

Swinging onto the back of Smokey, Dagon acts in accordance with his master and calls his beast from the sky. Starting toward the center of Kidron, Azzazel tells Dagon to go in the opposite direction telling every soul he comes in contact with that all must attend the queen's Soul Reapers Conquest match in Sodom one week from today. Looking back at his most trusted servant, he says, "Meet me in Skull Valley in one hour so that we can start making our way back to Sodom. And oh, by the way, remind the people that no excuses will be accepted for not being present in the coliseum."

The three amigos progressed down the hidden trail only stopping to relieve themselves when needed to. Betsie, Jax, and the roan looked like elephants following one behind the other as they traveled the beaten trackway because it is too small for them to spread out. Michal is familiar with the woods so she is the one leading the group to their first stop on the assignment they've undertaken for the Lord. A confluence of bridle paths join the trail they are on so she educated David on where they lead to. Being that they all flowed into the walkway they are on, David concludes that wherever they are going must be an important place in Hades.

They started out around midday and most likely could have reached the end of the path if they would've pushed the horses instead of walking them. Deep down inside, David wanted to get to where they're going quickly but the Word of God can sometimes bring opposition and therefore they may need the horses' strength to make an escape.

From the look of the overcast, nighttime is beginning to befall them. Trampling across the dirt, the ground beneath the horses suddenly starts to mesh with the grass. Michal sees that the path has come to an end and pulls back on the reins.

"Why have we stopped?" Orpah ask trying to look past David to see what's ahead.

"Because we're here, Orpah." Michal bids Betsie to go into the trees to the right so David and Orpah can come on side of her. "Just beyond those trees is Skull Valley that leads to Kidron," she said pointing her finger.

"Skull Valley?" David ask not liking the sound of its name.

Michal catches his reaction to the name of the valley. "Relax, David." She chuckles. "It's only called that because a long time ago a lot of souls died there in a great war over Kidron."

"But why fight over Kidron?" David inquired.

"Because Kidron is surrounded by high cliffs on every side except for a gully with Zaqqum trees running along the backside of the city. Skull Valley is the only way in and is the only way out of the city. Anything you need you can find there. From food, to water, witchcraft, weapons, fortune-telling, and healing if you are hurt severely. These things are just a fraction of what the city has to offer so you can see why people over the centuries have tried to seize it for their selfish gain."

David looks toward the trees and then to the disciples God has blessed him with. "Well, ladies, I think we've found the perfect place to start our ministry." David kneed Jax forward. "You know, Michal. Out of all the great qualities Kidron has, I didn't hear you say that they have the Word of God. And I think it's about time they've heard it there."

Directing Jax into one side of the small patch of trees and out of the other, David finds himself off to the side of the main road of Skull Valley. Orpah manifest behind him and Michal arrives shortly behind her. All three of them decide to carry on along the side of the road so that no one on the main road can see them unless they happen to cross paths.

Ahead of the pack, David stops when Jax embarks upon a man-size culvert under the graveled road. Surveying the sky, he finds it best to stop there and continue on into Kidron in the morning. "Stay here while I check this culvert out for safety," he said swinging down from the saddle.

David draws his sword and steps inside without having to duck. He walks about six feet inside in complete darkness and pushes his way back to the other side of the culvert that has been sealed off by a heap of dirt. Also, someone has placed a big boulder in the center of the drain so that he or she could hide behind it if someone entered unannounced. Everything David sees adds up to the old drain being a safe and unexposed habitat for his companions to rest at.

Magically appearing back onto the terrace, Orpah asks David why is it that they've stopped. He gladly tells her his reasons about how it will be better for them if they persist into the city of Kidron in the morning instead of at night. David is their leader, so Michal and Orpah comply without hesitation.

"Orpah and Michal, take the bedrolls and anything else we need inside while I double back with the horses and tie them to a tree on the hidden trail we've been riding on." David grabs all three horses' reins and begins walking toward the path that brought them there. As the ladies are entering the culvert, he yells, "Looks like we're camping here tonight so make yourself comfortable," while laughing because the two of them probably haven't slept on the ground in a very long time.

It took Azzazel more than an hour to meet Dagon in Skull Valley. Implementing Queen Jezebel's orders throughout Kidron took longer than expected. Making his way through the city, Azzazel noticed that the majority of the townspeople were inside their homes out of fear of him and Dagon being around.

The mission he's been on to capture David didn't call for the queen's shofar so he gave Dagon the okay to leave it behind. Had he had had it, he could have blown it and everyone would have had to come to the center of the city or suffer the consequences for their disobedience. On that account, Azzazel is left having to go door to door relaying the throne's decree personally.

On the way to exit Kidron, Azzazel stopped by Areopagus's house and placed him over making sure the city was empty one week from today. He also tells him that if anyone doesn't adhere to attending the coliseum, Areopagus is to report it to the queen so the perpetrator can be brought to justice. Keeping to his schedule, he promised his wife, Azzazel races under the dim sky to meet Dagon.

"I'm ready to go now, Dagon," he said as Smokey walked up on Dagon in Skull Valley. "Sorry for the delay but it seems our presence made the locals not want to come out and mingle among us." A devilish grin curves at the corners of his lips. "Why don't you fly ahead over the main roads to see if you can spot any travelers? If you do, be my guest to let them know what the queen has ordered. As for me, I'll meet you in Gomorrah at midnight where we will rest and proceed at first daylight."

Dagon nodded his head to the king while pulling back on the pterodactyl's reins. The strength in his pet's wings brought him high in the sky in just two or three flaps. Azzazel continued on the main road while staring at his reliant servant until he was out of sight.

Surrounded by massive rock walls, he rides Smokey compliantly down the long uneven road of Skull Valley. Finally, the rocks come to an end and the trees make up for where the high cliffs used to be. Wanting to extend on without any complications, he decides to make water before pressing forward to Gomorrah. "Give me a minute or two, Smokey," he said sliding off his beast back. "I shall be back shortly."

Orpah was the first to hear rocks tumbling down the hill from the road on top of them. Alacrity to the possible threat approaching, she taps David and points toward the entrance. David hears the crunching of rocks underneath someone's feet and gestures to his friends to go to the far back wall at the end of the culvert. Michal and Orpah listens while David silently follows them.

At the back of the culvert, he pulls out his sword and the two ladies place arrows in their bows. Like a panther waiting patiently for their prey, they sit ready to strike the shadowy figure in the hat standing in front of the man-size drain. Azzazel steps inside the dark pipe to relieve himself while mumbling something about David. Michal has met the king on many occasions and puts his voice to the hat he always wear.

"Look, Pastor Grace," Michal whispered. "This is the day the Lord has given you your enemy into your hands for you to deal with as you wish."

Then David crept up unnoticed behind the boulder and pulled Azzazel's handkerchief from under his breastplate. Azzazel finished his nature's call without having a clue of how close he came to becoming the worm of torment's late-night snack. David crept back to the back of the culvert while Azzazel left and climbed the short hill to the main road. Back into the saddle, he pats the back of Smokey's neck to give him the signal to change gears to speed away.

Orpah speaks, "Pastor Grace," she said lowly until she knew for sure the king had truly departed. "Why is it that you didn't end his life as if he had no doubt ended yours if he had been aware you were in here?"

"The Lord forbid that I, a man of God, do such a thing to a helpless soul that is incapable of defending himself. Believe me, my sisters in Christ, if the time comes and I must fight or perish, then I will fight without thinking twice about it." David sheaths his dagger. "I know it's probably not making any sense, Orpah, but the times I speak of wasn't tonight. Because if I had or had you had done such an unjustly act, then we, who are followers of Christ, would have been no better than Azzazel."

"You're right, Pastor Grace, I don't understand but I trust your judgments in what you have decided to do tonight. For you have shown me this day that you are truly the man of God that you say you are."

"Thanks, Orpah, and I pray as we walk this walk we have chosen, the two of you become enlighten on what the Bible means when it speaks of God's grace. Undeserved favor and undeserved love."

19

Vex. In the dictionary, Webster defines vex as to annoy, to trouble or afflict, to baffle, or confuse. This is the state the witch and the soothsayer are in as they sit around their table giving thought to the three cards that were brought forth during Azzazel's tarot card reading yesterday. His wife Asherah asked could the random cards of the shepherd's crook man been coincidental but Areopagus shuns the thought immediately because his cards have never lied to him before.

Areopagus comes to his senses and shakes off David's and Azzazel's destiny and taps his right shoulder with his fingers. Blackbird discerns his trainer's summons and jumps from his perch to the shoulder tapped. First daylight's bottom lip is almost over the horizon so before being subject to a penalty for not forwarding the king's memorandum, he begins the notifications to the queen. Just as he is writing the first words, repetitive hard knocks on the door disturbs his reference to throne duties.

Asherah opens the door. "What is it?" she asks the man who is breathing hard on their doorstep. "And why do you trouble me and my lord at such an early hour."

"Areopagus!" he shouts looking over her shoulder. "It is I Jabin! Please come quick," he said regaining his breath. "For there is a man clamoring forbidden proclamation throughout the city of Kidron."

Areopagus hurriedly follows Jabin to the well on the Eastern side of Kidron. His wife is right on their heels as the two men jostle their way through the flock of people to get to the front. Orpah and Michal are standing next to the well keeping an eye on the multitude while David stands on a bluff a few feet from the ravine.

"Repent! Repent, for the kingdom of the heaven is at hand and near all of you today! Repent! I say repent, so that you can be saved!"

Areopagus's ears are aghast with lawlessness. "You, Mr. David, should be ashamed of yourself for bringing such curses down upon this city from the throne of Queen Jezebel."

David is surprised to hear the inscrutable man who has stepped from the crowd knows his name.

"Yes, Mr. David with the gauntlet on his hand. I know who you are and I also know that there's a certain king by the name of Azzazel looking for you."

David continues to shout. "Repent! Repent, Kidron, and be saved on the day of judgment from the realms of hell. Repent!"

"Be quiet, you fool!" Asherah scowls. "Who are you to tell us what we should do when our souls are already condemned."

"In the words of Isaiah the prophet, 'I am a voice crying in the wilderness, prepare your souls for the Lord. And all those who believe in Jesus Christ and repent shall see the salvation of God.'"

Michal walks to the bottom of the hill to address the people. "Please listen, Kidron, before you cast discrimination against Pastor Grace for giving you the opportunity to have eternal life. For just as you, we too." Michal points to Orpah. "Did not want to hear or believe what he had to say. But after telling us the truth and showing us the truth in the Holy Bible, we have come to realize that we can someday be with God if we accept his free gift in his only begotten son Jesus."

"Well said, my beloved sister in the Lord," David said radiantly because Michal and Orpah continue to astonish him on their accelerated growth in the Lord.

"What is this gift you speak about and what do we have to do to receive it?" a man's voice asked from the center of the crowd but he already knew the answer because he personally knew Jesus.

David raised the Bible above his head with both hands. "Repent, I tell you! Repent of your wicked ways that this vile world has put on your shoulders to do. Most assuredly I say to you, unless one believes in Jesus Christ and be born-again he cannot enter the kingdom of God." The assemblage of people had expressionless looks on their faces when David said they must be born-again. "Do not marvel that I said to you, you must be born-again. For the Word of God says that there are things in this world that we do not understand and yet we still believe in them. So is everyone who is born of God. The things I preach to you are true and I testify today before you of their truths. If they were not so, I would not be standing here boldly speaking to you what the laws of Hades strongly protest. I stand here today because I've been born-again and what better way to declare my faith to my Lord than to lead someone else to the joy I have come to trust in. For God so love the world that he gave his only begotten son, that whosoever believes in him should not perish but have everlasting life." David lowers his Bible and look at the uninterested faces throughout the crowd. With words of compassion, he says, "I say this to you, Kidron, because God made him who had no sin to be sin for us so that in him we might become the righteousness of God."

"Born-again, he says." Areopagus spits to the foot of the bluff. "Who do you think we are, Pastor David Grace, that we are to believe we are going to be born-again, and life in Sheol will be happily ever after?" Areopagus looks to the people. "My fellow citizens of Kidron, I ask you today not to be deceived by this irreverence teaching this man and his followers are speaking to you. Right now, as he speaks, the temperature has risen a few degrees from the blaspheme this man has brought to our town." Areopagus fans himself. "Don't you feel it? Because I sure do, and if I do, that means the queen does as well. Honestly, do we want her displeasure upon us after working so hard to keep her content with the way we have been running our city?"

"My husband is right. Why should we bring the Devil's Advocates' wrath upon us by defying Lord Satan? Let us also be mindful that in six days we are all to be in Sodom for the Soul Reapers Conquest match." She pauses and points her finger toward the locals. "And if the queen even has a hint of us listening to this deranged man today, we may find ourselves in the jaws of her ferocious pet hyenas, Apollyon and Abaddon the destroyers (For this is what their names means.).

A man steps from the horde of people. "What should we do then, if we decide to believe in this Jesus Christ?"

David joins Michal and Orpah by the well. "Anyone who has two shirts should share it with the one who has none and anyone who has food should do the same. I say to you, repent of your sins, my brother, and let the love of God guide you from this day forward until we are caught up to the heavens to be with his son Jesus."

The man's heart is sadden because he denied the truth of Jesus firsthand and his denial in the Son of God is what sentenced him to Hades. "I believe, Pastor Grace, that Jesus died for my sins and I ask him to please forgive me for appealing to Jerusalem to nail him to the cross," he said tersely ashamed of the innocent blood he allowed to be shed during his priesthood.

David is about to speak but Areopagus speaks first.

"Joseph Caiaphas!" Areopagus called out with rage in his voice. "Surely you of all people are not going to believe this unwanted man's lies about being born-again. I expect this defiance from the women or some of the lesser men of integrity but not you, who are considered one of the patriarchs in the history of the prince of darkness."

"My apologies, Areopagus, for the choices I am making today." Caiaphas lifts his head to look Areopagus in the eyes. "But since the day I stepped foot in this hellish place, my soul has been laden with turmoil for crucifying a man who only sought for mankind to love one another as you would love yourself."

"You do know what this mean, Joseph? For I have no choice but to have Blackbird report this rebelliousness to the queen."

"Do as you please, Areopagus. My decision is final."

Areopagus yells to the crowd. "Anyone else?" He looks left to right to see if someone will be foolish enough to step forward. "Would anyone else dare to defy the gaveling hands of Queen Jezebel?"

The swarm of people began to disseminate because all of them knows Areopagus is Jezebel's eyes and ears over Kidron. Also, King Azzazel's presence yesterday has startled them enough to continue obeying the Devil's Advocates' orders or he will make them burn for eternity. One by one and two by two, the citizens went their way until two men are left standing in the open grounds next to Caiaphas.

"Pastor Grace." One of the men walked to speak to David while the other man who spoke up earlier in the midst of the gathering trailed behind him. "Just as my neighbor Caiaphas, I too have been battling within my soul for giving the orders to my soldiers to ridicule and kill a man who only crime was proclaiming he was the Son of God."

The man who followed him to the well shoulders were shrunk and as he approached he dragged his feet dispirited for allowing the devil to use him as a liar before and during Jesus's unlawful trial. "This Jesus you speak of I knew and walked with, Pastor Grace," he stammers. "And the words you speak, Pastor, I've heard many times before but did not believe in them." The man stands straight up confident that he is about to make the right decision. "Pastor Grace."

"Yes, my brother."

"If you will have a sinner like me, I would like to be born-again and be your disciple."

Areopagus tore his garment at the center of his collar down to his waist. "Blaspheme! This is outright blaspheme I tell you. Caiaphas, see what you have done? Not only are you but also Pontius and Judas are also joining this treacherous revolt!" he exclaimed grabbing his wife's hand. "Asherah, let us leave these grounds before this disease of disobedience pervade us into becoming one of his disciples." Walking some ways off, Areopagus stops and says, "My apologies to you, Caiaphas, but from this day forward your soul is in the hands of the queen."

Could this be true? David thought. "Could these three men be: Judas the betrayer of Jesus, Caiaphas the accuser of Jesus, and Pilate the executioner of Jesus asking for forgiveness of their depraved sins? Surely they must be like Artemis and Cybele, possibly going by false names to deceive the next soul in Hades. But if Michal and Orpah are who they say they are, then these men can be too."

"Pastor Grace," Orpah said tugging his chain mail. "Are you okay?"

"Huh?"

"I said are you okay, Pastor?"

"Yes, yes," he said as the veneration of the three men in front of him begins to fade away. "I'm okay. I guess I got a little beside myself at the sight of our new brothers Caiaphas, Judas, and Pilate giving their lives to the Lord." David extends his hand and shakes each man's hand in agreement to their first steps of faith toward the path they have chosen to walk on. "Today, Caiaphas, Judas, and Pilate, I give you my right hand of fellowship in the grace given to you becoming a new man. The road you have chosen will be rough but the reward for being on it will be great when you see the glory of the Lord in heaven. These are your sisters, Orpah and Michal, and they will lead you through the sinner's prayer and afterward I will baptize you in the name of the Father, Son, and Holy Spirit. God bless you and we look forward to you growing in the Lord as you add to your faith."

When Orpah and Michal were finished taking care of God's business, Pilate offers his home so that they all can take a load off of their feet from the few hours of standing. David took the thought into great consideration and decided it would be best to leave the well to baptize them just in case Areopagus tries to cause a public disturbance.

Pilate's residence is unusual because it was only a cave on side of a cliff until he broadened it to make it his dwelling. It took him years of chipping away at the rock to make the inside what it is today. Among Kidron's citizens, his abode is the only home that is safe on all sides except for the entrance from intruders. A rock is rolled from left to right for the door when he is going or coming, and when he is home a red curtain hangs loosely to the ground. Inviting his new friends in to rest, Pilate gestures for them to make themselves at home and sit wherever feels comfortable for them.

David doesn't waste any time baptizing them. The ladies sat on rock chairs carved in the walls of the cave while David poured water from the sphere down on the heads of each man as they stepped forward at his request. Since it is Pilate's home, he felt it was common courtesy to go last to be doused with the cooling water. Shivering, they all stood and listened as David told them what the Bible says about the baptism of water represents.

"This day, my brothers, you have made a conscious decision to serve the Lord with all your hearts and all your minds. Henceforth, I ask that you listen to your souls and continue in doing good. Because we know that in all things God works for the good of those who love him, and who have been called according to his purpose. For those God foreknew, he also predestined to be conformed to the image of his son, that you might be the firstborn among many brothers and sisters. And those he predestined, he also called. Those he called, he also justified. Those he justified, he also glorified. Stand firm in your faith, my brothers. If God is for us then who can be against us. Now it is God who makes both us and you stand firm in Christ. In being baptized, he has anointed you, set his seal of ownership on you and put his love in your hearts as a deposit, guaranteeing what is to come." David makes an imaginary cross in the air with the Bible in the direction of the three men. "Be blessed, my brothers, in Christ. Be blessed. Amen."

"Amen," Orpah and Michal said together as they stood to give the men a group hug.

Resting, they all lounged around eating zaqs and drinking water from the sphere. Thoroughly dried from the Hades's heat, the spell of serenity prompt the three men to share their firsthand experience of when the Son of God was lifted up on the cross before the Roman and Jewish people.

The day his death occurred, their wrongs of what they did to Jesus was quickly upon them. Never, not until today, has any of them ever decided to confide in anyone about the man who died because of a lie. David and the women encouraged them to let it out so that the sinful yoke can be lifted off their shoulders once and for all.

Judas went first. "I remember when I first laid eyes on Jesus. It was my friend who brought me to him. He said to me, 'Come, Judas. Come and see this marvelous man who is healing the sick and speaking words of wisdom no man has ever heard before.'" Judas stared into space recalling how Jesus healed a paralyzed man by simply telling him to get up, take your mat, and go home. "It was on that day my friend urged me to follow Jesus. My friend went because he said that it was something about Jesus that drew him to him and he was determine to find out what it was. I went because I was at a time in my life when making ends meet was hard to come by. Immediately when I saw the lame man walk again, I knew people would pay unlimited amounts of money to be healed from their troubles. I was a prig when I met Jesus and I was going to be a prig when I walk with him. To me, this was my opportunity to get as much money as I can to regain my place in the community as a flourishing man. I made my rounds the weeks to come penny pinching here and penny pinching there. It wasn't much I had obtained during Jesus's teachings but it was enough to get me started in the direction of life I was look-ing for. I told my friend one day when Jesus had went out to a mountainside to pray during the night that tomorrow evening I was going to return to Judea to make up for the lost time I had been away. He told me that he understood and he wished me well on my journey. Morning came and Jesus woke all of us up to speak to us about his spiritual-discerning prayer. The vast number of men sat up while some stood to hear what Jesus had to say."

Judas begun to wail at the thought of what Jesus prayed during the night before. Michal sat next to him and held his hand to give him strength to carry on.

"He chose me!" Judas cried out. "Out of over seventy-two men and women he chose me to be an apostle as a witness to his life's story from the beginning to the end."

David is all ears to the personal history of Jesus's ministry when he walked this earth as the Lamb of God. Not only him but also Caiaphas and Pilate as well because they never knew Jesus the way Judas knew him.

"Why, Pastor Grace? Can anybody tell me why me?" Judas asked.

David puts his hand on Judas's back. "Because he loved you, Judas, and despite your shortcomings he wanted to give you a chance to make the right decision when the devil would try to have his way with you."

Judas dries his tears and continues, "From that day forward, Jesus began to put trust in me that I know he knew I didn't deserve. Like I said, I was a prig and yet he made me keeper of the money bag. None of the other disciples couldn't understand this because Matthew was a tax collector and he handled money on a daily basis in his previous life. They all knew I dipped my fingers in the money bag a time or two but no one said anything because Jesus appointed me as treasurer. Throughout Jesus's three years of ministry I watched him perform miraculous things. I even was empowered to do miraculous things, but for some reason my heart wouldn't allow me to accept that he was the Messiah the prophets wrote about."

Judas looks at the women and puts his head down. "Perfume," he mumbles but then speak up. "It was an alabaster of a year's wages of perfume that prompt me to betray the only person whoever trusted me, taught me, and loved me for reasons I couldn't understand. This poor woman poured an expensive jar of perfume on Jesus's feet when she could have sold it and gave it to the poor or better yet, me, since she was only going to waste it. When Jesus chastised me in front of the other disciples for asking why such a waste of money, I became angry and later slipped out from their company and went to Caiaphas to see how much money he was willing to give me to deliver Jesus over to him. Money!" Judas shouted. "Once again it was money that ruled my life and it was money that got me to give Jesus over to the Jewish council. Thirty pieces of silver is what Jesus's sinless life was worth to Caiaphas, so thirty pieces of silver is what I took."

Judas stands and walks to the curtain doorway. Ashamed about what he is about to say, he gives his audience only his back. "During our last supper together, Jesus sat me in the seat of honor to his right while the other disciples sat whenever they desired. After breaking bread and drinking wine that he said represented his body and the blood he will shed for the world, Jesus got up and took off his garment. Humbling himself as a servant, he washed all our feet and dried them with the towel that covered him. Jesus put back on his garment and told us he has given us an example that day on how we are to treat our fellow brothers in the future to be considered a servant of God. As customary to a meal of prestige. Jesus explicitly told his disciples that the one who is going to betray him is the one who will dip his hand in the dish with him according to the customs. No one understood what he was saying because a veil was over their hearts and eyes. As we dipped our hands in the bowl together, he handed me the sauced bread and outright told me, 'What you are about to do, do it quickly.' The other disciples thought he was telling me to go buy something for the festival but in actually he was saying, 'It's too late, Judas, for Satan has already entered you.'" Judas turns around. "When I returned, I returned with a kiss to Jesus's cheek that signaled the soldiers with me that this is the man who Caiaphas demands to be brought to him. Later I recognized my wrongs of condemning innocent blood and returned the money given to me. Soon after, guilt took hold of me and I took my own life in a field with a rope around my neck." Judas rubs his throat. "When I came to, I was here in Sheol for my lies, deceit, and for murder."

Caiaphas stands and faces Judas. "Please forgive me for appealing to your weakness for money so that you would betray your master." Caiaphas looks at David and then back to Judas. "I too have cursed myself by corrupting the Jews to spill innocent blood. My story may not be as elaborate as yours, my brother Judas, but I do have a story," he continued while taking a seat. "The day I heard of Jesus of Nazareth I was wroth that the people said that there was a man teaching them the law of our forefather Moses. After assembling the Jewish council, I asked have anyone heard of this Jesus and if so what school did he go to, to be considered a rabbi. None of my council or the council of the Sadducees couldn't vouch for his teachings. Shortly after our confidential meeting, I sent men to ask him who testifies of his knowledge of the law of Moses, and to my amazement, he said his father in heaven testifies of him. Blaspheme. I thought, because Jesus said he is the Son of God. I then knew that this lawlessness must be contained before his words get beyond my hands of control. My council came up with a plan to catch him in his words, but no one from each of our camps could find fault in his speech. As a matter of fact, he made us look like fools in front of the people as we left worse off than when we came. Then Jesus began to become a thorn in my flesh as he ate on the Sabbath, worked on the Sabbath, and healed on the Sabbath. The people began to listen to his message and started receiving him as the Messiah, sent by God. When witnessing the people going against our Jewish customs, I decided to call a secret meeting to plot and kill

Jesus before they actually tried to make him king of Israel. My argument to the Jewish council was that if we don't destroy Jesus then the Romans will come and take away our temple and our nation. That year, I prophesized words that I didn't know where they came from. I said, 'It is better for us that one man die for the people than the whole nation perish.' My prophesy opened the council's eyes to agree with me, and on that day, the trap was set for Jesus to step in." Caiaphas walked to the corners of the cave and stood alone. "Crucify him!" he shouted making the words echo off the rocky walls. "'Crucify him' is what I yelled when Pontius Pilate, the governor, asked the Jews what shall I do then with the one you call the king of the Jews?"

Caiaphas thought about what he is about to say next. Stepping into the center of the cave, he said, "It wasn't until the sky became dark for three hours, the curtain tore that separated the holy of holies from the rest of the temple, and the Jewish council told me that deceased men and women were walking throughout the town, is when I knew I made a grave mistake and could not fix it." Caiaphas wipes faint tears from his eyes. "You know what's sad, Pastor Grace?"

"Tell me, Caiaphas. We all are all listening," David replies.

"That it took Jesus dying for nothing at all for me to believe that what he daily professed was the truth. I, Caiaphas, high priest of the Jewish nation, crucified the son of the living God."

Michal and Orpah sat and listened to the history of the man they have put their trust into to bring them in the presence of God. Both of them cried to how Jesus was done unjustly for only wanting to bring the world together as one nation under God. David briefed them to his knowledge about the day he died on the cross, but these guys were actually there and watched his terrible death with their own eyes. Even David could only listen to them speak from their perspective of how they denounced the truth that walked on the earth when they were alive. As Pilate got up to speak, David thought, *Three men, three different actions, and three different ways Satan used them to get rid of his one problem in Jesus.*

"I am Pontius Pilate, governor of Judea, only answering to Chief Tiberius Caesar, commander over a legion of centurion soldiers. And yet I couldn't release a man who I had found no fault in during an unjustified trial." Pilate paces the floor in his home with his hands behind his back. "I didn't know what to think when Caiaphas and the Jews bombarded their way into my presence early in the morning. Surely I thought they were mad for bothering me at such an early hour. I was tempted to display my governing power and have them thrown out but the uproar concerning the man they drug in by the shackles captured my attention. Curious to what this lowly man had done, I allowed the Jewish council to speak. Every crime they shouted against Jesus wasn't a crime at all. It was almost hilarious but being that I was a high official in the Roman Empire I had to keep my composure before the people. Trying to get to the bottom of the accusers' accusations, I separated them to question Jesus alone. I asked him, 'Are you the king of the Jews?' He replied, 'Is that your own idea or did others talk to you about me?' When I asked, 'What is it you had done?' he didn't answer the question. Instead, he said, 'My kingdom is not of this world. If it were, my servants would fight to prevent my arrest by the Jewish leaders.' I didn't know how to respond to his remarks so I just plainly asked him, 'Are you a king or not?' Jesus answered, 'You say that I am a king. In fact, the reason I was born and came into this world is to testify to the truth. Everyone on the side of truth listens to me.' 'What is truth?' I retorted. 'What is truth?' I asked him again and again but didn't get any more replies from him after he declared his testimony. I then gathered the Jews and told them I found no charges against him. I even went so far as to send him to my rival Herod Antipas but he too couldn't find him guilty of a crime and thereafter sent him back to me."

Darkness starts to set in inside the cave from the day passing. Pilate uncovers the lamps along the walls so that his company can have some light.

"During the Jewish festivals, the Jews and I had agreed upon a custom to release a prisoner to their liking. Three times I tried to sway them to release the king of the Jews but they chose Jesus instead. The only problem, it was Jesus Barabbas, the murderer, and not Jesus of Nazareth, the Christ. My wife even stepped out of her place as a woman and came to me during the trial and said let Jesus be because she had suffered a great deal that day in dreams concerning him. I loved her and respected her boldness to reprimand me but my duties is to Caesar and not my wife. Yes, I had the power to release Jesus but the Jews' persistence that he should die outweighed my righteous judgment. Finally, I gave in when Caiaphas cried out, "Crucify him! We have no king but Caesar!" I had no choice but to sentence him to death after I heard that because one of Jesus's charges was that he claimed to be a king!" Pilate rubs his eyes trying to wipe away the vision of the bloody Jesus barely standing after he was flogged. "He never said a mumbling word."

"What's that you said?" Orpah asked.

"He never said a mumbling word in his defense after our conversation. It was as if he willfully wanted to die the horrible death he was soon to endure." Pilate sits down and draws three crosses in the dirt with his finger and puts a halo over the one in the middle. "He could have protested his innocence, he could have acted stubborn or as if he had no strength, but he didn't and instead carried his own cross until his knees gave away from under him. I watched from the windows of my domain Jesus hanging in the distance.

And if that wasn't enough, the Jewish council asked that he be killed and taken down because of their festivals. I sent word to my soldiers but after a devastating earthquake they found that he had already died. Impossible, I thought because the other two guys was still alive. But after proper verification, it was in fact true that Jesus, the king of Jews, had died. From first glance one would think the Jewish council problems was over but three days later I received a report that the man I washed my hands on finding no charges against had risen from the dead. My soldiers said an angel came down from heaven and rolled back the stone which covered his tomb. When the angel's glory was gone, Jesus was gone along with him." Pilate laughs in unbelief. "Can you believe that, my brothers and sisters? After all that tumult the people uplifted, the man we all put to death had risen from the grave."

Dave stood and held out the Bible for everyone to touch it as he walked throughout the cave. "Today, my brothers and sisters, we have heard the full gospel of what this great book talks about from Genesis to Revelations. This day, even I have learned knowledge about our Lord and savior Jesus Christ that I wasn't aware of. I sit in awe at hearing Judas speak on how he walked with Jesus, how Caiaphas falsely accused Jesus, and how Pontius Pilate sentenced him to be nailed to the cross on account of the people. It was God who brought us together tonight and it will be

God who will see us through to the end. To Michal and Orpah, be blessed beyond measures, my sisters. And to our new brothers in the Lord, may God guide you into all truth until we all meet in heaven." David shakes the three men's hands. "The moral to all what we have learned tonight is that Jesus walked, died, and rose from the grave for the sins of the world." David holds up his Bible and shouts, "He has risen! Praise God for Jesus has risen! Amen."

"Amen" came from around the room from all six people. Pilate, being mindful of the hour, opened his doors for his guest to rest for the night. After settling his guest into their bedrolls, Pilate and Caiaphas talked among themselves on what to do next. Judas had already acknowledged that he will join Pastor Grace's quest to bring the Word of God to all souls they encountered in Hades. They, on the other hand, had not thought about David's mission until now.

Leaving everything behind is what vexed them both. The life they have been living in Hades has been good because the people looked up to them for what they did to Jesus. The past is past, and David said all has been forgiven in heaven. Judas and the women are leaving everything behind to walk the walk they have chosen. Wanting to be real about their faith in Christ, they understand that they must do the same. As they settled in on the floor of the cave, they both agree that tomorrow they will become a disciple and help David in whatever way he needed them to.

"He has risen! Praise God for Jesus has risen!" is all Pilate and Caiaphas remembered as they drifted off full of joy to sleep.

20

In the Bible, Proverbs 18:24 (NIV) states, "One who has unreliable friends soon comes to ruin but there is a friend who sticks closer than a brother."

Friends. Friends is what David can surely say he has today. Not just any kind of friends but friends like Proverbs 18:24 says he should have. Back on the hidden trail, David is basking in the friendship with the two women and three men he now calls his brothers and sisters in Christ. Orpah, Pontius, Judas, Michal, and Caiaphas have left everything they have to pick up their cross and be a disciple in helping him spread the Word of God. David is the only one who hasn't left nothing behind because he had nothing to leave. Therefore, he appreciates what the people surrounding him is giving up for the words of wisdom he has ministered unto them. *Friends,* he thought, strolling along on Jax's back. "Friends that sticks closer than a brother."

It's been four days they've been riding and at the rate they are going they should reach Sodom by tomorrow night. They could have gotten there sooner if they had Smokey's lighting speed or took the main roads, but Areopagus recognizing who he is made him cautious about his journey to the Soul Reapers Conquest match. He is also cautious because he didn't want anything to happen to him or his pupils until everyone who is coming from all over Golgotha hear the message of grace he has prepared to preach in the coliseum. Besides, what better way to enjoy the company of his friends than a good trail ride before the unknown happens when they arrive at their destination.

The four-day course of travel went quite well for all of them. Michal and Orpah were able to revisit their log cabin to say their final good-byes to the home they built from scratch. Caiaphas, Judas, and Pilate listened between stops as David read to them everything they wanted to know about the book he called the Holy Bible. And David detoured to the Field of Blood to speak to the great Leviathan for encouragement in what he is about to endure in two days when he stands before Golgotha.

It wasn't that he was scared to face the people in the coliseum, but it is because he desired some of the Leviathan's wisdom on how he should bring forth his message without anyone getting hurt. Sadly, the Underlings nor the Leviathan would not reveal themselves unless they sensed danger on their land, so the six of them went on their way after about a half of an hour of waiting.

David is leading the way down the small path because there is only one way to go. Michal is their guide and she and Orpah are in the middle of the riders just in case danger approaches them. She says the passageway they are on ends at Gomorrah, so from there it will be practically no time to ride to Sodom which is next door to the small town.

Pilate grew up a Roman soldier before he made governor of Judea. His knowledge of being in battle is why he is at the rear with his trusted spear in his hand. Judas is in front of him with his sword, and Caiaphas is behind the girls with his walking stick that is six feet long. Besides the sound of the animals in the woods shuffling through the trees, nothing has tried to come up against them since they agreed to bring God's word to the capitol of the region.

"Pastor Grace."

David turns around to see what Michal wants. "Yes, Michal. Is everything okay?"

"Yes, but I think Betsie here is a little bit thirsty. Do you mind if we stop to give the horses some water? If I'm not mistaken, Gomorrah is still a ways off." Michal runs her fingers through Betsie's mane and pats the side of her neck.

David looks down at Jax's trotting as if he could walk another three to four days without stopping. "Whatcha say about that, Jaxy boy?" Jax's head bobs up and down from the motion of his body walking and the bit chimes in his mouth. David chuckles and takes the nods as if Jax is saying yes. "Michal, I think what you are asking is a done deal according to Jax and Betsie agreeing to that it's time to recharge their batteries for a minute or two." David looks back at everyone behind him. "What do you say, guys? Should we just rest here on the trail or should we go into the woods and make camp?"

Enchanting music begins to travel through the air softly from deep within the forest. The music is only but a whisper and if they hadn't stopped they wouldn't have heard it because the horses' hooves would have muffled the notes as they passed by.

Being that he didn't get an answer to his initial question, David swings down from the saddle to ask his friends personally as a group. "So what will it be, guys? Should we just rest here or...?"

Orpah shushes David. "Sorry, Pastor Grace, for shushing you but do anyone else hear the music coming from that direction." Orpah points toward the right side of the path.

Everyone fine tunes their ears to the direction Orpah says the music is coming from.

"I think I hear it, Orpah," Judas said guiding his horse a few feet off of the walkway. "Yeah, she's right, guys. It sounds like a flute playing in the distance."

Suspense fills David as he walks to where Judas's and his horses are standing. When he reaches them, he goes a little farther into the trees so that if he does hear what Orpah and Judas are hearing, he will not be mistaken where the sound is coming from.

A harp and the clanging of a cymbal stop him dead in his tracks. "I know that sound," he said to himself, thinking about the day he entered Hades. "Kog!" he yells while running back to Jax.

"Kog?" Michal asked the other riders as David places his foot in Jax's stirrup. "Pastor Grace, who is Kog?"

"Just someone who helped me understand why I didn't make it into heaven and gave me a crash course on being in Sheol." David pulls Jax's reins to the right and puts his heels in his flanks. "Come on, guys, I have someone I want you to meet," he said waving his hand so that they would follow him. "If we hurry we can find him before he stops playing the music. Yah!" he shouts to his steed before jetting off through the wilderness.

The music quit almost as soon as they found its source. Sitting on the back of their horses in the forest, they all look through the tree trunks and branches for the cabin David said the music came from. Pilate is the most skilled at finding things from his days of war, so he devise an old plan called divide and conquer.

"Let's split up," he said. "Since we know the music came from this direction, I say that two of us go that way, two go that way, and two go that way." Pilate gives the direction he wants each pair to go with his hand. "It's right here, you guys. The reason why we are not seeing the cabin is because of the loss of light and the trees. The best way to go about this is to walk in each direction counting to two hundred." Pilate pauses to think if that will be enough time to find what they are looking for. "Yeah two hundred should be enough time," he repeats. "Wherever you are when you count to two hundred stop and you should see this cabin Pastor Grace says is around here. If not, turn around and meet us back at this point."

David chimes in to help with the search. "What Pilate says I feel is the best way to go about locating Kog's cabin. Michal, you come with me. Orpah, you go with Pilate, and, Judas, you go with Caiaphas. Now listen carefully! If anyone of us find that cabin we are immediately to turn around and meet back at this assigned spot. Please do what I say and do not approach the cabin without me. My friend Kog is a very cautious man!"

Pilate sees David is finished with his speech. "Remember, count to two hundred and stop, look, and return back to this location to meet up with the rest of us. If no one has nothing else to add, let's ride."

313

Judas and Caiaphas are the two who found the cabin tucked away in the woods. Counting their horses' steps off backward from two hundred, they were at four when Caiaphas's horse stopped abruptly. Judas, being the younger of the two, curiously wanted to explore the wooden structure. But Caiaphas quickly rebuked him before he could engage in his curiosity. Listening to his elder, Judas stays in the saddle and follows Caiaphas back to where they rode to tell the rest of the pack about their find.

"We found it!" Judas blurts out. "We found your friend's cabin you are looking for!"

"He's right, Pastor Grace. It's about two hundred yards that way." Caiaphas turns his horse in the direction he wants his friends to look.

Judas's excitement gives David the willies. "Please tell me that you two didn't go to Kog's cabin because he doesn't like unexpected guests hanging around his property."

"I assure you, Pastor Grace," Caiaphas said. "We did exactly as we were told after the cabin came into our sight."

"Great." David begins to ride in the direction Caiaphas and Judas went. "Follow me and be careful. In a few minutes, we'll be knocking on a bear's beehive who will do anything to protect his honey."

The horses brought them to the area his friends spotted the cabin. At a standstill, Judas motioned with his finger that Kog's place is just beyond the trees in front of them.

David puts his hand up as if to tell the gang to stay while commanding his horse to the grounds in which Kog's cabin is sitting on. "Whoa, boy," he said pulling the reins when Jax's nose gets close to the door. Sliding down from the saddle, he looks around to make sure Kog is not waiting to snap his neck like he did the guys who tried to ambush him a half a century ago. No one jumps from behind the trees, or down from the roof so he balls his fist and raps on the wooden door.

"Kog, it's me your friend David! Are you busy because if so I can catch you on the next go around?" David pauses to take a deep breath hoping Kog remembers him. "Kog, are you home? I just thought I'll stop by to say hello to a familiar face." David waits and surmises Kog doesn't want any company. "I'll be going now!" he shouts. "Good-bye, Kog, and thanks for helping me when I came from heaven!" David gets back on Jax and is about to leave when the door suddenly swings open pulling in some dead leaves from off the doorstep.

"Who are you, and why are you at my door?" Kog steps out with a sword in one hand and a morning star in the other. David looks at the weapons, and his mouth for some reason will not move. "Look here, Mister. You got five seconds to speak up before these spikes in this here ball finds its way to the side of your head." Kog lifts the morning star. "Five, four, three…"

"Kog!" David holds up his hands to show he's unarmed. "It's me David Grace!"

Kog acts like he is about to swing the medieval weapon. "I don't know no damn David Grace!" he drawled.

"Sure you do. I came from heaven by myself and stayed the night with you." David recalls how he woke up on the hard ground with a note the next day. "You told me not to trust no one and that the last person who came through heaven's gate alone was you."

David's words jog Kog's memory to the night he banged on his door. "Oh yeah." Kog scratches the side of his head. "David Grace, yeah, now I remember you." Kog laughs thinking about how scared he was when he got inside his cabin. "You are the scary-ass white boy who tried to move in with me, but I guess you figured out the hard way that wasn't going to happen."

David and Kog share a laugh together. "Yeah that was me all right but as you can see I made it."

"How long it's been? Three, what, four months?"

"Not exactly. Try three weeks."

"Damn, feels like eternity since I've last seen you. Maybe it's because I see souls all day every day. Hell, I thought you were the group of guys that left here earlier doubling back to try some funny business. That's why I didn't open the door at first." Kog looks past Jax and sees David's friends standing in the distance. "Who are they and are they with you?"

David looks toward his friends. "They are with me, Kog. They are my friends."

"Friends!" Kog shouts. "What did I tell you about friends?"

"I know, Kog, but a lot has changed in my life since we last saw each other and if you have a minute I'd like to share with you how the man you see before you is not the man who left your home oblivious to whether he will survive to see the next day."

Kog shakes his head hoping he is not going to regret what he is about to say. "Tell your friends to hitch their horses around back and come inside." Before David rides off to tell them Kog's remarks, Kog bellows, "And this new life of yours better not be no BS or my foot is going to be seeing all's of ya out the front door!"

The women are ready to rest from their day of travel. When hearing that Kog has opened his doors to them, they were the first to reach the hitch rail and hop off the backs of their horses. As the men rode in behind them, Michal took the horses' reins and tied the men's horses up one by one next to each other. Everyone walked around front except for Judas. Being the youngest of them all, he stayed behind to water the horses and feed them zaqs for nourishment. David told him that Jesus is proud of him for being a faithful steward for the gospel and for standing up for Christ despite their current state of affairs.

David was already finished ministering the death, burial, and resurrection of Jesus to Kog when Judas joined them from tending the horses. Kog listened respectfully to the Word of God but seeing souls enter Hades every day has harden his heart to anything concerning being in heaven. His rejection is because, if Jesus is so good and loving why would he send people to a place where he is not present? David and his companions tried to explain but Kog continued to stick to what he believed in.

"Kog, we appreciate you listening and we appreciate your honesty. It would be a blessing to all of us if you were to accept our Lord into your heart but only you can do that and you have your reasons for making your decision. Our job—" David points at his followers. "Is to bring forth the Word of God in spirit and in truth so that no one can have an excuse on the day of judgment when Jesus ask them what did you do with the cross? Our job is not to coax the Word of God on anyone, so with that being said, I thank you again for listening to us and for being honest. God bless you, my dear friend Kog. God bless you."

Kog stood and pumped David's hand. "If that's it, can I get a look at that Sharia sphere you say has cold water in it because I don't know about you but I'm thirsty as hell." Kog winks at the ladies. "Get it, as hell."

Laughter filled the room from Kog's corny joke and limpidness. David's friend couldn't help but to admire Kog's earnestness to the message preached to him today. As Kog took his seat, his paunch shook up and down as he slapped his knee to his own witticism.

"Sometimes I just kill myself with my silly ways," he said taking a big swig from the sphere and wiping his mouth with the back of his hand.

Pilate and Caiaphas kicked back while Kog told the story of how David was scared out of his wits when he opened the door to greet him. Judas and the girls exited to check on the horses when Kog was saying that David was as green as a cactus on a rainy day when it came to survival in the afterlife. He honestly said he felt sorry for him the next day when his cabin disappeared to the next location he was supposed to welcome the next soul doomed for eternity. "I bet you felt like an asshole when you woke up to that brief letter I wrote you, huh?" David nodded his head as Kog continued on being old jaunty and talkative Kog.

Rest time is over and Pilate is the first to identify the shifting of the obscured light weakly shining through the opened door. If their appointment in the coliseum is to be met when the doors are opened, they will have to be on their way soon.

"Pastor Grace." Pilate stands and walks to the door.

"Yes, Pilate."

"My apologies for interrupting you and your friend catching up on the past but as you can see." Pilate looks toward the sky. "We are now at the peak of our day and we need to be leaving soon or we will not have time to prepare when we arrive in Sodom."

"Sodom!" Kog exclaimed. "What business do you have in Sodom?"

David places his hand on Kog's shoulder and stood. "God's business, my friend," he replied while putting the sphere and Bible inside the satchel. "At this time, day after tomorrow, Queen Jezebel has called a mandatory-present gladiator match. And we, my friend, are going there to be the main attraction when we get up in front of all Golgotha to preach what thus sayeth the Lord." David looks to his brothers in Christ. "Caiaphas and Pilate, if you may, will you go outside and let the others know we will be leaving here shortly?"

"Yes, Pastor." Pilate looks at Caiaphas and nudges his head toward the door and exits.

Contrite from Kog not accepting Christ, David hugs Kog before Kog can detest. He tries to back away but David embraces him tighter. "Thanks, Kog, for everything. I don't know where I will be if you would not have given me the run down on Hades." David releases Kog and puts his hands on his shoulders while looking him straight in the eyes. "Today has been a glorious day for me, my friend. Even though sorrow befalls me for your name not being written in the book of life, I know you have heard and understood that Jesus Christ died for your sins. Therefore, my friend, you have hope on your side to repent before judgment day. In two days, I will be facing the most important trial of my life for the sake of the gospel. I wish I could reasonably say I will someday see you again but being frank with myself I most likely will not survive the hands of the queen. Please don't feel uptight when I say this, Kog, but I love you and may God continue to guide you to the souls exiting heaven's doors."

Kog feels sentimental to David's sincere words but then toughens up. "Enough of this mushy stuff, David. You know I'm an old lumberjack and it takes a lot to get through this thick piece of wood I call my skull." Kog knocks on the side of his bushy head. "If it makes you feel any better, I'll never forget what you and your friends said here today." Kog slaps David on the back as he is going to the door. "Be careful, David, and you may not believe me when I say this but I applaud you for standing up for what you believe in. Goodbye, Pastor Grace, and good luck."

Kog closes the door and took a seat back in the chair he was sitting in. Meditating on the sincerity of David's message, his soul feels some light shine in the void inside him. "Jesus, I remember it like it was yesterday when you sentenced me to Sheol for my sins. I didn't agree with your decision then but I now see that you know me better than I know myself. Seeing David today and his friend's happiness in Hades made me realize that it has to be some truth in what he preached to me concerning you. Please forgive me for rejecting your word up until this time. I ask that you forgive me of my sins, and I ask that you come into my life from this day forward. I promise Jesus I won't let you down and that from now on I will tell everyone that I meet that they can be in your presence again if they repent and accept you into their hearts. Amen and thank you for making me keeper of the gate."

They all left Kog's home with their minds set on Sodom. Soon, they will be in front of a multitude of people in the coliseum. The name of the event is the Soul Reapers Conquest match, and when David and his disciples present themselves to Golgotha, reaping souls is exactly what they are going to do. Only not by watching the bloodshed of others that will reap souls to burn in the lake of fire, but by the shedding blood of Jesus that will reap souls to dwell in the kingdom of heaven.

21

"David!" a woman's voice shouts over the mass of people.

David and his followers are standing outside the entrance of the corral they've housed their horses in for today. The normal fee to house a horse in the corral is a half a zaq a day, but since space is limited due to the gladiator match, the man in the booth is charging a zaq per horse. Judas is the treasure keeper so he is the one paying the wages while the rest of the gang is watching the swarm of people get in line to enter the coliseum.

"David!" a slender hand raises above the heads of the crowd and waves. "David, it's me Artemis from Gomorrah!"

The herd of people begins to separate as the woman pushes her way through them the best way she can. When she pops out from the crowd, David grimaced when Artemis forcefully makes her way in front of him.

"Hello, Ms. Artemis," he said averting his eyes because he knows it was her or Cybele who told Azzazel about the compass to Sharia.

Artemis comes right out and speaks the loss in her heart. "David, Azzazel and Dagon killed Cybele!"

David's mood changes from disgust to concern. "What? I mean why or what happen?"

"The day you left they broke into our loft and threatened our lives. Queen Jezebel had already given the order to kill Cybele for not showing up in town square when Dagon blew the shofar. When we woke up, Azzazel was choking me while Dagon had his demon hands around her throat." Artemis starts to cry. "I'm sorry, David, but King Azzazel was looking for you and seeing me and Cybele's life pass before my eyes, I screamed out that you had the compass to Sharia so that they can leave us alone." Artemis hangs her head between her shoulders. "She's dead, David. Dagon still killed her despite me telling them about you. Azzazel said that it was an order from the queen."

"I, I, I don't know what to say." David embraces Artemis and puts her head in his shoulder. "I'm sorry, Artemis, for not being there to help you. I thought you betrayed me to Azzazel but now I see that you were trying to save you and your sister's life." A tear rolls out the corner of his eye and down onto Artemis's face. "How selfish of me to think that way about the two of you when from the time I met you, you were nothing but kind to me."

"I miss her, David," Artemis takes her head off his shoulder. "Life as I knew it in Hades is not the same anymore. She trusted me to protect her just as I trusted her to protect me." Artemis wipes the tears from her eyes and her face becomes angry. "At first I didn't give a damn about the queen's Souls Reapers Conquest match but since I know Jezebel is going to be in the coliseum, I wanted to tell her face to face that she can go to hell for taking Cybele's life from me."

What Artemis is saying is true about why she came to Sodom. Except for the fact that she is also there to lend a helping hand in Queen Jezebel being tossed into the lake of fire. Since the day the worm of torment took Cybele to hell, she vowed to see Jezebel belly flopped into the torturous lake right behind her or die trying. If Queen Jezebel dies then she will fulfill her vows to Cybele. If she dies instead, then she will be back with her sister were she feels she belongs.

"There, there, Artemis," David said placing her hand in his. "No matter what we may think, our God in heaven is a good God and he knows Cybele's heart."

Artemis is taking aback by David saying the name God in Hades. "God? Since when are you a man of God again, Mr. I'm not a pastor anymore?"

David looks at his friends who are wondering what Artemis is talking about. "Artemis, when we first met, I was a man entering Hades not knowing where my fate will begin or end in the afterlife. That morning when I left your home, I decided to take Cybele's advice and find Sharia. My journey was long and rough but in the end I found the path to the watery place inside a golden door that opened unto heaven. It was then, when I realized God has been with me all that time and he is still with me as we speak." David looks to Michal and Orpah and they shake their heads in agreement. "This is why we are here, Artemis. We are here to let all Hades know that Satan may be the prince of Sheol but those who believe in Jesus will no longer be confined to Sheol and store up eternal riches in heaven."

"Pastor Grace, the line is growing shorter and we need to get inside the coliseum to be ready to speak when everyone is seated."

"You're right, Caiaphas," David said glancing toward the entrance. "Why don't all of you go and get in line while I tell my friend Artemis what we are about to do."

When they all left, David tells Artemis that he apologizes for not being able to stay and console her more than he wishes to. He also goes on to inform her of how he plans on preaching the gospel in the coliseum. After everyone in Golgotha is seated, Queen Jezebel will give the stragglers throughout the region some extra time to present themselves or they will be subject to discipline for disobeying her edicts. Pilate is the one who brought this to his attention so David felt this is the best time frame to bring forth his message to the people. Artemis thinks their plans is a suicide mission, but who is she to question him when she didn't plan on leaving the coliseum alive either. With pissing Jezebel off in mind, it didn't take her long to say she will join the revolt against the throne of the region's capital.

People of all shapes and forms are attending the Souls Reapers Conquest match. You name the race and they were there. Men with men, women with women, married couples, single men, and single women. They all piled into the rows and rows of seats to see the death that will soon be on the coliseum's field if everything goes according to Jezebel's plans.

Two men sat at the entrance as witnesses to those who attended and for those who didn't. One was an eyewitness who had a photographic memory in case the other witness's gifts were perhaps not working properly. He is the one handing out stones to every soul walking in. The stones are for when the queen or king gives the command to stone any man on the battlefield who doesn't want to fight or decides to quit before he or his opponent is dead. That goes for women too?

The other witness is not an eyewitness. He is more like a soul witness because he has a special gift that connects him to every soul within the Golgotha province. After everyone passes him and the doors are shut, he can feel and supernaturally visualize the souls' whereabouts who is not inside the coliseum. Between these two witnesses, no one can get pass a mandatory-present ordinance from the queen.

Pilate leads the group when they got inside the colossal brick structure. The coliseum is Roman built so he knows his way around the building practically with his eyes closed. Guiding his friends through the vast halls, Pilate leads them to a side entrance that is normally used if someone on the battlefield had to make a dashing escape.

During the execution from the front entrance to the entrance to the battlegrounds, Artemis ducked off inside a room while the rest of the outfit kept going. It wasn't until Pilate did a head count that David noticed she was gone. Standing there among his disciples, he remembers their earlier conversation on how Artemis wanted to see Jezebel face to face. Being that he's come too far to get to this point in the ministry for Christ, he decides to let her go her way and steps into the shadowed area with the rest of the pack. "May God be with you, Artemis. Be careful."

"Are you ready, Pastor Grace?" Pilate asked with his right shoulder to the door ready to push on David's command.

David looks for Artemis to show up at the last minute but she doesn't. "Yes, Pilate, I'm ready as I'll ever be."

"What about you ladies?"

"We're ready, Pilate." Orpah speaks for the both of them. "Caiaphas and Judas."

"I'm ready, Pilate," Caiaphas said.

"Me too," Judas replied ready to run when the door swings open.

"On three!" David shouted putting his shield on his back while everyone gets prepared to enter the ground floor of the coliseum. "One, two, three!"

Pilate shoves the door open and they all run out into the center of the circled battlefield. The seats are full but no one opens their mouths to David and his followers down below because they thought that they were the preshow before the main event. All six of them have their weapons in their hands to defend themselves if anyone tries to apprehend them for being on the field. Not a soul runs up, so David sheaths his dirk and pulls out his Bible from the satchel. Turning around slowly, he waves a salutation to the suspended faces staring at him from the assemblage.

David shouts, "Greetings to all Golgotha and welcome to the Souls Reapers Conquest match!"

The crowd claps, stomp their feet, and screams to being present in the coliseum for today's events. David lets them holler until everyone calms down.

"Today, we are all assembled to see death fall upon this very field I'm standing on. I say, why should we come together to see our fellow brethren die, when we can come together to see our fellow brethren live."

David looks at the quiet faces wanting to protest but no one knows if Queen Jezebel has allowed him to speak. "Right now you're probably asking yourself, 'How can one live if he's already dead?' My answer to you will be Christ. Jesus Christ to be exact." David holds up the Bible. "There are those who rebel against the light of Jesus, who do not know his ways or stay on his paths. The eyes of the Devil's Advocates watches for dusk, they think, no eye will see them so they keep their faces concealed. It's sad, but they want nothing to do with the light of Jesus. For them, midnight is their morning. They make friends with Satan, the terror of darkness. As heat and drought snatch away the melted snow, so does the graves snatch away those who have sinned. My name is Pastor David Grace, and I stand before you to tell all of you about the definition of Grace. God's Riches At Christ's Expense."

David knows he's pressed for time so he goes right into his message. "In the beginning was the word, and the word was with God, and the word was God. He was with God in the beginning. Through him all things were made that has been made. In him was life and that life was the light of all mankind."

The multitude is quiet so David's voice carries to the top rows of the coliseum. "Jesus Christ is the light and he

is the word the Bible speaks about. He is also the fullness
of God's grace, the fullness of God's truth, and the fullness of God's glory, who came from the father. Praise be to
God and father of our Lord Jesus Christ, who has blessed
us in the heavenly realms with every spiritual blessing in
Christ. For he chose us before the creation of the world
to be holy and blameless in his sight. In love, he predestined us for adoption to sonship through Jesus, in accordance with his pleasure and will to the praise of his glorious
grace, which he's freely given us in the one he loves. In
Jesus we have redemption through his blood, the forgiveness of sins, in accordance with the riches of God's grace
that the father lavished on us. As for you, you are dead in
your transgression and sins, in which you follow the ways
of this world and of the ruler of the kingdom of the air the
spirit who is now at work in those who are disobedient.
All of us also lived at one time, gratifying the cravenness
of our flesh and following its desires and thoughts. Can we
honestly say that we were not by nature deserving of God's
wrath? But because of his great love for us, God, who is
rich in mercy, made those who believed in Christ, alive in
Christ even when they were dead in transgressions. It is by
grace you will be saved. It is by God's grace that we are in
Sheol and not burning in the lake of hot sulfur. Our God
is all merciful and his gracious love makes him forgiving
and long-suffering. In the book of Nehemiah, the Bible

says that when Israel left captivity from Egypt, God led them to the Promised Land by a pillar of cloud by day and a pillar of fire to give them light by night." David looks up to the sky. "The Bible also says that he blessed them with shoes on their feet, clothes on their backs, tents to live in, and food to eat."

Pilate looks to the queen's box to see if Jezebel is coming out to take her seat. No one appears from the stairwell leading to her booth so he lowers his guard and continues to listen to David.

"I don't know about all of you, but when I look up during the day I see light gray clouds and when I look up at night, I see clouds of fire giving me light. When I look down, I have shoes on my feet, and on my body clothes on my back. Whenever I'm hungry, I can eat from the tree of Zaqqum freely, and if I desired too I can have a home to lay my head in every night when I go to sleep."

The crowd can't believe what they are hearing but David's persistence keeps their ears receptive to what he is saying.

"God has been good to us, Golgotha. We may not see it because our eyes have been blinded with corruption, but we can't deny that he has been good to us and spared us from the lake of fire until judgment day. The world as we know it declares the glory of God. The skies proclaim the work of his hands. Day after day they pour forth speech. Night after night they reveal knowledge. They have no words. No sound is heard from them. Yet their voices go out into all Hades, their words to the ends of the world. I pray that you will become rooted and established in love, may have power, together with all the Lord's people, to grasp how wide and long and high and deep is the love of Christ, and to know his love that surpasses knowledge, that you may be filled to the measure of all the fullness of God. I pray that you may know the hope to which he is calling you, the riches of his glorious inheritance in his holy people, an incomparably great power for those who believe. That power is the same as the mighty strength he exerted when he raised Christ from the dead after being crucified for our sins. When he raised him, God placed all things under his feet and appointed him to be head over everything for the church, which is his body, the fullness of him who fills everything in every way. Now me, I became a servant of this gospel by the gift of God's grace given to me through the working of his power. Although I am less than the least of all the Lord's people, this grace was given me: To preach to those in the graves the boundless riches of Christ and to make plain to everyone the administration of the mystery of our Lord's life, death, and resurrection that brings us back into the presence of the father. Now what I am commanding you today is not too difficult for you or beyond your reach. It is not up in heaven, so that you have to ask,

'Who will ascend into heaven to get it and proclaim it to us so we may obey it?' No, the word is very near you, it is in your mouth and in your heart so you may obey it. God opposes the proud but shows favor to the humble. Humble yourself, therefore under God's mighty hand, that he may lift you up in due time. Be alert and of sober mind. Your enemy, the devil prowls around like a roaring lion looking for someone to devour. Resist him, stand firm in your faith and the God of all grace, who called you to his eternal glory in Christ after you have suffered a little while, will himself restore you and make you strong, firm, and steadfast. To him be the power forever and ever, amen."

David steps back in line with the rest of the group and makes them all join hands. "See, I set before Golgotha today life and prosperity, death and destruction. For I command you today to love the Lord your God, to walk in obedience to him, and to keep his commands, decrees, and laws then you will live and the Lord your God will bless you with eternal life in heaven. But if your heart turns away and you do not repent, and if you continue to be drawn away to bow down to Satan and worship him, I declare to you this day that you will certainly be destroyed. This day I call, my brothers and sisters in Christ, as my witnesses against you that I have set before you life and death, blessings, and curses. Now choose life so that you may live and that you may love the Lord your God, listen to his voice and hold fast to him. For the Lord is your life, and he will bless you when the book of life is opened with his grace. Please, if anyone desires to be born-again and live a new life in Christ, come forward and my friends will let you know what you must do to be saved." David raises both of his hands and vehemently yells. "Repent! Repent Hades and ask the Lord to forgive you of your sins!"

The majority of the people were silent. Except for the whispers that murmured among one another, nobody decided to speak up or stand up to David's message or his invitation for their souls to be saved from their sins.

Down below on the field, they all gazed to the seats surrounding them, praying that at least one person be bold enough to accept Christ and gain eternal life. Some of the people wanted to inquire more information about the grace he spoke about but no one within a hundred miles radius would dare think twice about defying Jezebel's guillotine-chopping hands.

Meanwhile, in the stairwell that leads to the queen's observing box, the Devil's Advocates are making their way to their seats. Azzazel comes out first and extends his hand for his queen to sit in her throne next to his. Dagon stands to her right with his lance while Areopagus and his wife Asherah, King Anubis and his successor Athaliah, and the two witnesses from the entrance to the coliseum have a seat behind her. All eyes turn to face the throne as the crowd stood up to honor the queen's supremacy. She, in turn, raises her hand for everyone to be seated but before she can lower it, Areopagus sees David and some of the citizens of Kidron on the battlefield.

"Blaspheme!" Areopagus shouts pointing his finger toward David. "My queen, that is the man I told you and the king about who were blaspheming our lord Satan in Kidron."

"And look, my husband, Caiaphas, Judas, and Pilate has joined them in their defiance to the throne of Golgotha!" Asherah said with a sneer.

Callous, the queen is shocked to see that someone has defiled her authority. "Who are these peasants, my king, and why are they disrupting my annual Soul Reapers Conquest match?" she asked imperiously.

"My queen, this is the man with the iron glove who has the compass that leads to Sharia. Areopagus says that he is also the man stirring up strife telling the souls of our region to repent and love one another as you will love yourself."

"Love? What is love?" she asked stolidly.

The queen pauses to think and then her eyes become wide with excitement. Looking to the crowd, she gestures for the people to sit down while whispering in her husband's ear. Azzazel grins deviously because Jezebel has let David's fate fall in the hands of her pet hyenas.

"Today, Golgotha, we have been shown favor by our lord Satan to view a massacre of anyone who decides to go against the laws of this land!" Jezebel raises her scepter. "Release Abaddon and Apollyon!"

22

A hubbub of thunder pushed its way from the stone seats after Jezebel bellowed for her crazed hyenas to be released. King Azzazel jumps to the top of the wall that surrounded the throne's box and motions with both of his hands for the congregation to yell louder. His gesturing roils the crowd, making them scream so loud that a slight draft crosses the face of David and the stomping of their feet causes chips of brick to fall off the outside of the ancient structure.

Perfectly balancing himself, Azzazel spreads his arms like an eagle before doing a front flip down to the ground and sticking the landing. Dagon leaps over the wall behind Azzazel and causes dust to rise under his feet from the heaviness of his weight and body armor. As Azzazel is getting ready to pull the lever to raise the hyenas' cage, King Anubis and Athaliah appears from the stairwell to get in on the bludgeon and mutilation of the disobedient citizens standing on ground zero of the coliseum.

"Abaddon and Apollyon!" Azzazel shouts between the metal bars of the cage. "Destroy!"

The hyenas come charging out on his command with their huge doglike bodies and two rows of teeth sprinting at full speed to the center of the arena. Azzazel, Anubis, Dagon, and Athaliah storm behind the monstrous beasts ready to put to death anyone who is left breathing after the hyenas' annihilation attack.

David and his disciples have their feet pressed into the black dirt with their shields up and their weapons drawn awaiting the assail heads on with complete courage. All of them knew this day was coming when they decided to walk with Christ in Hades. And all of them knew from the words David spoke that in order to live in Christ you must die to gain eternal life.

Orpah and Michal are the first to respond to the assault coming at them. Quickly pulling arrows from their quivers, they placed them in their bows and released. Michal's training from her father, King Saul, has her reactions, reflexes, and mechanics a lot faster than Orpah so she is more brisk with the draw.

Her arrow finds its target in the mouth of Apollyon followed by three more to the center of the animal's chest. The four blows are fatal, killing the beast instantly. Orpah, however, is not so effective. Her arrow went over the head of Abaddon and she couldn't recover fast enough to reload her string. The missed discharge will soon after cost her dearly, and the dreadful creature would rip apart one of her brothers in the Lord.

"David, watch out!" Judas screamed as the loosed hyena moved across the surface of the coliseum floor swiftly and upon David in no time.

Judas pushes David as hard as he can when the creature leaps toward David and his toothy jaws are inches away from David's face. Abaddon's teeth finds Judas's arm suspended in midair so his slobbery jaws chomps down on his arm like a bone.

The bite makes him fall backward screaming in agony as Abaddon tears his arm out of the socket and tosses it across the field. Placing his huge paws upon his midsection, Abaddon proceeds to dig his teeth into Judas's chest. Every organ inside of his upper body is ripped out instantaneously. Some of his insides are eaten while the rest lay stretched out on the ground next to him. No one is able to come to his aid because Azzazel and his crew have started to duel with the rest of them.

Orpah is the only one not occupied with an assailant so she is the one who must try and stop the mutilation of Abaddon's attack. With all her strength, she pulls the string on her bow to her breast, takes aim, and let's go. This time, her arrow strikes her target on the side behind the beast left shoulder. Judas is barely conscious when the hyena leaves his maimed body to pursue his attacker.

Azzazel draws his sword from its scabbard to strike down David, but David pays no attention to him and runs over to Judas who is in excruciating pain. The crowd screams for blood when they see David not upholding Azzazel's challenge.

"Thank you, brother," David said while falling to the ground and grabbing Judas's bloody hand.

"No, thank you, my brother, for allowing me to once again walk with my Lord and savior Jesus Christ." Judas coughs up green blood and turns his head to the side so that it can run out of his mouth. "Pastor Grace."

"Yes, Judas." David grips Judas's hand tighter because he sees that his friend is losing consciousness.

"When you—" Judas coughs again but this time the blood doesn't block his passageway from allowing him to speak. "When you see Jesus..." he stammers. "Could you please tell him I'm sorry for...for..."

The sentence Judas tries to get out doesn't come into fruition. Judas's hand becomes limp, and David plants in his mind the little words Judas spoke, and his heart finishes his request for him. "He already knows, Judas. Our Lord already knows," he said closing his friend's eyes with two fingers.

"Is he dead yet?" Azzazel asked poking Judas's corpse with the tip of his blade. "I'll never smite a general tending to his wounded soldiers in battle."

David rises to his feet and unsheathes his dagger. "Please don't insult my brother by acting like you care." David traverses to his right with his mouth trembling in anger. "If it's a fight that you desire, Azzazel, then it is a fight that you shall get," he said as he locks his fingers around the hilt of his sword.

Azzazel lifts his sword and swings with all his might. "To the death!" he yells, as his blade collides with David's at full force.

To the right of them, King Anubis has challenged Pilate in today's warfare. Both Pilate and Anubis show power with their spears as they thrust and block each other's blows in combat. Anyone other than Dagon in Hades, Pilate probably would have overcame them with the dexterity he has in warfare. But King Anubis is no amateur when it comes to the game of thrones, so whatever Pilate dishes at him, Anubis shields and dishes right back.

Across the way, Athaliah and Michal are going at it like two cats fighting over their master. Only it is not their nails they are using to scratch each other's furry skin until one quits and leave but the sharpness of each other's blades that will sever limbs until one of them falls and dies. Tracing and traversing, they both strike, purry, careen, and some-times step back in respect to one another's skills.

They are both an even match because of Michal's upbringing and Athaliah's bloodline of terror she exhibited to become the successor of King Anubis. Slits of blood are all over their bodies as they dice each other up and down waiting for each other to make a deadly mistake.

Orpah's hands are full fending off Abaddon. The arrow she shot in his side has had no effect on slowing the beast down from wanting to leave her in pieces like Judas. Each time Abaddon charged her, he clawed her with one of his paws. The last pass he made at her he scratched the inside of her thigh causing her to fall to the ground barely escap-ing the snapping of his jaws. A defensive blow to his head with her sword is what kept Abaddon from taking her apart as he circled back around laughing like his brothers and sisters in the wild.

Orpah regains her footing and faces Abaddon who has blood dripping from his eye. The stare of death in his good eye tells her that playtime is over. Rushing at her with all the power in his legs, Abaddon seeks to end this woman-against-beast conflict that has blinded him. Abaddon is too big for her to confront when charging at full speed, so she does what her instincts tell her to do and run for her life.

The wall that enclosed the arena is ten feet tall, Orpah's best bet is to try and leap and grab the top of the wall and climb into the bleachers. In doing so, she will have an advantage at bringing down the beast with her bow and arrow. Her plans quickly changed when she looks back and sees Abaddon on her heels trying to grab at her ankles. Adding up her options, Orpah decides to run up the wall and then does a backflip over the head of Abaddon. The ferocious hyena tries to follow her but when she flips behind him, he is left with his front paws on the wall and his back exposed to the double-edged sword that awaits him.

"This is for my brother Judas," she grumbles angrily, pushing and twisting her blade deeper into his back. "And this is for the shot I missed when your ugly face came roaring out of your cage." Orpah pulls her sword out and drives it down to the guard until Abaddon's lifeless body is spread out like a skinned animal rug.

Caiaphas is no match for Dagon's strength. The only reason he's lasted this long is because of his speed and knowing when to move when Dagon tries to pierce him with his lance. Each time Dagon thrusts his weapon, Caiaphas is inches away from being stuck with its metallic tip. Not once has Caiaphas tried to strike back because in actuality he's not a combat person. In his mind he has done well with the demon brute and for that reason he decides to try his luck and lashes back the next time Dagon drives his pointed shaft at him.

Caiaphas stays as far back as possible and times his attack precisely. As soon as Dagon impelled his weapons, he blocked his attack to the side while rolling his body up the long shaft and striking Dagon in the helm with his walking stick. The blow had so much momentum behind it that his walking stick broke into a small stub. Dagon doesn't bulge at all from the belt he just encountered. Caiaphas's craftiness which kept him alive up until now worked from a distance, but within Dagon's arm's reach, he is as good as dead.

Dagon drops his lance and grabs Caiaphas by the throat. With both hands, he lifts Caiaphas off his feet, leaving his legs dangling like strings hanging loosely on a garment. Dagon remains silent as Caiaphas defends himself with weak punches while being strangled. Staring into Caiaphas's eyes through his spiked bucket helmet, Dagon feels the vitality leaving his victim and therefore tosses him to the ground. He does so because choking your opponent is not as exciting as watching the horror in a man's eyes when their body is being divided into two by his most trusted battle-ax.

Caiaphas is grasping for whatever air his windpipe can find when Dagon stands over him with his old-fashioned wood chopper in his hands. Groveling with the little strength he has, he pleads for mercy hoping Dagon will show some sign of emotion for human life. The only sign he gets is a shiny ax raised high above Dagon's head.

Caiaphas looks into the eyes of his demise and tries one last time to get to his feet. As he is pushing himself off the ground, Dagon comes down with all his power on top of his skull splitting it in half like a log about to be thrown into the fire. Dagon thought, *My queen shows no mercy,* as he picked up his lance and leaves his ax embedded in his victim's forehead.

David's high school fencing experience has held up quite well against Azzazel. Back and forth they exchanged blows to each other's upper body, only to come away with minor cuts and bruises because their armor protected them both. Azzazel could have ended the fight long ago but he wanted to give the viewers something to remember when they leave the Soul Reapers Conquest match. Every strike from David that could have been lethal, he careened and caromed leaving David with small cuts in unprotected areas on his body. His latest cut was delivered to his ear when he swung with all his might leaving his head at risk to be smitten. Azzazel couldn't help but capitalize on the defenseless act that is put in plain sight by his competitor.

"I must say that this has been fun." Azzazel diagonally slice the air until his sword finds David's. A loud cling followed by the sound of metal echoes through the space between them as Azzazel twirls his blade in a circle. "But unfortunately one of us must exit this bout triumphant and unfortunately that one of us is not you."

Azzazel's wrists movement spins faster and stops. David's wrist can't keep up with Azzazel's swift hand movements and therefore his dirk fumbles in his hand. He flicks his wrist as David is trying to get a grip on the hilt but within seconds his dagger is lying on the ground too far for him to retrieve.

"Aha, Mr. Grace. It seems Areopagus's tarot card readings concerning us have proven to be false." Azzazel puts the tip of his blade in his rival's neck. "My apologies for not entertaining you further but my queen is a very impatient woman." Azzazel looks over David and sees that his bare hand is void of a compass. "Since we both desire that this duel comes to an end soon, I ask that you be so kind and take off the mysterious iron glove."

David hesitates but then slides the gauntlet off his hand and throws it beyond Azzazel.

"Now could you please show me your palm?"

David turns his palm up.

"Hmm? What have we here?" Azzazel takes off his hat and rubs his head. "Two things," he said, pressing the point into his neck deeper. "One, you never had the compass to Sharia to begin with. Or two, you already found Sharia and have hidden it nearby." Azzazel looks at the leather strap arching over his shoulder. "Let me guess," he says quickly, cutting the strap and bringing his sword back to David's throat. "Pick it up. Pick it up and don't try anything stupid or your followers will watch you bleed out like a pig before them."

David picks up the satchel slowly and hands it to him.

"Ah," he said pulling back the leather flap on the bag and looking inside. "What do we have here?" he asks scooping the sphere out of the satchel and dropping the bag to the ground. "What is this strange ball of obscure color I have in my hand? Could this be what I think it is?"

David tries to grab for the sphere but Azzazel holds it out of arm's reach. "It's nothing, Azzazel. Nothing that concerns the likes of you."

"I beg to differ," he replies applying pressure to the blade to let David know not to make any sudden movements again.

Dagon steps behind David with his lance in his hand. His massive body is so close to David, that he can feel the hot air of Dagon's breath ruffling the hairs on the back of his neck. Orpah tries to come over and help but he waves her off to keep her out of harm's reach.

With Dagon behind David, Azzazel steps back to examine the puzzling ball further. His eyes are somewhat under a spell as he rolls the sphere around his hands to see what makes the aqua ball work. His fingertips find the handle which pulls out the spout. Right when he is about to pull on it, something catches his eye down below in his peripheral vision.

"What's that?" Azzazel asks pointing at the open satchel on the ground as he bends over to investigate. David thinks he's talking about his Bible, but then wonders how could that be, because the latch that covered the Bible was buckled when he tossed it to the ground. "Where did you get this?"

David looks at the hands of Azzazel and notices that he has the handkerchief in his hand he took from him while he was in the culvert.

"From you, Azzazel."

"But how? I have been searching for you high and low and not once have our paths crossed each other's until today."

"Probably not in your eyes, but in actuality that is not exactly true."

Azzazel steps forward and gets face to face with him. "Speak now!" he yells. "Tell me how you obtained my handkerchief in your possession or die the worst possible death that you can imagine."

"One week from today, my Lord Jesus delivered you into my hands when you went to relieve yourself in a culvert in Skulls Valley we were hiding in. While you were inside taking care of your business, my companions wished for me to end your life but when I approached you my heart wouldn't allow me to. I said, 'The Lord forbids that I, a man of God, do such a thing to a helpless soul that is impalpable of defending himself.' Also, I couldn't find it in myself to smite a once king of God's people, Israel. Not only just any king but also a king who defeated the Arameans according to the Lord's word through the prophets."

"Who told you this?"

"The Holy Word of God that the world calls the Bible told me this, King Ahab, the husband of the sinful Jezebel."

"I…I don't know what to say. For truly you are a more noble man than I for sparing my life." Azzazel looks at the handkerchief in his hand and remembers the last card he pulled in his fortune-telling reading. Even though he is a wicked king, he is still a king who honors the knight's code when it comes to battle. Which is: When one spares a life in time of war, that person's life is forever in debt to the one who graciously allowed them to live. With the knight's code in mind, Azzazel kneels to one knee and gives David the sphere of Sharia. "Forgive me, man of God, for inflicting on you and your followers so much grief. According to the knights of the round table, from this day forward my life is forever in your hands."

Pilate is still fighting with Anubis when Azzazel surrenders his sword. Unaware of what's going on, he continues to fight so that he can avenge his brother Caiaphas who fell by the hands of Dagon. His anger opens his eyes to see more clearly and move his feet more swiftly and thrust his spear with better precision.

Anubis was not prepared for the power of Pilates's blow when he delivers a strike to his head. His reflexes block the blow up top but Anubis's body is left open for attack. Pilate channels every ounce of his strength he can find and drops his spear quickly and drives it with all his might. Anubis must have blinked in disbelief because he never saw the iron point coming to the left side of his chest. Pilate's strike was fatal and Anubis falls dead with blood dripping from his punctured heart.

The multitude snarled and booed when they saw Anubis fall at the spear of Pilate. Queen Jezebel is enraged with what she is seeing on the field coming from the enforcers of her region and silences the crowd. "Dagon!" she shouts through the stillness of the coliseum. "Kill them all! Starting with the king!"

Dagon was entranced when the queen gives him the command to kill Azzazel. His brain is already baffled at the sight of his master bowing to the man they've been seeking to destroy since the first day they found out he had the compass to Sharia. Now, from a higher authority than the king, he must fulfill Queen Jezebel's orders because his loyalty is to her throne first and to King Azzazel second.

Azzazel picks up his sword and stands when Dagon steps back to create space to foin his lance. David turns around to see what has captured Azzazel's attention but is shoved to the ground by Azzazel for safety. "Dagon, stand down! This is an order from your king!"

Dagon pauses in confusion to comprehend what should he do. Jezebel, however, demands obedience and overrides his thoughts of hearkening to the king. "Dagon, no!" Azzazel hollers as he looks down the medieval weapon propelling toward him at unbelievable velocity and power.

The strike landed in Azzazel's abdomen. His iron breastplate was made from one of the best craftsmen in Hades, but even its strength is no match for the pressure being driven by Dagon's supernatural power. David is horrid at what his eyes are seeing. Backpedaling out of danger, he can't help but stare at the head of Dagon's lance sticking out of Azzazel's back.

Azzazel, now obligated to the welfare of David, doesn't fall in defeat because his endurance of being a true soldier won't allow his knees to buckle. Adrenaline fills his veins and rises to his brain and then down to his muscles. The blood from his wound acts as a lubricant as his legs begin to charge up the shaft that is still in Dagon's hands.

Pilate takes advantage of Azzazel's counterattack and advances on Dagon who has his back to him. Leaping into the air, Pilate looks down and sees there is a breaking point in Dagon's armor. Twirling his spear to position the tip to hit his target dead on, he comes down hard on the nape of Dagon's spine between his helmet and breastplate.

Azzazel catches the tail end of Pilate's fury. Right when he is shoving his sword underneath Dagon's chin, Pilate's spear comes through Dagon's neck and into his collarbone. Azzazel never saw the blow coming and fell backward with the dead weight of Dagon on top of him.

David runs over to make sure Dagon isn't breathing. Pilate is already standing over him when he gets there and tells him that he is dead. Azzazel is coughing up balls of blood, squirming to be free from being pinned to the ground by the death on top of him. David asks Pilate to help him roll Dagon off Azzazel on the count of three and after utilizing what's left of their strength they finally turn Dagon face up.

"On this day, King Azzazel, as my God and brother is my witness, I, Pastor David Grace, relieve you from any debt you feel you have for me,"

Azzazel looks up in agony and replies. "Where you go from here, most noble David, I beg you that you never forget that I, King Azzazel, honored the knight's code down to my last breath. Farewell, Pastor Grace, and take your people as far away from Queen Jezebel as possible."

His head falls over eye level with the black dirt on the floor of the arena. As he waits there for hell to subdue him, he shows no fear because of all he's done in his past life, this life, and if he can, the life to come.

Michal is bleeding severely. Athaliah has cut her real good on her ribs and on the bicep of her striking arm. Athaliah is about to go in for the kill but as she raises her sword she is distracted by Pilate, David, and Orpah running toward her. Looking past them, she notices King Anubis, Azzazel, and Dagon have fallen in battle. Outnumbered four to one, she decides to retreat and runs back to the stairwell.

Orpah picks up an arrow from the ground and puts it in her bow. Taking aim at Athaliah's back while fleeing the arena, she pulls with animosity in her shot and gets ready to release. Before she can let go, Michal limps over and puts her hand on her shoulder. "Let her go, Orpah. She's not worth it." Orpah feels her friend's touch and drops her bow crying for the loss of her brothers who died to redeem themselves before the Lord.

Two men and two women are left standing on the blood-stench terrace. Coming together in the middle of the field, they all tear their clothes for bandages to dress each other's wounds. As they are standing there looking over each other, something tells David to look up. In the throne's box, Artemis is creeping up behind Jezebel with a knife in her hand. He wants to shout for her to stop but if he does he'll give Artemis's position away.

Areopagus and the witnesses from the gate has their attention on the field just as Jezebel's. Asherah, however, is off to the side and catches Artemis raising her knife to stab the queen. "My queen, behind you!"

Jezebel pulls the jeweled egg on her scepter and a small dagger comes free. Extending her arm, she spins quickly and slices Artemis throat wide open. "You fool!" Jezebel yells looking down on Artemis's bloody body that fell over on its side. Jezebel turns around carefully while avoiding the pool of blood that is spewing toward her shoes.

"Golgotha!" she shouts to the crowd who is now yelling to get in on the action. "Today we have witness the fall of great men to those who have not kept the laws of our land! I am honored to say that some of the enemy's soldiers have fallen as well but in the eyes of our lord Satan, justice has not been served!" Jezebel takes a stone out of Areopagus's hand and raises it. "The stone you have in your hands, I command you this day to make it rain down on the field until no life is left in any of their unlawful bodies!"

Queen Jezebel raises her scepter and everyone in the bleachers raises their stones also. When she lets her scepter fall, the sky becomes a deluge of black rocks. David and his disciples join hands because the exit is too far to make a run for. "Lord, remember us when you open the book of life," he prays closing his eyes to the rocky showers that will soon cover them all.

23

"Bravo! Bravo!" The sound of a man's voice whoops through the man-made storm followed by loud claps. "Encore! Encore! Bravo! Bravo!" The voice shouts again louder drawing the coliseum's eye toward him.

Orpah opens one eye and then the other hoping that a hard rock doesn't hit her in the face. The voice she heard was intriguing because of its peculiar tone and the power within it. Standing in the main entrance of the arena floor is the most beautiful man she has ever laid eyes on. His beauty makes her smile and feel comforted because the aura surrounding him is that of a savior.

"Pastor Grace, look, an angel has come to rescue us from the evil Jezebel." Orpah points her finger to the winged being a ways from them. "Our hard work for Jesus has paid off and he has protected us from a tortuous death."

David and his steadfast friends look up to the stone cloud sitting above them. Their gaze of suspense to why they're still breathing is diverted to the light coming from the splendid creature acting like he owns the place. Michal and Orpah want to run to him for stopping the rocks from beating down on them, but David tells them to remain where they are.

David shouts. "Who are you?"

The angelic being raises his hand to the black cloud and moves his hand from left to right. "You can call me Lucifer for now." The cloud above them parts like the Red Sea and the stones in the air drop off to the side striking no one. "Well, at least while I'm in my God-given body from birth."

"Lucifer!" David's eyes widen with fright.

"Who is Lucifer, Pastor Grace?" Michal ask looking at his fearful expression.

"He is the devil or shall I say Satan. The prince of Hades and hell."

"How can this be? He doesn't look like an evil person," Michal replied.

"Yes, David," Lucifer replied and pauses. "Can I call you David or do you prefer that I call you Pastor Grace." Lucifer puts his forefinger and thumb to his chin. "Uh, I think I'll call you David because Pastor Grace sounds too formal. Any who, like I was saying before I was rudely interrupted by my own thoughts. I'm not such a bad guy. At least your disciples don't think so."

"Everyone, stay back! This is just one of his many tricks to get people to believe in him. The Bible says in 2 Corinthians 11:14 that Satan can transform himself into…"

"An angel of light." Lucifer finishes off the Scripture before David can. "Yes, Michal, what your Pastor Grace is saying is true. As a matter of fact what you are seeing before you today is just one of my many forms I take on according to what the occasion calls for. Sometimes I'm a lion because Jesus likes to liken himself to a lion. Or sometimes I'm my present self which is what everyone calls the devil. We all know about the cunning serpent I was to get Eve to sin against God. These are just a few beings I take on. Believe me, there's more but we'll get into all that on a later day. Today, I've decided to show my face because of Mr. David Grace here doing what he's been doing in my domain. So today, that is what I'm here to address."

Lucifer begins to walk toward the center of the ring. His bare chest looks to be malnutritious but not because of lack of eating but because that's the way God made him in the beginning. His wings are a glowing white and as he walks the light from the atmosphere reflects a rainbow of colors throughout his feathers. The colors are unique because they appear to be chrysolite, emeralds, topaz, turquoise, and jasper adorned all around him. His feet are bare as well and each step he takes, stones and debris along the ground repel from his path from the energy emanating from within him.

"Hello, David," Lucifer said showing a little curtsy while displaying a golden wreath sitting atop of his Golden Fleece hair. "I'm pleased to finally meet you." David steps back and is about to tell Lucifer what's on his mind but Lucifer continues speaking. "Please save your words of flatter because the pleasure is truly all mind." Lucifer looks over the dead souls lying in the dirt all around them. "First thing's first," he said snapping his fingers, causing the worm of torment to appear in the entrance he was recently standing in. "My apologies for the mess of bodies upon the ground. I would have sent my pet to escort them to hell earlier but I was having too much fun watching all of you kill one another. By the way, great shot, Michal, when Apollyon came out."

Lucifer looks in the direction of the invertebrate animal sitting still like a pet awaiting his master's command. The creature's wormy body is sizzling hot with smoke from traveling the depths of hell and its senses of death and pain are heighten to the fallen souls on the field. Lucifer points his finger upward and the soul-thirsty worm raises his midsection ready to feast on the four bodies that died today.

"Take everyone except Azzazel," he said calmly turning his finger in a circle. "His disobedience was totally uncalled for so therefore I'll deal with him personally when all this is over."

The worm of torment makes his rounds gobbling up the dead starting with Caiaphas. Queen Jezebel knows that the worm will soon come for Artemis's soul and orders the two witnesses to toss her to the ground. Artemis's lifeless body is quickly picked up and rolled over the wall making her hit the coliseum floor like a sack of bones. Azzazel still has a hint of life left in him and watches Dagon's armored body get swallowed up whole next to him. The crowd circling inside the stoned bleachers chant for more blood to be shed when Artemis is taking last and disappears with Satan's pet burrowing his way to hell.

"You monster!" Pilate yells wanting to smash Lucifer's face in but Michal and Orpah restrains him.

"Calm down, Pilate," David said. "Judas, Caiaphas, and Artemis all knew what they were getting themselves into when they stepped foot inside these doors. All we can do is pray for their souls and continue to fight until we meet them again in our next life."

"Yes, calm down, Pilate. Listen to your pastor," Lucifer said sarcastically. "I come in peace, looking to present to all of you a proposition for the zeal you have for God's cowardly son Jesus."

"Jesus is not a coward!" Michal shouts in Jesus's defense.

Lucifer shifts his eyes over the battlefield. "Well, if what you say is true, where is he? Was it not I who saved you from being stoned and dying the second death? Is it not

I who is here to make sure you lived to see another day in Hades? Yes, Jesus does have a lot of power, but down here his power is useless to what I'm capable of doing. Every day I challenge the Son of God to face me and he doesn't answer me. That's why I do what I do throughout the world and the graves. It's a shame how he leaves the people of earth to stand up for him after they have accepted him into their hearts. He calls it trials and tribulations. I call it pure cowardliness. Honestly, is that the kind of God you want to serve?"

"Let us be, Lucifer. Anything you have to say we are not trying to hear it." David steps out from among his disciples. "Don't you think that before we vowed to stand up for Jesus that we knew you were coming to stop or deceive us into thinking what we were doing is wrong? You would think that you would've tried some other tactics but I see that you are still the same snake in grass you were in the garden of Eden. Like I said before, let us be, Lucifer. We've all said our prayers and our hearts are ready to dismiss whatever you are trying to get us to accept, see, or understand from you."

Lucifer laughs to David's brave speech. "I admire you, David. I admire you for having the balls to stand up against everything I've decreed for eternity in Hades. Since the day you entered Sheol, I've been keeping my eye on you. I wondered how long you would last after the thirsty souls in the graves found out you had a compass to Sharia. But as time went on, you seemed to overcome obstacles and one day turn into two and two days ended up becoming three and so on and so forth. What really got my attention is when you started preaching God's Word despite knowing that everything you were doing is totally against everything I stand for."

Lucifer clasp his hands together and points them at David. "Oh hell, let me just cut to the chase. I want you to join me, David Grace. Why, you may ask? Let's just say it is because you put a smile on my face for doing to me what I do to Jesus every day. You, David Grace, is what I've been waiting on to come through Hades's doors. Someone who can infiltrate the enemies' camps and lead other soldiers to join their revolt. Magnificent! Truly, all I can say is magnificent. I couldn't have done it better myself. Today, I offer you and your followers a peace offering. No harm done, no harm taken," he said looking at all of them and then back to David. "Join me, David, and we will do mighty things together."

David pushes his hands from in front of him. "Our Lord Jesus came down from heaven, walk the face of the earth, and died on the cross for the sins of the world. While he was here, he said in Luke 9:23 that whoever wants to be his disciple must deny themselves and take up their cross daily and follow him. Today, Lucifer, me and my brothers and sisters in Christ have taken up our crosses knowing that in doing so that we will have pain, suffering, and possible death." David looks to Jezebel, then to the silent crowd, then to his companions, and then back to Lucifer. "The answer to your question is no, Lucifer. In Jesus's name we came to the Soul Reapers Conquest match, in Jesus's name we stand, and—"

"In Jesus's name we will fall if needs be!" Pilate shouts raising his spear to the sky.

Lucifer begins to plead his case. "But don't you know I have the power to send you back to earth and be back with your precious wife Amy. If its riches you desire I can make King Solomon, who was the richest man ever, look like a goat herder on side of you. Whatever it is that your mind can think of I can give you if only you will join me and reverence me as your lord."

David steps back in the midst of his brethren and quotes Jesus's words from Matthew 4:10 out of the Bible. "Away from me, Satan! For it is written: 'You should worship the Lord God, and him only you shall serve.' My answer is final.'"

Lucifer is taken aback. "How dare you speak to me the same way that coward spoke to me when I came to him in peace?" Lucifer's eyes fills with fire and his body changes from ivory white to a galvanize gray, starting at his feet and ending at the top of his head. His sun dawn hair becomes pitch black and seven horns rise from underneath the strands and pushes the gold wreath to the ground.

All the horns combined forming a crown to show his majesty over the graves. "I can't believe you insulted me with Scriptures in my own kingdom!" Suddenly his beautiful wings turn to midnight and his smooth skin becomes rough as leather. "My patience with all of you has come to an end! He opens his right hand and an onyx trident appears in it. "Enough with Lucifer! Now it's time for you to meet the devil that my pride and wickedness has made me in to. Satan, lord over hell, Hades, and death!"

Lucifer, now Satan, points his trident at David like he is about to zap him with some mysterious power. Pilate steps in front him and holds up his spear and shield to show Satan that in order to get to David, he would have to go through him first. Michal and Orpah comes around to the front of him as well. Both of them put up their shields ready to defend David and themselves from the rage Satan has in his eyes for them.

"You know what?" Satan said wanting to abolish them all to burn in the lake of fire. "The four of you are not even worth my power. Since your disobedience has gotten the attention of Golgotha and today is the queen's Soul Reapers Conquest match, I say, let the games continue on as promised." Satan points his trident toward the entrance where the worm appeared. "David Grace, meet Goliath!"

David parts his companions with his hand and steps forward. "Goliath," he said, looking to the entrance hoping it is not who he thinks it is.

Satan smiles with a fiendish expression and shouts, "Goliath Jr., come forth!"

Goliath Jr. emerges from the dark tunnel onto the fighting grounds ready to bash, crush, and kill whoever his master has summoned him from his region to destroy. A true champion from birth, like his father, Goliath Sr., who King David slew in the Bible with a sling and a single stone. His height was six cubits and a span (which is about ten feet). He had a bronze helmet on his head and wore a coat of scale armor of bronze weighing fifty thousand shekels (which is about 135 lb).

On the front of his legs, he wore bronze greaves, and a bronze studded mace was slung on his back. His mace shaft was like a weaver's rod and the iron points that were studs was sharp enough to pierce an elephant's skin with ease. His steps were slow but each one he took covered at least five feet of the ring's dirt surface. He had one eye because he was born with a defect. Therefore, the people of his region labeled him as a cyclops because of his deformity.

Goliath's long strides stop when he is towering next to Satan.

"Who is it, my lord, that you have brought me to this faraway land to destroy?" Goliath's voice sounds like the lion's roar on a quiet night in the jungle.

"Goliath, meet David."

"David!" Goliath shouts. "Is this the David who slew my father on the battlefield in front of my people?"

Satan looks up at Goliath and shakes his head no. "Sadly, my boisterous servant, he is not the King David who killed your father. But he is a David representing the same God who King David represented on the day your father fell."

"You're talking about the God of the tribe of Judea and Israel?" The God whose name and power continued throughout the ages to put a foot on my people's neck and wouldn't let up until all nations knew that his presence was among his people."

"What you are saying, Goliath, is true." Satan points his trident back at David. "So now you know by your own words what your lord desires." Satan walks off to the side. "Goliath, destroy this fool who comes in the name of his lord. When you finish breaking him apart, I want you to spread his limbs along the ground so his followers can see what a foolish mistake they have made by professing the name of Jesus in my realm."

"Yes, my lord. What you ask, it will be an honor for me to do," Goliath said with a deep laugh while pulling his studded mace from the center of his back.

David turns around and tells his disciples that the battle with Goliath is his. All of them tried their hardest to persuade him differently but he lets them know that the only help he needs died on the cross over two thousand years ago and is now seated at the right hand of the Father. The women are scared for their pastor because Goliath is so huge of a man. Pilate sees that his friend will not be dissuaded and thereafter tells his sisters in Christ that the fight doesn't belong to them but to Pastor Grace only.

"Pastor Grace, it's been an honor being your disciple for the Lord," Pilate said, shaking David's hand and embracing him. "No matter what happens, my friend, I want you to know that to the death we will all die fighting for what we believe in."

"Thanks, Pilate, for humbling yourself to do God's work in Sheol. God bless you and if death seems to find me, please know that I love all of you."

David gives Pilate his satchel and walks all of them away from Goliath. Before he turned to face the giant, he made sure they were all far away as possible from intervening with the fight he has gladly taken on.

As Goliath steps forward, David raises his shield and dirk to strike back upon his attack. David said to Goliath Jr., "You come against me with your studded mace and bronze armor, but I come against you in the name of the Lord Almighty, the father of my Lord Jesus Christ, whom you have defiled. This day the Lord will deliver you into my hands, and I will strike you down before all Golgotha! All those gathered here will know that it is not by sword or spear that the Lord saves, for the battle is the Lord's. This day, Goliath, you will fall and every soul present will see that my Lord has given you and whatever else Satan throws at us into our hands."

Goliath replied, "Am I a dog, that you come at me with your puny sword and shield and words of blasphemy toward my lord Satan, prince of Hades and hell." And Goliath cursed David by his gods. "Come here," he said, "and I'll give your flesh to the vultures and the wild animals of Sheol."

As Goliath moved closer to attack him, David ran quickly toward the battle line to meet him. Goliath, with his hands wrapped around the handle of his mace, twisted his hips and swung with all his might. The yellow cross on David's shield must have been like a target to him because the head of his mace hit it dead center where the lines cross. The power within Goliath's swing lifted David's feet from underneath him causing him to fly through the air and slide when his back hits the solid ground.

Goliath is on top of David in a matter of seconds. His stride is slow but since his foot span is so wide it's hard for any opponent to run from him. Before he can gather his thoughts to regain his footing to fight, Goliath comes down hard with his mace upon him again. The shield in his hand across his chest catches the bludgeon force and saves him from a strike that was for sure deadly.

David's hand is crushed from being in between the shield and the chain mail that covered his upper body. The vibration from the iron studs smashing the shield runs through his arm, and up to his head making him feel like he is standing inside the Liberty Bell when it was struck on the day of independence.

Truly shaken, he rolls to his left from one of the three giant boots trying to stomp him into oblivion. The sound of Goliath's foot pounding the dirt as he rolls out of the way for his life jogs his memory and brings his mind back to the battle at hand.

"Stand still so I can break you," Goliath said as David jumps to his feet.

The shield in his battered hand falls to the ground. Goliath's strength has marred it to scrap metal so he is left with only his dirk to parry the giant's attacks. Goliath's exertion in trying to end the battle quickly has taken some power out of his swings. This time when he swings his mace it's a little slower so David ducks the strike and runs around to the backside of him.

Being a man of war, Goliath foresaw the smaller man's schemes to use his speed and agility against him who is the bigger opponent. His timing is like clockwork as he balls his fist and roundhouse punches David to the side of his head. Like his hand being smashed by the gigantic mace, David's jaw is knocked off the hinges and the bone that protected his right eye sinks into his face.

Orpah and Michal closed their eyes and look away when he falls over onto a bed of stones that were thrown from the bleachers. Pilate wants to go and help him when a scream of agony spew from his mouth from the stones cracking his ribs when he landed on them. Quickly thinking, he decides to stay put because if he shall fall alongside David, then his sisters will be left all alone to fight Goliath and Satan by themselves.

Satan is watching the one-sided battle from the air. While David is lying there hanging on for dear life, he flies in circles around the coliseum rousing the crowd to cheer for Goliath, his gladiator of justice. Chants of, "Death! Death! Death!" comes from the multitude when the giant advances on David to tear him into pieces the way Satan ordered him to do. David hears the crowd's sentencing cries and a vision of Goliath Sr. falling to his knees in defeat runs through his mind as if he is on the field when King David slung the stone in the name of the Lord Almighty.

Goliath bends down to grab him. "What did I tell you, puny dog?" he asks lifting him with one hand by the neck of his chain mail. "You should have listened to Goliath when I said I was going to give your flesh to the vultures and wild animals of Sheol."

Blood is dripping from David's mouth and only one of his eyes is working properly. Hanging limply in the air, he plays possum as Goliath drops his mace and reaches back to punch him into hell. Right when he has cocked back to punch, David raises his hands high above his head and drives a round stone deep into Goliath's eye with all the muscle he has left inside of him. The blinding blow causes Goliath to release him instantly.

David lands on his feet and picks up his dirk. Remembering his plan of attack from earlier, he runs to the backside of Goliath again. Goliath is too busy stepping around blindly, unaware that David is on the weak side of his armor. With the sword in his good hand, he cuts Goliath's joints where the thigh and calf meet.

The sharp blade slices his ligaments severely. Wobbling for balance and stamina, he falls to his knees and tilts his head back to pull out the stone stuck in his eye. The bronze helmet he wore thuds to the ground after it slid off his head. David drops his dirk and picks up the heavy mace and faces his enemy who is now at his eye level.

"Just as your father fell by a single stone, today you, Goliath Jr., have fallen by a single stone also." David's words are hard to speak because of his broken jawbone. "This very day I will give your carcass to the birds and wild animals of this world so that all who have seen you fall will know that Jesus Christ is Lord over heaven, earth, and hell!"

David uses the core of his strength and swings the mace like a sledgehammer down on his skull. Immediately, spurts of green blood shoot out his head where the iron studs left holes in his shattered face. As Goliath fell forward dead, David stepped out of the giant's way and fell to his knees, tired from the long day of war. "Thank you, Jesus, for your strength and for giving me the victory," he said as the world around him begun to spin in circles from exhaustion.

"Pastor Grace, Pastor Grace, wake up," Pilate said, cuffing David in his arm and shaking him.

"Is he dead?" Orpah asks kneeling to get a closer look.

"I can hear a heartbeat!" Michal exclaims, lifting her head off his chest.

"Pastor Grace," Pilate said again tapping him repeatedly on the unbroken side of his face. "Pastor Grace, you have to get up before Satan approaches us."

David's face moves a little and his lips mumbles something as his eyes slit to the three faces he will lay down his life for any day. Fully conscious, he smiles to still being alive in Hades and sits up in Pilate's arm. Pilate stands and Michal takes one arm while he takes the other. Being mindful of his wounds, the three of them pulls David to his feet so that when Satan strikes again, they can do whatever possible as a group to face him head on.

"Thank you, my brother and sisters," he said, standing with his arms around their shoulders for assistance. "Who's next?" he asks jokingly with a mouthful of blood drooling down to the ground.

Pilate lets the joke fly over his head. "You did well, Pastor Grace. You did well," is all he can respond while keeping his eyes on Satan angrily staring at them from above.

The people of Golgotha sat quietly to the sight of Azzazel, Dagon, Anubis, and Goliath Jr. dying at the hands of the men and women standing on the field. During the battle, they all sought the deaths of David and his followers, but now that they have defeated Queen Jezebel and Satan's best warriors, the majority of the assembly had a change of heart. Seeing David take a severe beating from the giant and coming out triumphant brings the multitude to their feet. A man standing in the nosebleed section starts to clap and then one by one the people in the stadium begin to clap with him. The claps of victory irks the ears of Jezebel and the chants of "David!" sends Satan's tolerance to below zero.

"Enough!" Satan shouts to the stoned bleachers making the hairs on the people's head flutter from the power within his voice. After silencing the crowd with the threat of his trident, he looks down to the foolish souls who has excited the people into possibly rising up against him in his kingdom. "It's time to end this dismay and I swear by myself that you will burn for eternity regretting the day God formed you in your mother's womb."

Satan comes down from the sky and lands with full force. His landing splits the ground beneath his feet and travels throughout the coliseum shifting the foundation of the stadium. Decorative stones around the top of the brick structure breaks off and kills some of the people.

Panic runs through the bleachers when Satan's body becomes engulfed in flames. Outraged beyond measures, he lifts Azzazel with the power of his hand and throws his trident at him. The pitchfork shows no mercy as it divides him into two and returns back to him. David and the rest of his gang take heed to the power Satan has and decides not to put up a fight but to stand firm trusting in the Lord.

"Where is your God now, David?" Satan asks pointing his trident at his enemies. "Call his name and see if he comes to save you from my hands?" The fire surrounding him grows brighter as he channels his power to flow from within him and into his trident. "Good-bye, David Grace."

As Satan's power charges his trident to disintegrate the followers of Jesus, a white dove with an olive branch in his beak flies to the ground from out of nowhere. Satan knows the dove is not from this world and the sight of the feathered creature brings his thoughts of destruction to a halt.

The bird is at David's feet so David picks the dove up to examine it.

Looking over the bird, he pulls the olive branch from its mouth and recalls how Noah sent a dove out of the ark and it came back with an olive branch in its beak. The olive branch was to show Noah that God remembered him throughout the flooding of the earth.

"What is this?" Satan asks, staring at the foreign bird. "A dove? Is that all your God can do?" he shouts to the gray clouds above him. "Coward! You should have believed me when I told you Jesus was nothing but a coward." His trident turns a glowing red. "Sayonara, David. See you in hell."

A bolt of fire shoots out the trident and stops before it reaches David. Suddenly the sky becomes luminous as sunlight and a beautiful, brilliant light pushes its way through the clouds and spotlights down on the four souls professing Jesus is Lord. Jezebel and the rest of the crowd points their fingers wondering what's going on. Satan, however, continues to try his hardest to destroy David, but the light surrounding him and his followers is acting like a force field.

"No," Satan said to himself. "How can this be?"

Standing there in the light, Michal, David, Pilate, and Orpah look at each other with smiles of joy. The dove that is perched on David's finger takes off and flies around the coliseum so that everyone can see it. After making its rounds through the arena, the dove flies to the heavens and is never seen again.

Everyone's attention is to the sky so no one notices that the four of them are being lifted up by the light retracting back to its source. Satan turns around disbelieving what his eyes are seeing. But just as David recognized the power of Satan and decided not to continue on fighting, Satan recognizes the power of God and decides it would be useless to try and stop the light that cannot be penetrated.

And then the display of God's gracious hand is over. Like a light switch turning on then off, the abnormal light is gone and the people the light came for is gone with it.

24

Specks of gold glitter are in the white clouds all around them. When they left Hades, they were all side by side until Pilate, Michal, and Orpah begin to be drawn abruptly toward a higher power. David noticed the change in their speed when he remained on his back soaring through the air while his disciples were turned upright. He wanted to scream, "Wait for me!" but within a blink of an eye, his friends zoomed off and he is left all alone.

"No, don't leave me! Come back! Please come back!" David screamed reaching his hand out hoping someone will take hold of it.

Lying there in the beautiful light, he tries to move his body into a sitting or standing position but can't. Whatever has a hold on him won't allow him to move and has pulled the brake lever on his glorious trip to the gates of heaven. As he is praying to be joined again with his brothers and sisters in Christ, the bright clouds around him begins to show images of a scene he's unfamiliar with. The images appear and disappear before his eyes can fully grasp the picture that is being displayed to him.

What is that? he thought.

All of sudden the images stop and the clouds surrounding him becomes bleached white. Staring into the clouds which now looks like a blank screen, the image that was flickering comes back and remains clear. No longer suspended in God's glory, David's eyes focus on a number of ceiling squares directly above him. A warm light to his right shines through a window and brushes the side of his face. Blinking once then twice, his eyes travels to four corners and he thinks, *Room. I'm in a room.*

David sits up but lies back down because his head feels like somebody hit him with a 2 × 4. He tries to express his pain but the tube in his throat makes him gag when he is trying to speak. The feeling in his legs and arms come back as panic to his current conditions enters his brain.

Frantically moving his hands, he reaches for the plastic tube shoved down his throat. Slowly, he wraps his hands around the circumference to pull it out, but before he can, he notices something with a wire is attached to his index finger. Quickly, he brings his hand to his face and as his mind is fathoming what his eyes are seeing, his ears open to the sound of a mellow beep.

A hospital, he thought looking around at the array of electronic monitors and IV lines winding down to his arm. *Why am I in a hospital when I am dead and supposed to be in heaven or Hades?* David decides not to pull the tube out his throat and begins to search for the button that calls the nurse. The red button he is looking for is on the railing of the hospital bed. "Oh well, what else do I have to lose?" he asked himself wondering what is going to happen next after he pushed it.

Nurse Heidi is sitting in the nurses' station with the other roving nurse, Ms. Acu'na, when she gets the alert from room 826. Two patients are in room 826 and both of them are incomprehensive. One is Nate Roberts who was a Jon Doe until yesterday when his fingerprints popped up in more places than one throughout the state of Illinois. A month ago he was shot in the head while running out the back door of a man's house. Ever since then he has been in a coma fighting for his life awaiting the day to wake up and stand trial for twelve counts of burglary. The other patient is David Grace and he has been on life support for the past week after being in a severe car wreck.

After looking over the ICU visitation sign-in sheet, Nurse Heidi sees no one has signed in to visit any of the two patients. She wants to disregard the nurse's call alert but her nurse's duties call for her to check on the patients she is assigned to no matter what the circumstances.

Standing, she walks down the waxed hospital floors and turns the door handle to David's room. Gasping with disbelief, she drops her clipboard and walks over to the wide-eyed patient who was pronounced dead a week ago.

"Mr. Grace! How, what?" she exclaims incredulously before running out the door to get the doctor.

Hospital floor level 8 is racing with a swarm of people trying to see the man who miraculously woke up after being diagnosed brain dead and being put on life support for personal reasons. The hall is crowded with janitors, housekeepers, nurses, and any other employees you can think of. Nurse Acu'na is guarding David's door so that none of them can barge their way in to disturb her patients.

Dr. Jackson is his doctor, and she appears from the elevator and begins making her way through the throng of people leading to room 826. Nurse Heidi is directly behind her asking everyone to please let the doctor come through.

"Good afternoon, Mr. Grace. I am your physician, Princess Jackson, and might I say that you have defied all medical books in this age and the ages to come. Before I proceed to tell you what's going on and why is there a crowd swarming outside your door; I want to ask you, do you comprehend what I am saying? Blink once for yes, or nod your head. Whichever is less painful for you will be all right with me."

David looks up at Dr. Jackson and her long dark curly hair and smooth chocolate skin is the same as the Princess Jackson that was secretary/treasurer of his church. Stupefied to how and why Princess Jackson is a doctor, David forgets to respond to her question.

"Mr. Grace, can you hear me?" Princess pulls out a penlight and shines it into his eyes. The light wakes him up and David blinks rapidly, nods his head, and raises his hands. Dr. Jackson smiles and said, "Okay, Mr. Grace, I can see that you understand me." Dr. Jackson checks his vitals and concludes that besides the concussion on his head and the bruise on his left hip that he is practically fine. "Mr. Grace, Nurse Heidi is going to call your wife Amy and give her the good news about your miraculous recovery. As for your health, I am confident that nothing is wrong with you to keep us from removing the ventilation machine from your lungs. Since your wife is the one who decided to put you on life support, I would appreciate it if you would wait for her to remove it. Unless, you really want us to remove it at this moment?"

David shakes his head no and winced from the pain shooting through his body. Dr. Jackson notices the change in his facial expression and that his skin is a little wan.

"Mr. Grace, I know you're probably in a lot of pain from the accident. Nurse Acu'na here is going to give you a morphine pump that you can push a button to administer when you are in need of relief." Dr. Jackson takes out a syringe and a bottle of Demerol to help him with the soreness in his body. "Mr. Grace, this will help you sleep and when you wake up everything is going to have a more sense of normalcy," she said, staring into his gray eyes getting heavier and then shutting into a world of darkness.

Amy is lying in a reclining chair when David woke up. Her eyes are closed and her blond hair is draped across half her face. Something is different about her but the beauty of her presence is too becoming to try and figure it out.

This room is different from the room he shared earlier with Nate Roberts. Where he's at now, he is the only patient in the room and all the electronic gadgets, except for the heart monitor, are gone. A sharp pain from the colostomy bag and urination catheter being removed runs rampant through his lower body when he raises the back of his bed to sit up.

David looks at Amy who looks like a woman who is exhausted and has finally found the peace she's been searching for. Her sleep is sound and looks to be well needed that he doesn't want to disturb her. He decides to let his wife rest because he has a lot of unanswered questions on his mind.

Questions like: Why doesn't he have three bullets in his chest? Why Princess Jackson is his doctor? Why Nate Roberts, Nurse Heidi, Nurse Acu'na, and room 826 he was in sounds so familiar? And why was his doctor saying he was in an accident? *What kind of accident?* he thought looking for the button Dr. Jackson prescribed for him to push if he felt any pain.

"David honey, you're awake." Amy folds her legs and the recliner turns back into a chair. "David, oh, David, I missed you so much." Amy puts his face in her hands and kisses him repeatedly. "I love you, David."

"I love you too, Amy. I don't know how I got here but however I did I'm glad to be in your arms again."

Amy starts to cry when she hears her husband's voice. "David love, I cried and prayed and then cried some more. I asked God every day to watch over you and to allow you to fulfill your dreams to become a pastor of his Word in heaven."

David faintly remembers Amy's prayer when he heard her in Hades. "I think I heard you, Amy, but I thought I was imagining it because I was having a hard time in Hades."

"Hades. What's Hades?"

"It's a purgatory for those who didn't make it into heaven go before they go to hell."

"Hell! Why would you go to hell?"

David's mind takes him back to standing before Jesus and being judged righteously. His entire ministry he lied to his supportive wife about what he was doing but when he stood before the throne of truth, his lies had caught up with him. Letting out a deep breath, he looks Amy in the eyes and said, "Because I was using our church for my own selfish gain and leading one of our members on to do things for me that wasn't right in the eyes of God."

"Our church." Amy steps back to take in all what David just said to her.

"Yes, Amy, our church, the Temple of Christ."

"Are you okay, David?" Amy bends over to look David in his eyes. "You look okay except for your skin is still pale."

"Amy, did you hear what I just said about me stealing from the church?"

"I heard you but I think we should get Dr. Jackson in here to see if you have any brain damage from the accident."

David doesn't grasp the last part of her sentence right off. "So you're not mad, and you forgive me?" he asks as the word *accident* pops back up in his mind. "Hold up, what is this accident everybody keeps talking about?"

"David, you were in a car accident last week on your way to the courthouse to get your DBA license for your church the Temple of Christ."

"A car accident a week ago. When was this, what five years ago? I'm sorry, Amy, but I would think that I would remember if I was in a car accident."

"Baby, let me call Dr. Jackson."

"Why?"

"Because five years ago we weren't married. As a matter of fact, five years ago we didn't even know each other."

"What are you talking about? What year is this?"

"Two thousand and ten and today is the 10th of August."

Dr. Jackson came in soon after Amy sent the nurse to go and get her. "Amnesia is common when receiving a hard blow to the head and being unconscious for the time David was not with us," Dr. Jackson said to Amy while checking his vital sign again. "So how are you feeling, David?"

"Health wise, I'm fine I guess, but my wife here tells me that the last five years I remember in my head is not real and that I'm not a pastor of a successful church in Beaumont, Texas."

"Beaumont!" Amy chimes in. "Baby, we are in Chicago, Illinois. We never made it to Texas because you were hit by a truck."

Dr. Jackson raises her hand to stop any more confusion. "David, last week according to several eye witnesses and a red light camera, you ran a red light and was struck by an oncoming truck while you were making a left turn. A man by the name of George Freeman pulled you from the car and laid you in the street until the EMTs showed up. While waiting for medical assistance, a lady by the name of Ja'Nice Walker ran over to help Mr. Freeman because he was screaming you were unconscious, and you didn't have a heartbeat. Ms. Walker performed cardiopulmonary resuscitation on you for over ten minutes trying to get a pulse. It was her mouth-to-mouth first aid experience that kept oxygen in your lungs that we are able to have this conversation today. When the EMTs arrived they took over and picked up where Ms. Walker left off. Finally, after hard work and dedication for you to live, EMT Debra Paxton and Frank Garcia found a pulse. It took almost fifteen minutes to get your heart beating again and on life support. Their reasons for putting you on the ventilation machine was because your brain activity ceased from the lack oxygen. I pronounced you brain dead when I examined your brain with the best of our hospital equipment and saw that your brain wasn't responding at all on any of our tests. After revealing my diagnosis of your state of being to your wife, she became emotionally distressed and therefore was not in any shape to concur with what I had told her. Later that day, her friends took her home and the day after she said she would like to keep you on the machine until all your loved ones said their final good-byes. The IV bags were only to assist you to sustain life until you were taken off life support. You were given a nutrition bag, antibiotics for infection, saline sugar solution, and the drug Dopamine to control your blood pressure." Dr. Jackson looks over David's charts. "I think that about covers everything, Mr. Grace. You are now up to date on this past week of your life. I hope what I have told you have given you a better understanding of what you have been through."

Amy takes David's hand and begins to cry when Dr. Jackson finished speaking. "Today, my love, is the day I was going to give the okay for you to be taken off the breathing machine." Amy kisses David's hand and puts it to the side of her face. "God is good, my love, and he is still in the answering-prayer business."

David lays back and stares out the window thinking about all the people who helped save his life. Ironically, everyone Dr. Jackson named he met when he was Pastor Grace on life support. "It wasn't real, Lord?" he asks out loud shaking his head.

"What's that, honey?"

"It's nothing. I was just telling God that what I went through while I was on life support felt so real."

Dr. Jackson walks to the door. "If there's nothing left for me to do here, I have some patients I need to attend to. You two have a good day and tomorrow I will release you to go home."

David remembers something as Dr. Jackson is opening the door. "Dr. Jackson."

"Yes, Mr. Grace," she replied expectantly.

"You wouldn't happen to have a handsome twin brother by the name of Prince Jackson, would you?"

"Why yes, how do you know that?"

David thinks about how loving and forgiving God is and a smile curves to the bottom of each of his earlobes.

"Oh, it was just a lucky guess. God Bless you, Dr. Jackson, and thanks for taking good care of me."

Deacon Samuel and Deacon Cotton came the next day to take him home from the hospital. Amy called Deacon Samuel the night before to ask him if he can bring her husband home when he is released. Their apartment was a mess from her staying at the hospital every night and from her going to work every day to keep her mind off her life's tragedy. When Deacon Samuel gladly agreed, she told David she would be gone when he wakes up so that everything will be in order when he goes home.

"Good afternoon, Deacon Samuel, and thanks for coming to take me home." David rolls the tray his last meal was on out of the way and shake his grandmother's and his friend's hand.

"Good afternoon to you too, David, and besides the bandage around your head you look 101 percent better than the last time we saw you."

"We?" David said looking toward Deacon Cotton.

"Pardon me, I'm William Cotton. I'm also a deacon at the church Deacon Samuel goes to.

"My apologies for not introducing him to you when I came through the door. Let's just say I am too overjoyed at God's healing power."

"Amen," Deacon Cotton replied.

"Amen," David said right after him.

A nurse brought a wheelchair while the two deacons were telling David about all the people from their church coming daily to pray for him. All he can do is listen to how much people helped Amy get through her time of grief. Placing his arms around both of their shoulders, he stands and balances himself with the two strong men helping him. The feeling in his legs are a little unstable from being in the bed so long. Finally his blood circulates to his lower body and his feet takes their first steps in over a week.

"Steady, David," Deacon Cotton said as he is lowering him into the wheelchair.

The electric doors spread apart when they sensed the three men approaching them. Bro. Chuck is out front in the church van waiting with the side doors opens. The van is equipped with sideboards for the elderly members of their church so David steps on them to get inside.

"Thank you, Mister."

"Chuck. Bro. Chuck is what everyone calls me."

"Right," David said thinking about the Bro. Chuck who drove the shuttle bus for the Temple of Christ."

Bro. Chuck runs around to the driver's side and jumps inside as his friends are buckling their seat belts. Adjusting his rearview mirror, he looks at David in the reflective glass.

"You look good, David. Glad to have you back with us," he said as he pulled off heading toward his apartment.

Amy is waiting on the steps of their apartment with open arms. A welcome-home wreath is on the door and a yellow-and-purple ribbon is twined around the metal railing down to where he is standing.

"Welcome home!" she shouts giving her husband a big hug and a passionate kiss.

"Thanks, honey. You've been so good to me." David gets a little teary.

Amy looks up at Deacon Samuel. "Deacon Samuel and Deacon Cotton, do you mind helping me get him into our home?"

"I don't mind and I'm pretty sure Deacon Cotton doesn't mind either."

"Oh thank you both. You, two guys, are the best," she said hugging each one of them.

The two of them slowly helped David get to the sofa closest to the door. Amy hastens over with a big pillow and puts it behind her husband's back. The two men of God wished they could stay to be of more help but after he was settled into his seat, they told the happy couple they had church matters to get back to. Amy is cooking a beef stew and asked would any of them like a bowl for the road. Deacon Cotton declined but Deacon Samuel said he'll take two. One for him and one for Bro. Chuck in the van.

"Why thank you, Amy, for the blessed hospitality," Deacon Samuel said when she handed him the Styrofoam bowls.

Amy shakes both of the men's hands for going out of their way for her since the day David was in the car wreck. "It's the least I can do for all of your help and prayers for me and my husband."

"We were only doing our duty for Christ," Deacon Cotton said. "So all the thanks shall belong to Jesus."

Deacon Samuel looks over at the picture of his grandmother on the wall. "You know, David, they say that every prayer prayed according to God's will is answered at its appropriate time." Deacon Samuel walks over to the picture of Pastor Thelma Grace and smiles. "If there's nothing else we both know, we both know that Pastor Grace never stopped praying for God to keep you safe under his wings of grace until you become the man of God you're called to be." He pauses and thinks about the prophesy he prophesized over David's life. The thought of all what has happened to his friend gives him the assurance that his prophesy will soon come true. "Keep Christ first and I look forward to someday hearing you preach. Good-bye, my friend, and thank you, Amy, again for the beef stew."

Not having no one call him Pastor Grace feels awkward when he only hears his first name spoken. Shaking off the weird feeling, David takes his freehand and puts it over

Deacon Samuel's. "Have a blessed day, Deacon Samuel and Deacon Cotton, and tell Bro. Chuck I said thank you for driving me home."

When they were gone, Amy fixed her husband a bowl of beef stew. David said thank you and after seeing he was comfortable she left and went ran him a hot tub of water.

Sitting alone reverie to what he's been through, his eyes looks up at his grandmother smiling down on him. The last time he saw her was in heaven and she told him, "I believe in you, David. I always believed in you and I know that you are going to do the right thing when the appropriate time is presented to you." Up until this time, he thought his grandmother was talking about not falling into temptation when he entered into Hades. Now he realizes that she was telling him not to fall into temptation when he becomes Pastor Grace.

Epilogue

"Now I know that none of you, among whom I have gone about preaching the kingdom, will ever see me again. Therefore, I declare to you today that I am innocent of the blood of any of you. For I have not hesitated to proclaim to you the whole will of God. Keep watch over yourselves and all the flock of which the Holy Spirit has made you overseers. Be shepherds of the church of God, which he brought with his own blood. I know that after I leave, savage wolves will come in among you and will not spare the flock. Even from your own number men will arise and distort the truth in order to draw away disciples after them. So be on your guard. Remember that for three years, I never stopped warning each of you night and day with tears."

"Now I commit you to God and to the word of his grace, which can build you up and give you an inheritance among all those who are sanctified. I have not coveted anyone's silver or gold or clothing. You yourselves know that these hands of mine have supplied my own needs and the needs of my companions. In everything I did, I showed you that by this kind of hard work we must help the weak, remembering the words the Lord Jesus himself said, 'It is more blessed to give than to receive.' When Paul of Silas had finished speaking, he knelt down with all of the elders of the church in Ephesus and prayed."

David scanned over Acts 20:25–36 for a third time and closed his Bible. The alarm clock went off at seven while he was reading but he'd turned it off because the last time he rushed to the courthouse he was struck by a pickup truck and died. Meditating on the Scriptures, the Word of God enlightens his spirit to the truth within them. It is as if the Apostle Paul is speaking directly to him as he writes words of wisdom on how a pastor should oversee the church by leading by example. Tears of Jesus's blessed love begin to form in his eyes as he thinks about where he's been and how God has given him another chance to get his life right.

Amy wakes up. "Good morning, baby," she said with a groggy yawn.

"Good morning, my love."

Amy looks at her husband with his back to the headboard and his Bible in his hands. "What's wrong, baby, are you okay?"

"I'm okay, Amy. Just thinking about when I was on life support."

"It's over with now. God has healed you and allowed you to see another day."

"Amen," David said, wiping his eyes.

"What time is it?"

David looks down at the clock on his nightstand. "A quarter past seven."

Amy quickly sits up. "A quarter after seven!" she exclaimed. "But, baby, we're going to be late getting to the courthouse."

"So be it then," David said calmly. "If we are late, then we are late." David grabs his wife's hands. "All I know is that the last time I rushed out of this apartment to get my DBA license, I was one breath away from never seeing your pretty face again. Come now, let's get dressed so that we can be on our way."

All dressed and ready to go, Amy and David stood in the middle of their bedroom floor doing a mental check of all they will need to bring to the county clerk at the courthouse. Amy opens the white envelope in her hand and makes sure she has his two forms of ID and the fee needed to patent the name of the church he is going to start in Beaumont. When they both agreed that they have everything, Amy began to walk out the door but David pulls her back to him.

"I love you, Amy Grace."

"I love you too, David Grace." She smiled.

"Always have and I always will," he replied, locking his lips around hers the way he did on their wedding day.

Soon after David was released from the hospital, his job called and said that the Coca-Cola plant in Beaumont, Texas, has an opening in the department he works in. Coca-Cola also said he had two weeks to be in Beaumont and on the job, so therefore he needed to get all his business in order or they will fill the position. The next day, Amy put her two weeks' notice in and called her friend Tabitha to tell her the good news. It was as if God was pulling the strings on everything because Tabitha said the apartment she lives in has two apartments available and they were waiting for her application.

The August sun is out this morning. Last night's forecast said today is going to be a hot one but the ripples of thick clouds in the sky decided to say something different. The windows are down as the two of them talked and enjoyed the breeze of the speed of Amy's car on the Chicago expressway. Rush-hour traffic is down but it's there so the acceleration of her car is more tolerable than if they had left earlier than what they did.

Exiting 159th, Amy points to where David was hit by the truck when he ran the red light. He slightly shudders when she makes the left turn on green the way he should have according to the law. All he could do is shake his head to his reckless behavior that by the grace of God didn't cost him his life. Amy senses the change in his spirit and rubs his knee to comfort him.

"God loves you, David Grace," she said, turning the steering wheel into the courthouse parking lot. "And your purpose in this world is far greater than what me or you can imagine."

David and Amy stand hand in hand in the winding barriers zigzagging down to the license clerk's window. Men, women, and children wait patiently for their turn to be next. It's eight forty and the line is mediocre as the morning rush has subsided and the locals have returned to work. Step by step they move conversing on how they can't wait to tackle the beginning stages of getting the church off the ground. Before reaching the window, they come to an agreement that their new residence will have to do for their services until God blesses them with a building. David thought, *Wow, it feels like I'm having déjà vu,* as the man in front of him left the window.

"Good morning," Amy said to the clerk.

"Good morning, my name is Alice and how can I help the two of you today?"

"How are you this morning, Ms. Alice?" David asks.

"I'm fine and thanks for asking."

"My name is David Grace and this is my wife Amy. This morning we are here to get my DBA license for the church I will be starting in Beaumont, Texas."

"Okay, but the license I will issue you will only be valid for the state of Illinois."

David doesn't know how he let the states licensing procedures slip his mind and apologizes to the clerk for his ignorance.

"David honey, why don't you get the license for Illinois just in case our journey in the Lord leads us back to Chicago?"

"That's a great idea, Amy. I don't know what I'll do without you." David turns back to the glass window and speaks through the hewed circle made for communication. "Ms. Alice, my wife and I would like to go ahead and proceed in purchasing my DBA license."

Ms. Alice looks at Amy and David hands over each other's on the counter. Looking at the love they shared for one another in their faces and body language, she feels compassionate for them.

"I tell you what, Mr. Grace. Whatever name you decide to name your church, I will cross-reference the name in the state of Texas so that you will know if or if not the name is available when you get there." Alice pulls up the state of Texas license department on the Internet. "Okay, Mr. Grace. I'm ready, shoot."

David feels his wife's hand gently tightens over his. "The name of my church will be called the Temple of Grace."

Ms. Alice recants when David said what the name of his church is going to be. Shrugging her shoulders in curiosity, her fingers begins to rapidly press the computer's keys until what she is searching for pops up on the monitor. "There's not any church in Beaumont, Texas, by that name. Not that it would matter anyway because that is your last name," she said with a little edginess.

David pulled out the envelope from his pocket and presented all the information the county clerk asked him for to get his license. He also slid the fee needed through the rectangular opening at the bottom of the glass. Ms. Alice gladly accepted the payment but still at an impasse to the question festering in her brain.

"Mr. Grace."

"Yes, Ms. Alice."

"I'm sorry but I can't help myself in asking you this question." Alice looks to her boss's office to make sure they are not watching her. "Why are you naming your church the Temple of Grace, after yourself?"

"Yes, baby. Why are you naming the church the Temple of Grace instead of the Temple of Christ like we agreed?"

Alice and Amy both stared at him waiting for an answer. The past couple of weeks he has been trying to share with his wife his near-death experience but she always cuts him off when he tells her about Hades. Yes, his last name may be in the title of the church but the reason it is, is because of God's light shining down on him in darkness. From that day forward when people asked him about the name of the Temple of Grace, he will tell them that his church represents God's undeserved favor and God's undeserved love.

David looks at his wife and then to Ms. Alice and smiles toward the future he has in front of him. "I'm sorry, Ms. Alice, but my reasons for naming my church the Temple of Grace has nothing to do with my last name at all."

"Then what is it then?" Alice asked while handing him his license.

Knowing that answering her question will take days to explain, he smiled and replied, "Trust me, it's a long story," before stepping to the side and allowing the next person in line to approach the counter.

ɔn can be obtained
ɡ.com

'716
0020B/397/P

CPSIA information
at www.ICGtesting
Printed in the USA
LVOW01s153214
496336LV0